The enchanting realms Patricia A. McKillip crafts in such novels as Alphabet of Thorn *and* Ombria in Shadow *leave readers spellbound. Now the World Fantasy Award–winning author invites readers to attend a school of mystery and wonder . . .*

Brenden Vetch has a gift. With an innate sense he cannot explain to himself or describe to others, he connects to the agricultural world, nurturing gardens to flourish and in-stinctively knowing the healing properties each plant and herb has to offer. But Brenden's gift isolates him from people—and from becoming part of a community.

Until the day he receives a personal invitation from the wizard Od. She needs a gardener for her school in the great city of Kelior, where every potential wizard must be trained to serve the Kingdom of Numis. For decades the rulers of Numis have controlled the school, believing they can contain the power within it—and punish any wizard who dares defy the law.

But unknown to the reigning monarchy is the power possessed by the school's new gardener—a power that even Brenden isn't fully aware of, and which is the true reason Od recruited him . . .

"McKillip demonstrates once again her exquisite grasp of the fantasist's craft."
—*Publishers Weekly*

"Lyrical prose, well-limned characterizations, vibrant action, a sense of the wonder of magic, and a generous dollop of ro-mance . . . a story that will bind readers in its spell." —*Booklist*

"More enchantments and wonders."
—*Kirkus Reviews*

"A terrific fantasy tale starring a delightful protagonist, a vile villian, and an assortment of eccentric supporting char-acters . . . The story line grips . . . mesmerizes readers until the final spell is spun."
—*Midwest Book Review*

continued . . .

Od Magic

PATRICIA A. McKILLIP

ACE BOOKS, NEW YORK

THE BERKLEY PUBLISHING GROUP
Published by the Penguin Group
Penguin Group (USA) Inc.
375 Hudson Street, New York, New York 10014, USA

Penguin Group (Canada), 90 Eglinton Avenue East, Suite 700, Toronto, Ontario, M4P 2Y3, Canada
(a division of Pearson Penguin Canada Inc.)
Penguin Books Ltd., 80 Strand, London WCR2 0RL, England
Penguin Group Ireland, 25 St. Stephen's Green, Dublin 2, Ireland (a division of Penguin Books Ltd.)
Penguin Group (Australia), 250 Camberwell Road, Camberwell, Victoria 3124, Australia
(a division of Pearson Australia Group Pty. Ltd.)
Penguin Books India Pvt. Ltd., 11 Community Centre, Panchsheel Park, New Delhi—110 017, India
Penguin Group (NZ), Cnr. Airborne and Rosedale Roads, Albany, Auckland 1310, New Zealand
(a division of Pearson New Zealand Ltd.)
Penguin Books (South Africa) (Pty.) Ltd., 24 Sturdee Avenue, Rosebank, Johannesburg 2196, South Africa

Penguin Books Ltd., Registered Offices: 80 Strand, London WC2R 0RL, England

This is a work of fiction. Names, characters, places, and incidents either are the product of the author's imagination or are used fictitiously, and any resemblance to actual persons, living or dead, business establishments, events, or locales is entirely coincidental. The publisher does not have any control over and does not assume any responsibility for author or third-party websites or their content.

PRINTING HISTORY
Ace hardcover edition / June 2005
Ace trade paperback edition / June 2006

Ace trade paperback ISBN: 0-441-01334-1

The Library of Congress has registered the Ace hardcover edition as follows:

McKillip, Patricia A.
    Od magic / Patricia A. McKillip.— 1st ed.
      p. cm.
    ISBN 0-441-01248-5
      1. Wizards—Fiction. 2. Gardeners—Fiction. 3. Kings and rulers—Succession—Fiction.
    I. Title.

    PS3563.C38O425 2005
    813'.54—dc22

                                                                                2004065734

PRINTED IN THE UNITED STATES OF AMERICA

10 9 8 7 6 5 4 3 2 1

ONE

Brenden Vetch found the Od School of Magic beneath a cobbler's shoe on a busy street in the ancient city of Kelior. The sign hung over the door of a tiny shop that badly needed paint. Brenden gazed incredulously at the door, then again at the sign. Od, it insisted, in neat black letters, School of Magic. From the sign a shoe depended: a wooden clog, sturdy enough to sail, fastened to the sign with a dowel through its center like a mast.

Brenden hesitated. People jostled around him, strangers all of them, for he was a long way from home. Home was the rocky hills and cold, deep rivers of the north country, valleys patterned green and gold and all the colors of wildflowers for three short seasons of the year, while the blank white wasteland of the fourth seemed to last forever. He had walked down from there. The royal city, older than the Kingdom of Numis itself, had sprawled past its gates and stone walls centuries before. Brenden had spent the previous day just getting from its outer boundaries of fields and cottages, taverns

and markets, across one of its five bridges and within the
shadow of the walls of the inner city. The gates had long since
moldered away; streets ran through the walls where they had
once stood locked and barred against strangers and the night.
Nobody guarded them now; they let anyone in, even the likes
of the dusty, footsore traveler with nothing to his name but
an old leather pack, and little enough in that but seeds.

He had spent all but his last coins on a meal and a bed the
night before. He had been too tired to thread his way
through the bewildering maze of streets. Cobbles ran like
stone rivers underfoot, everywhere and anywhere, meeting
and parting, braiding and fraying without pattern. He had no
idea so many people existed. Making his way patiently
through them the next day, he glimpsed now and then what
looked like a great castle towering above the city. The king's
house, he assumed, its ramparts and lofty towers raised high
so that the king could see his enemies coming along the river
or over the distant mountains. The door to the school, he
was told when he asked, stood in its shadow. There was a
sign, saying very plainly what it was. Nobody mentioned
the shoe, but it had been fixed for an entire season in Brenden's memory.

Look for the door under the shoe.

He had not understood about the shoe; it had seemed, in
the context, some magical word. Well, there was the sign,
plain as a pauper's grave. And there was the shoe, looking
very like a shoe. He scratched his head and hovered, waiting
vaguely for another kind of sign.

I have been asked to come, he reminded himself to give
himself courage. I have been invited.

The invitation had come to him the same spring day on
which, a year earlier, he had seen his last of Meryd. That he

remembered vividly, for her going was etched in his heart. Not that he blamed Meryd. He'd gone wild, reclusive as an animal, she said, since his parents had died. That meant, by his calculations, she had put up with the worst of him for a year and half a season. His parents had died two years before at the bleak, muddy end of winter, from some strange fever that had swept through the village. He had tried everything to save them, every smelly, evil-tasting concoction he had ever cobbled together from root and leaf, bark and berry for human or animal. He managed to keep his brother alive, and most of the villagers who came down with it. But his parents had caught it first, and died while he was still flailing about in the withered world for a cure.

His brother Jode had left him as well, a few months after their deaths, to see what the world had to offer, he said, besides hardship and grief. He had tried to talk Brenden into leaving his sorrow behind in the silent cottage, and coming with him. But Brenden refused.

"What's here for you but ghosts?" Jode had demanded, not wanting to part with him, either. He was still stringy and pale from the fever, but Brenden saw the strength back in his eyes, and the determination. "Come and see the world."

"No."

He felt a hand on his shoulder as he stood in the doorway staring out.

"It wasn't your fault," Jode said huskily. "You did everything you could for all of us. More."

"I know."

"We'll go to Kelior, see what kind of cottage the king lives in."

"No." He heard himself then, words thudding out of him like stones. He tried to explain, his eyes on the slow night tide turning the distant hills purple, the low shrubs covering them soft as lambs' wool in the fading light. "I'd miss the wind."

"What?"

"I need it. The sounds of it. The smells."

"Wind's everywhere," Jode said bewilderedly. "Even in Kelior."

He couldn't see what Brenden saw: how the curve of the windswept hills, the random scents of fox and bog lily, the taste of grass, the dank grit of earth itself between the teeth held a mystery he needed to know. Why he needed, he had only an incoherent idea. But he tried to explain. "It was how I found what cured you."

Jode loosed him, came to stand against the doorpost opposite, gazing at his brother. His dark, lank hair hanging over his eyes, he looked like a wild hill pony, Brenden thought, and as stubborn. "I don't understand."

"I saw what I was using—I smelled it—I understood it in a different way. It was just some wild bulbs I put away for the winter. I must have looked at them a hundred times. And then I looked at them again, and they told me something they hadn't before."

"Talking bulbs."

"Things speak," Brenden said. His gaze slid away from Jode, back to the fields, their scents changing with the twilight, to the hills that rose, dark now and secret, against the dying light. "I need to learn to listen to them."

Jode was silent, staring at him. "I wish," he said finally, "you'd listen to yourself. You're gabbling. Are you feeling all right? I'm not leaving if you're coming down sick, too."

"I'm not. But don't go."

"I have to," Jode said restlessly. "All I see in here are ghosts. Her peeling apples, weaving, singing songs we heard in the cradle; him walking in, smelling of fields, whittling bone buttons for her in winter, whistling what she sings. Sang. And you wandering in and out like a ghost yourself, with barely a word to offer anyone. You stay and talk to your plants. I need some life in my life."

Brenden was silent. Tall and muscular from his peculiar habits of roaming and foraging, he had been worn down himself as well from the desperate winter. His hair, shaggy and pale as milkweed, collected stray burrs and bits of bracken. He looked, Jode had told him, like an old hermit. He was beginning to feel like one, with Jode leaving. He made another effort. "Where are you going?"

"South."

"To Kelior?"

"Maybe that far, maybe not." He touched Brenden again. "I'll let you know when I finally stop, in case you want to join me."

He left the next day. Brenden, alone in the cottage for the first time since he was born, found solace where he could, in things growing, in the season's changing, even in the wind's voice growing hollow and high in winter, like a gaunt old wolf. Sorrow was like sleeping on stones, he decided. You had to settle all its bumps and sharp edges, come to terms against them, shift them around until they became bearable, and then carry your bed wherever you went. He had pretty much arranged all the hard bulkiness of memory and grief into a balanced load when Meryd came into his life and the load, for a time, became immeasurably lighter.

She was also one of the things he had looked at countless times, until suddenly she changed under his eyes into something he did not recognize. She seemed to feel the same about him. They woke up one day and astonished one another. She turned from a gawky, sharp-shinned girl with perpetual scars on her elbows, into a young woman with skin like a peach and hair like never-ending night. For a while, she almost turned him human again.

She stayed with him, he knew, for as long as she could. Sometimes she was there in the cottage, sometimes not. So was he, drifting in and out of her life as she appeared and disappeared in his, the long year after his parents had died and Jode had gone. Some nights he spent in the bracken; some nights in bed with her. He never asked where she went when she left; he was only glad to see her when she returned. It was the only way, he realized later, he could have lived his life then, a stranger in it himself, exploring the borders of day and night, real and dream, death and life. He thought she knew that. He thought it was what she wanted.

But he was wrong.

"It's too sad," she had said, sitting bolt upright in bed in his cottage one night. "It's too sad around here. I can't bear it. I have to leave."

He put his arms around her, thinking she must be still asleep. He whispered into her hair, "You're dreaming."

"I'm not! You are!" She pulled away from him, her eyes as startled and vulnerable as a newborn's. "You never talk to me. You wander through my life like a ghost. I never know when I'll see you. Sometimes I think you'd never notice if I never came back, and so I stay away for days, and I'm right, you never notice! But I come back anyway."

He tried to hold her again, bewildered, making soothing sounds; she shook her head fiercely, her wild dark hair flying. "And then you leave, and I don't know where you are, and when you come back you never even tell me where —"

"Nowhere," he told her desperately. "Just out. Watching things. Learning—I told you—"

"Did you?"

"I thought you knew—"

"What? What do I know? You never tell me!"

"I'm sorry," he said, shaken. "When I'm out, I'm with things that haven't got a human language. Stones. Wildflowers. I just forget to talk, that's all. I forget the need of it."

"Well, I don't! I need your voice, I need words out of you—"

"I'll try," he promised recklessly. "I'll do better—"

"I can't," she said, her face turned away from him as she rolled abruptly to her feet and began to dress. "I can't do any better for you. I've tried and tried, and I can't any longer. I need to be with someone who needs to be human. You've forgotten."

He felt his heart crack as she took a step away from him; a word tore out of it, in a voice neither of them recognized. "No!"

For an instant it seemed as though she could not move; the word tangled around her ankles, held her by the hair, weighed down her bones. He felt something unfamiliar in himself: a stone that was part of the burden he carried. But it was not sorrow at all; it was a word he had never learned. The strange force drained out of him, left him confused. And then horrified as Meryd moved again with a faint cry. He glimpsed her white, stunned face as she glanced fearfully back at him.

Then she ran, leaving him her shoes and that expression to remember her by.

Where she went, he did not know; no one else seemed to, either. She might have fled over the hill to the next village;

she might have gone clear to Kelior. So her mother, whose life he had saved, told him when he went to ask about Meryd. Her mother's eyes did not blame him.

"Spring," she just said gently. "Spring took her. She went looking for something to make her smile. We can only hope she finds it, and that she tells us when she does."

He blamed himself. He lay awake night after night with that one, trying to find a place for this memory, this stone in his mind, trying to find a way to live with it. When a house full of past would not let him sleep, he left it, slept with the stars and the foxes. He wandered, trying to lose himself so that past would lose sight of him. He followed the lengthening days so far north that he caught up with winter again, unexpectedly, on Skrygard Mountain, an iron-faced, craggy peak so steep even the sun could not get over it to melt the snow along one flank.

Brenden smelled it before he saw it: the patch of white surrounded by trees taller than any he had ever seen. The silence of stone, of snow, seemed a word itself, one he could almost hear, in a language he could almost understand. He had left the wind itself somewhere in the meadows below, rollicking among the wildflowers. Here all was still. Something had spoken its last word here, perhaps eons ago, and the silence after the word ended still lingered over the place.

Or maybe, he wondered, listening, it was the silence just before the spoken word?

There were odd shapes scattered on the field of snow. Ancient dark, charred stumps they seemed, on the verge of turning into stone. Brenden, gazing at them, waited for memory or his eyes to sort out their lines, give them some familiar shape. They had no name in any world he knew. He shifted in the snow, beginning to feel the chill. Their silence drew at him. The strange, motionless forms seemed about to flick an eye at him, grow mouths, speak. He lingered, hearing the silence as an indrawn breath, just before thought turns to sound and forms the word.

Nothing spoke.

Maybe nothing ever had. He turned reluctantly, driven away by the cold, but still listening until he passed into noisy spring again and found his way back home. He took the silence with him, though; he heard it in his dreams, where a part of him waited patiently for the ancient dreamers to speak a word as old and slow as stone.

Gradually, as summer deepened, he swallowed his own bulky stones of grief and loneliness, and gave himself to the seasons.

He learned the language of plants by smell and taste; hunkered down on the earth, he listened to them grow for hours. He wandered in the wild woods, the empty heaths and bog lands, searching for things he couldn't name. He watched them, saw what animals ate this mushroom, that berry, that leaf. He took plants home and experimented, recklessly on himself, but very carefully on his animals. The world could live without him, but he couldn't live without his goat, his chickens, his sheep. He made himself sick a time or two, then cured himself. His garden and animals flourished. So did those of the neighbors who came to him for advice.

He made himself a reputation.

He hadn't been thinking about that or much of anything at all when the invitation to Kelior appeared. He had been sitting behind the cottage, eating a bowl of leek and lamb stew, next to a patch of garden he had just cleared. He watched spring rain clouds, purple and full-bellied, swooping over the valley. Spring reminded him of Meryd; he was

trying not to think of her, or of the strange force in him that
had made them both afraid of him. A stray gust of rain spat-
tered over him, into his bowl. He ignored it, used to whatever
weather chanced across him. The cloud passed on down the
valley; the sun brightened again. The stew, scraped from the
bottom of the pot, was days old and speckled with scorching.
His hands were filthy from digging. He never bothered to cut
his hair, those days, and he wore whatever he found around
the house, even his mother's skirts, which were useful when
he collected wild bulbs and mushrooms. When his clothes
and hair smelled rank enough to bother him, he went swim-
ming, fully clothed, in the nearest lake. He had forgotten
whatever manners he had learned, and paid scant attention
to the mute languages of his fellow humans, the expressions
and gestures that spoke as urgently as words.

He put his empty bowl on the ground, and a shadow fell
over him. He looked up; his breath stopped. It seemed, in that
moment, as though one of the strange, dark, faceless beings
had come down from Skrygard Mountain looking for him.

Then he blinked, or maybe the light shifted as the sun
came out from behind a cloud, and he saw the woman standing there. She was quite tall, almost a giant, barefoot and big-
boned as an ox. Her long hair, a mingling of ivory cloud and
smoke, swept nearly to her ankles. Nothing in her broad,
weathered face had passed anywhere near the realm of
beauty. It looked plain and durable and ageless, like a good
shovel or cauldron. Her long mouth lifted to one side in a
friendly smile as Brenden stared at her. Any number of animals seemed to be crawling over her. Mice peered from one
shoulder; a raven with a missing claw perched on the other.
Lizards clung to her hair. A ferret stuck its head out of her

cloak pocket. A great albino ox with a broken horn stood at a polite distance behind her, downwind, or Brenden surely would have smelled it coming. It carried an owl on its unbroken horn. A few mongrels, feral cats, and an old blind she-wolf sat waiting behind the ox.

"Brenden Vetch?" the stranger said in her rough, vigorous voice. Brenden nodded wordlessly. No one in his life had ever needed to ask before. The giant's eyes were gray as oysters, and as wrinkled around the edges. Gazing at them, Brenden remembered, very suddenly, what layers and depths a human eye could hold. In that moment he saw what those eyes saw: not a wind-gnarled tree or a weathered stone, but a young man who had mislaid himself.

He swallowed, found words from some forgotten hoard. "Is it about my brother? Do you have news of him?" Or Meryd, he thought, with a painful twist of hope, but he did not say it.

"I don't know your brother," she answered. She sat down on the ground beside him, carefully trailing her cloak across the grass so that stray mice or lizards would not get squashed. "My name is Od. I heard you are good with plants."

"Your name is—"

"Od. I would like you to work for me in Kelior."

"Kelior," Brenden echoed, mystified.

"I have a school there. It needs a gardener."

"A gard—In a city? What kind of a school?"

"A school of magic." Her long, sturdy fingers descended over the pile of wild bulbs he had stored over the winter. She picked one up, inhaled noisily its peculiar scent of lemons and sweat, and grunted. She put it down again. "It has teachers enough, but one of the gardeners, of the kind most difficult to find, left to spend her last years among her own people. So now I need you."

"Me? To grow turnips, you mean? Cabbages, such?"

Od shook her head. "I have those who grow turnips for the table, and those who grow herbs for medicines. What I lack is a gardener who grows for the purposes of magic."

"I don't know magic," Brenden said blankly. Then he remembered again the odd force that came out of him on a spring night a year before, the look in Meryd's eyes. He shifted uneasily, his mouth tightening.

The giant's eyes contemplated him, placid and shrewd, as though they saw into his mind. "You don't recognize it. But you use it. You listen to things. So do I. I heard your name on a wind coming down from the north country. It smelled of the magic of plants. You understand the ways of certain growing things that others don't. Especially of wild things. I would like you to take your seeds and your knowledge to my school in Kelior. Grow whatever you like there. See what you come up with. Come for a season. A year. You'll have lodgings; you'll be paid."

"I don't have—I don't know any magic I could teach others—"

"You don't have to. Stay as solitary as you like. Just continue at my school in Kelior what you're doing here, and the magic will come. When it does, you can teach the teachers what you've learned." She paused, waiting for an answer, stroking a mouse that had crept down her arm. The raven on her shoulder was grooming its feathers. A tiny gold lizard clung to her ear like a jewel. She said, when Brenden didn't speak, "I heal animals I come across in my wanderings. I'm better with them than with plants. Sometimes they travel with me for a time." Brenden looked at her mutely, waiting for something: a word left unspoken. The wizard spoke it. "You can leave your sorrow safely here; it will keep until you return. By then, maybe it will be bearable."

Brenden shifted, swallowing a sudden, hard edge of it. He had learned what he could from the hills and bogs; the winds' voices were familiar now. He could leave, he realized. Cut his hair, pack up his life, go south. Jode, he thought. Meryd. Maybe I'll find them there in Kelior.

He said, his voice trembling now at the thought of leaving, "I've nearly finished planting; I'll have to wait for summer's end. I can bring seeds with me then. I'll have to find places here for my animals, close up the cottage."

"Good," Od said. She stood up, a long way, it looked to Brenden, so high her windblown hair seemed to carry clouds in it. She gave him a nod and another smile as she slid the mouse back into her hair. "I'll see you in Kelior then, at summer's end. You'll find the school easily. Look for the door under the shoe."

And there he was in Kelior, with his pack full of seeds, odd roots and bulbs, dried mushrooms, herbs and petals, the odd potion he found worth carrying so far. And here was the sign for magic, painted over what must have been a cobbler's sign, a shop with windows so grimy he could barely see the dusty emptiness inside. He waited a bit longer, hoping that someone—wizard or student—would open the door first, so that he would know. But the passing multitudes ignored it, each face indifferent to the worn, shabby door and the traveler hovering indecisively in front of it.

He reached out, opened the door.

Inside was as empty, at first, as it had looked outside, not even a stray cobbler's nail or a wooden foot form on the floorboards. He closed the door behind him; the chaos of steps, voices, wagon wheels, horses' hooves faded. As he stood uncertainly, wondering where to go, the silence deepened around him. He found himself listening to it, breath indrawn, lips parted, waiting for the word that seemed about to roar into the place like a wind, and break into every birdsong, and wolf howl, and human cry of love and terror and wonder in the world. His skin prickled with apprehension and exhilaration; he took a blind step or two toward the heart of the silence, and found the word for it then in his own heart.

Magic.

There was another door.

This one was little more than a slab cut out of the wainscoting on the far wall and put back in with hinges and doorknob attached. Brenden crossed the room, through trembling drifts of fear and wonder that passed over him like plumes of warm and chill in lake water. He opened this door eagerly, wanting now to see the fearful, indescribable face of magic, hear the word it finally spoke.

What felt like a cavern yawned about him: an enormity of wood and stone, walls stretching endlessly upward, vast stairways on both sides of him flowing gracefully down to a dark marble floor. There were framed paintings and tapestries on the walls, carpets on the floors, lights like enormous heads of flowers suspended from the distant ceiling. He heard voices everywhere, upstairs, around corners, words glancing off the old stone walls, though not a face was visible.

The mysterious silence faded away; the word remained unspoken amid the relentless chatter and flurry within the walls. Brenden tried to hold it, but it flowed out of him, leaving him empty again and perplexed. Then he remembered the great castle with its lofty parapets and towers looming over the city, and thought in horror: I have blundered into the king's house.

But there was the sign over the door he had opened. And there was the shoe. And, suddenly, there was magic again, as someone melted out of air and nothingness to stand in front of him. Magic was a tall, dark-haired, darkly robed man, with a lean, impassive face, eyes as black as bog water, a mouth whose line the years had twisted somewhere between amusement and rue.

He contemplated Brenden expressionlessly a moment, from the hair he had pruned with garden shears to his scruffy sheepskin boots, then asked mildly, "What have we here?"

"I'm Brenden Vetch."

He saw no recognition in the still eyes. "Brenden Vetch," the wizard repeated, bemused but polite. "You've come seeking knowledge of the magical arts? Is that it?"

"No. Od asked me to come here. To garden."

"Od."

"Yes. She found me up north. I told her I'd come at summer's end."

The wizard's hand rose too abruptly, blurring a little before it closed on Brenden's arm. "What door did you open to get in here?"

"The one she told me to," Brenden stammered, alarmed at the sharp question. "The door under the shoe."

"Oh." The word was little more than a breath. "That's what brought me down, then. I felt something . . ." Then the wizard seemed to feel Brenden's impulse to back into the cobbler's shop and out the door; his fingers tightened and his voice loosened. "Please, you must come in. My name is Yar

Ayrwood. I teach here. I'll take you to Wye, who tends to the orderly workings of the school. She'll show you the gardens and find a chamber for you."

"But Od—Is she here?"

"I have no idea," Yar said, drawing him despite his misgivings toward one of the sweeping stairways. "No one has seen the door under the shoe for nineteen years." Brenden glanced back incredulously. There was no door where he had come through, only solid, richly paneled wall. "Which was," Yar continued, "the first anyone had seen of Od for seventy-nine years. And even then, nineteen years ago, it was only a glimpse of the back of her remarkable head, which had a pigeon on top of it. 'Look for the door under the shoe,' was all she said then in passing. I wonder how she knew we needed a gardener."

TWO

On that first day of classes, as always, the wizard Yar told his new students about Od.

"She came into Kelior out of nowhere midway through Isham's reign," he said to the dozen or so faces gazing at him in the dizzying heights of the tower classroom. "Isham, you may recall, ruled four hundred years ago. The last sighting of Od—that is, the last recorded sighting—was nineteen years ago. By which we might, with the application of the mathematical arts, begin to comprehend the astonishing longevity of Od.

"This city was completely walled, then. All its gates still existed and were barred and guarded at night; it hadn't yet outgrown its walls to spill across the river. Isham had battles raging on three sides of him. There were rebellious nobles from the west and south who wanted his crown, as well as a fleet of warships on its way down river from a neighboring ruler, who decided to take advantage of the chaos and snatch

Numis for himself. Isham did not believe in magic. But he very badly needed it, since he was about to lose his kingdom."

He paused. Most of the students had names as old as the battles; those who had come to study from neighboring lands likely had ancestors who sent a boulder flying over Kelior's walls or dragged a tree across the river to batter at its gates. Wherever they were from, they had all exhibited some talent for the magical arts, no matter how fleeting or illusory. The students from Numis were there by law, and, if needed, by the king's favor. Gifted students from other lands were there under the king's eye, their skills under Numis's control. None of the students from Numis, Yar judged, needed the king's help. They were the richly dressed, well-fed, well-mannered, carefully nurtured children of wealth and power who, if they had any thoughts, had already begun to conceal them. They were all listening—or not—with polite attention to the tale of the horny-footed wanderer.

"Enter Od. She was a rough-hewn, rumpled giant, by all accounts, who never wore shoes or cut her hair. She had a habit of rescuing animals in trouble, so she traveled in strange company. That day she purportedly had with her a great black bull whose eyes had been burned out, a crippled raven, a dove mourning its mate, mice in her pockets, any number of abandoned dogs as well as a cat and her litter of kittens on the back of the bull." Expressions were surfacing, Yar noted; a couple of the students looked as though they had caught a pungent whiff of Od and her followers. "She made her way into the king's council chambers, where Isham was listening to the dismal news from his messengers and the bleak opinions of his advisors. No one stopped Od from entering. The guards who admitted her confessed later to a peculiar feeling at the sight of her, though they couldn't, in that perilous moment of history, remember the word for hope.

"The king and his advisors stared at Od. She pulled a stray mouse gently out of her hair, and said, 'I want to start a school in Kelior.'

"'Now?' Isham demanded. 'This city will be under siege in two days; my counselors are advising me to flee, and you want to start a school?'

"The cat had begun to scratch among the maps and papers on the table. Od lifted it off, set it among the ashes in the fireplace. 'I have an urge,' she told Isham, 'to settle for a while. My feet are tired. This city has a good heart.'

"'It's about to die,' Isham protested bitterly.

"'I'm good with things about to die,' Od said. 'If I rescue your city, will you let me start my school?'

"Isham gazed in wonder at the calm, ox-boned giant with small animals crawling up her hair and the raven on her shoulder picking fleas out of its feathers. "'If you rescue my city,' said the king, who had no hope, so he had nothing to lose, 'I will be your first student.'

"And so Od sent a powerful current upriver that sank the invading warships; she sent winds that blew the rebel armies into complete confusion, where they were lost for three seasons and only found, barefoot and starving, in the middle of winter. By then, Od had started her school, and the king, astounded by her power and craving it for himself, was the first student to pass under the cobbler's shoe to learn magic."

The students glanced at one another. The detail never failed to prod a question out of someone.

"What cobbler's shoe?" asked a young man with golden hair and a supercilious expression very like his father's. "We came through the main gate. I don't remember passing under a shoe."

"Then you didn't," Yar answered briskly, and cocked a brow at the others. "Anyone? No one? You'd remember if you did."

"But what does it mean, Master Yar?"

"In those early days, Od began her school in an old shop a cobbler had abandoned when he fled the city out of fear of war. Isham, though he had no talent for magic, left his pride at the cobbler's door out of gratitude and a keen desire to try to learn what Od knew. So, you can see, from the very beginning there was that strong bond between wizard and ruler which strengthened through the centuries until Od's school became, in Cronan's reign, part of the king's palace. 'To pass under the cobbler's shoe' for most students is simply an expression, meaning that because of your talents or your potential you have been accepted into Od's school."

A girl with the shining black hair and pale skin of a northerly realm was gazing at him out of narrowed green eyes. "You passed under the shoe," she said abruptly.

Yar's mouth crooked wryly. "I was too poor to get in through the gates. That's another meaning."

"And there's still another meaning," she insisted. She did not say what; she waited for him to explain himself. But he did not care to. The lesson was about Od, and the adventures of that young man who Yar had been seemed very long ago.

"Od," he prompted. "Think Od."

"But you—"

"That's a story for another day."

"But—"

"Is Od still alive?" someone interrupted. "I mean now, not

nineteen years ago. If no one sees her, how does anyone know?"

"She makes herself known now and then," Yar answered nebulously, not wanting to reveal news of Od's latest appearance to the students before Wye told the other teachers. "You'd think she'd be dead and buried by now, yes. But as soon as we assume that, we get a visit from her, or from someone who has seen her, or we are sent a new piece of writing, describing a strange land she is wandering through and the remarkable animals she has discovered there."

"In what land did she study," a young man descended from warriors asked shrewdly, "to learn how to rout an army?"

"She taught herself."

"She never went to school?"

"She never mentioned one. About breaking the siege of Kelior, she only wrote that she had never attacked an army before; she had no interest in war, but reflecting upon Kelior's plight, she saw how wind and water might be useful weapons."

"But the power itself," the young man persisted, his eyes alight with possibilities. "Where did she get such power?"

"That, she must have been born with. I doubt that we'll ever know the extent of those powers, since she mostly uses them on ailing animals."

"Will we be taught that?"

"I assume you mean warfare, not healing a crippled magpie," Yar said mildly, stifling his weariness for the subject, which came up as regularly as the gates opened to new students. "If you have a gift for wizardly warfare, believe me it will come under the sharp scrutiny of the king and his counselors. You will be taught how best to use your powers for

Numis. You will never leave Numis to go roaming out of curiosity and wonder, as Od does. You will be considered too valuable a weapon. If you are permitted to leave, it will be to fight Numis's battles. If you go without the king's permission, you will be considered a traitor, a renegade, an enemy, and the wizard who tracks you down and rids Numis of the threat of you will be rewarded." He smiled a little, thinly. "So be careful what you wish for. The rulers of Numis have never forgotten how close Isham came to losing the realm, and they have learned to see enemies everywhere. Even within the walls of this school."

The warrior's son only shrugged slightly, undaunted. "If I had such power, why wouldn't I use it for Numis? I would want to use it for someone. I don't understand how Od could discover how to wield the wind like a weapon and not want to do it again."

"The kings have let Od roam," another student commented. "They aren't afraid that she'll use her powers to attack Numis in the service of another king."

Yar nodded. "It's a subtle distinction. She proved her loyalty and friendship to Numis by rescuing Kelior and by keeping her school here. No one wants to risk offending her by trying to restrict her freedom. She might just laugh and vanish out of Numis forever. Then the rulers of Numis would have to look for her behind every threat to its borders."

"I don't want to become a weapon," a young woman said aggrievedly. Her voice held the lilt of a neighboring kingdom. "Master Yar, aren't there other magics in wind and water besides death?"

"Oh, there are," Yar said, relieved to get out of the bottomless quagmire of power and politics. "There are, indeed.

Let's adjourn to the library to see what Od herself has written about that."

He led them down from the great central tower in which he taught and lived in comfortable chambers overlooking the busy complex of rooftops, arches, parapet walls, buttresses, turrets, huge glass domes, gardens perched on high flat roofs above the city to catch the light. Yar could see very easily into the private gardens of the royal household. But as King Galin pointed out, it was futile to try to keep anything private from wizards. That worked both ways, Yar had learned early in his years there. The king kept a close eye on the school, which rulers of Numis had come to regard as highly and as jealously as their private coffers. Whether it was a flaw of innocence or of ambition in Od's character to have placed her school in the shadow of the king's house, nobody knew for certain. After several centuries the wizards had stopped arguing about it, so not to offend the king in whose house they had somehow come to dwell.

Yar left his students under the eye of the librarian, who was gathering Od's fragile scrolls and letters off the shelves for them to decipher. He was about to take the quickest way up to the rooftop gardens to warn the new gardener of an impending invasion of students, when a vague form intruded, disturbing his concentration before he could vanish. He gathered himself together again, blinked the world back into view, and found Valoren Greye in his way.

Yar was not surprised. The formidable young wizard, a former student recently raised to the position of king's counselor, seemed to be everywhere at once when new students entered the school. He was the nearest King Galin had to eyes in the back of his head, and took his responsibilities with what Yar considered an inordinate amount of zeal.

Yar, who could remember a time years earlier when Valoren knew how to smile, regarded the lean, somber, butterhaired counselor quizzically. "What is it?"

"I've been asked by the king to cast an eye over the new students, begin to get to know them, so that if problems arise, we'll be aware of them early."

Yar nodded briefly, understanding the problems to be anything that ultimately might threaten the crown on Galin's head. "I haven't seen any."

"You weren't looking for them."

"No," Yar agreed, reining in a flash of annoyance. "But after nineteen years here I have learned to recognize a few things on the first day."

Valoren absorbed that without comment, continued gravely, "I thought it would be simplest if I came to one of your classes, listened to your students. You, of course, would be aware of my presence."

Yar sighed noiselessly. "They're in the library now. After that, I'm taking them up to the gardens. Many of them are so well brought up they have no idea where a pea has been before they find it on their plates, or that a weed growing out of the midden can cure what ails them."

Valoren's eyes, almost as pale as his hair, contemplated that dispassionately; he commented, "They would not reveal much of themselves in either place. After that?"

"After that to the labyrinth, then to the royal menagerie. They'll come back to my chambers after the midday meal, where I'll give them some idea of what they'll be taught for the next few years and what they might be expected to do with it."

Valoren gave a slight nod. "Good. I'll be there, then."

He turned; Yar watched him narrowly a moment, wondering if the brilliant, humorless Valoren was the culmination of everything he had been taught at Od's school, or if he would have grown that way, anyway. Coming to no conclusion, he made his way up, with a thought and a step, to the gardens, where the new gardener, potting bulbs to bloom in the spring, nearly reeled off the roof at the sight of him.

"I'm sorry," Yar said quickly. "I wasn't thinking."

Brenden drew an unsteady breath and let go of the roof wall. "I'm not used to magic."

Nor to heights, Yar suspected. The city swirled endlessly about them to the edge of the world, it seemed. Yar wondered if the young man could see as far as the home he had left. Something in the bleak eyes told him no: he was too far from everything he had known.

"I came to warn you that I will be bringing students up here this morning. Only a few," he assured Brenden, who looked alarmed at the thought of having to explain something. "A dozen or so. You can ignore them. I know enough to show them the difference between balm and rue."

Memory melted across the young man's taut face. "It takes living to know that," he said tersely. "Not magic."

Yar nodded. "Magic," he answered wryly, "is how you use what, in spite of all your good intentions, you learn."

The gardener mulled that over. "That's fair. Most of the time you don't intend. Life just happens. And there's no way around it."

Yar was silent, curious. Curiosity led his thoughts astray; they brushed the memory the young man had opened: a moment when something shapeless, unwieldy, and enormously powerful in him had roused itself and revealed its face.

Startled, Yar's thoughts scattered. He found the gardener's eyes on him, heard himself say as if to something wild, "If you can't bear the stone walls here, tell us before you leave."

"I think," Brenden said tentatively, "it will be all right. For the while."

Yar returned to his students. He took them under the school to see the labyrinth, and up to the rooftop gardens and greenhouses, and to the king's menagerie in the royal gardens, from which the teachers borrowed when they needed an animal to make a point. In the labyrinth he watched their faces, anticipating which students might require rescuing from their curiosity in the middle of the night.

At midday, he dismissed them to eat and study. He felt the summons of a calm, orderly mind, and went up into the highest tower to talk to Wye.

As usual during the day, she sat in her chambers, surrounded by books and papers, accounts, requests, letters from distant lands, sealed notes from the king. She had been at the school most of her long life. Her skin and hair were ivory, her eyes black, still and secret. Her aged face with its strong bones, which had once been beautiful, had not changed a line, Yar thought, in the nineteen years he had been at the school. After those nineteen years, he could scarcely remember the young, eager face he had worn when he walked in under the shoe.

Wye finished a word in whatever she was writing and raised her eyes. They knew each other very well; he sensed trouble immediately, an inner conflict, confusion. She returned the pen to its holder and sat back in her chair.

"Yar," she said, her voice very soft for some obscure reason, "I have come to a decision."

"Yes?"

"About the gardener." She paused, lowered her eyes, shifted a paper an inch on her table, while he waited, unenlightened. "Have you mentioned to anyone how he came to be here?"

"You mean which door he came in?"

"Under the shoe," she said, nodding. "As you did. And directed there by Od."

"No," he answered, still baffled.

"Well, don't. Not to anyone. Especially not to Ceta."

His brows went up. Ceta, in whose lovely river house he dwelled for much of the time after the sun went down, had close connections by family to Valoren and by marriage to the king's court. What she was not to know, he realized suddenly, neither was the king. His lips parted, closed again. He sat down on a corner of Wye's sturdy worktable, gazing at her questioningly.

She shifted under that gaze, but met it without blinking. "He is, after all, only a gardener," she said firmly. "The king does not interest himself with gardeners at the school. That's my business."

Yar remembered the enormous, untapped power, much of it disguised as grief and loneliness, he had sensed in the young man potting bulbs. "Is it?" he breathed, fixing her again with a bog-water eye. "Is it, indeed?"

"Od sent you here through her secret doorway, and look where it got you."

"You don't need to remind me."

"Teaching the children of the rich and powerful how to become more powerful for their king and his court."

"Perhaps that's what Od intended."

"Do you believe that?" she asked, her voice so unexpectedly wistful that he searched himself before he answered.

Memory beckoned; he walked a little way down a forgotten path, where air had taught him, and light, and dirt, and dark. He had wrested his own magic out of necessity. Dark was not an abstract on a page in a book, but something to become, to eat, to battle, to breathe, to take apart before it took him apart, and to refashion, only when he had defined it, into a word again with which he could live in peace.

"But that was a long time ago," he whispered. He saw Wye again, waiting for his answer, her eyes oddly vulnerable. He said simply, "No. I believe that I failed the powers I had. I didn't realize, as the years passed, how these walls that keep us safe and comfortable have also put such limits on our vision. We teach from the books the kings and their wizards have permitted us to keep. We teach the word for dark. We have forgotten the night."

"Brenden has not forgotten," Wye said, her voice web-thin again.

"No."

"You felt it, then. All that power."

"Yes."

"He barely knows he has it. No one need know. Od sent him here for a reason. I know what this school would make of that power. What I want to see is what he might make of himself. So."

Yar nodded. "I am mum," he promised, rising from her desk, "on the subject of shoes."

Wye picked up her pen again, paused before she dipped it. "He could use someone to talk to," she suggested. "You might look in on him now and then, when you have more time. Explain things to him if he finds the courage to ask. He might tell you more about himself."

"Why me? Why not you?"

"Because I didn't pass under the cobbler's shoe. Because he is like you."

Yar laughed softly. "Maybe once. A long time ago. But I'll do what I can."

He spent that evening, as usual, with Ceta, amusing her with the day's small incidents and the peculiar questions he had encountered. Daughter of a northern lord, Ceta had been given the house by her father upon her marriage to a noble with country estates, who preferred living near the king's court. The marriage, Ceta confessed to Yar, had been mainly one of duty; when the young noble died unexpectedly, she was not entirely bereft. She refused to marry again, using grief as her defense. Yar had met her several years before in the king's private library, where he had gone in search of a missing book of Od's and found the lovely widow, a perpetual student of history, immersed in it. Now they sat together on furs and rugs in the deep ledge of a window overlooking the river, nibbling spiced meats, pickled vegetables, olives, cheese and flat bread with their fingers. Below them on the broad river ships and boats with their lamps lit sailed serenely past on water reflecting the lavender twilight.

Behind them books and scrolls lay scattered on opulent, ancient carpets from lands whose names Yar was not entirely sure he knew how to spell. Ceta, who wrote with a clear, lucid style and researched with enthusiasm, was gaining a reputation for scholarship. The king had asked her to write a history of Od and her School of Magic, with emphasis on the influence the Kings of Numis had on its growth and renown. Yar had grown used to walking through the changing tide line of books and papers on her floor.

"I ran across a very old piece of her writing today," she told Yar, when he spoke of his students' difficulties with

Od's eccentric accounts of magic. "About some outlandish country—"

"What was she doing there?"

Ceta wrapped an errant strand of long, dark hair around her finger and brooded out the window. She was very tall, lanky; her folded legs barely fit across the ledge. One bent knee hung out the open window, attracting insects with the yellow, perfumed silk fluttering down from it. "Oh, I remember," she said abruptly. "It only sounded like some outlandish realm. She was actually traveling in Numis, but so far north that I didn't recognize the place she described. The manuscript must have traveled with her for some time. I think her mice tried to make a nest out of it."

She picked out the plumpest olive, nibbled around its seed. Yar leaned back, watching a gnat tangle itself in her drifting hair. "Is there a point," he inquired mildly, "to your tale?"

She spat the olive pit into her hand and tossed it out the window. "Only that you made me remember it. And that she bothered to write about it."

"Write what?"

"What she saw. Whatever that was. I'd never heard of it." She uncoiled her legs, slid off the ledge to her piles on the carpet. "I'll find it for you."

Yar watched her long fingers play among the scrolls. "Here it is—No. Here." She picked up a battered, rolled manuscript so stained and crumbled it was difficult to open.

"It looks," Yar murmured, "as though she sat on it."

"It is very well traveled." She brought it to him; he frowned down at the faded words growing more elusive in the deepening twilight.

"'In the shadow,'" he read haltingly, "'of Skrygard Mountain, I found them. They had no faces. Blind and mouthless, old stones, old weathered stumps. Still they saw without eyes, without words they spoke. They wait. I found a crippled owl in the snow and took her down with me.' "

"I can't imagine," Ceta interrupted, "what they might be. Do you know?"

Yar shook his head, moved by the passage, but not knowing why. "It's a haunting image. I have absolutely no idea. Did you ask Wye?"

"Yes. She suggested I ask you."

"What about your cousin Valoren?"

She shrugged lightly. "Valoren learned everything he knows at the school. If you and Wye don't know what Od is talking about, why would he? Od might have written more about them; maybe something else will turn up. It's not important. It must not be, or everyone would understand it."

"I suppose so," Yar agreed, distracted by her labyrinthine pacing among her papers. "I suppose not."

She raised her dulcet, genial voice, and called, "Shera— Lights!" Then she returned to the window, took her seat. She studied Yar as her housekeeper lit the lamps and candles, each burning reflection darkening the river behind it and drawing their faces more clearly out of the dark.

He said ruefully as a candle illumined her blue-gray eyes, "I should leave soon." Wye preferred the teachers to spend nights at the school while the new students adjusted. Some of them had terrible dreams. Others discovered gifts they never knew they had, and their experiments could be alarming. Yar had known students to lose themselves in the labyrinth, sneak into the king's menagerie, blow things up.

Ceta's long mouth slid awry again. "Ah, well . . . I have a cousin in your classes, did you know that?"

"A student?"

"Yes. Lord Tenenbros's daughter Marcia. Valoren's sister."

Yar made an ambiguous noise. Another student bound to the service of the king . . . He found Ceta's eyes on him, disconcertingly limpid.

"You disapprove."

He sighed noiselessly, spread his hands. "I have no alternatives to offer. The very walls of the school are owned by the rulers of Numis. Why should they not train wizards to their own advantage?"

"Why not?" she asked him, genuinely puzzled. "You offer no alternatives, but sometimes I think you see them. Or you think you do. Are you getting restless in your comfortable life?"

"Perhaps."

"Then perhaps you should leave teaching for a while and offer your own services to the nobles of Numis." He did not answer; she added after a moment, "Have I offended you?"

"I was thinking thoughts of insurrection."

She laughed, but breathlessly; her hand went out as though to cover his mouth. "Don't. Not even in jest. Anyone would think you've been spending time in the unruly Twilight Quarter."

He put his hand on her ankle, toyed with the thin gold chain around it. "Is the Twilight Quarter still unruly? I haven't been there for years. Not even to retrieve a student exploring the delights of the forbidden. Students have grown so cautious, these days; they never do anything wrong anymore."

"Why should they? They are expelled if they are caught in that quarter."

"I wasn't expelled."

"You weren't caught."

His thoughts strayed from his own past to the gardener, with all that unruly power kept in check only by ignorance.

"What is it?" he heard Ceta ask.

"Nothing. A student crossed my mind."

"Oh." She rose, calling again, lightly, "Shera!" as she took a candle in one hand, and his hand in her other, tugging him into her flowing wake of scent and silk.

Walking back to the school later, down the street that followed the broad river until an ancient wall sent the street curving away from the enclosed Twilight Quarter and uphill toward the Royal Quarter, Yar chanced upon a second marvel.

There was a confusing roil of activity around the Twilight Gate, an archway through the thick wall which led to the upside-down world within. The peculiar quarter slept by day and lived by night; there was always a flow of traffic in and out of the gate from moonrise to dawn. But this train of bulky wagons strung with odd lights, drawn by oxen with ribbons on their horns, seemed unusual, surrounded as it was by jugglers tossing what looked like falling stars and crescent moons, by drummers and pipers creating a fanfare for the wagons, elaborately costumed riders on horseback patiently following the slow carts. Performers, Yar thought as he passed them, and wondered how far they had come.

A swirl of color caught his eye. A woman rode past him, and he stopped. She seemed surrounded by coils of light, his confused eyes told him. Then he amended that to streams of finest silk, flowing from her wrists and hair and ankles, held by various figures in voluminous skirts who spun, now and then, forming circles as round as the moon with their skirts, as the streamers of silk in their hands fashioned their own dance around the rider.

She turned a little in her saddle to look back at Yar. Her exquisite face seemed real and unreal at once: a porcelain mask, or skin so pale she might have been kin to the moon. Her eyes caught torchlight, blazed a warm, lucent amber, then faded dark as eyeholes in a mask. Her hair, a long, rippling flow behind her, seemed to have caught the jugglers' stars in it like a great, dark net.

What are you? he thought amazedly.

She turned her face away from him at the question. He stood there watching the swirls of light and shadow weaving around her until she passed into the shadow of the gate and he could move again.

THREE

Arneth Pyt sat surrounded by cold, white, windowless marble walls in his quarter warden's chamber; he was staring at a list of street wardens on duty that night and wishing he were one of them. On a side wall, an ancestor of the king's, fully dressed in armor and looking as though something had bitten him under his cuisse, glowered moodily down at Arneth. Through the partially open door, he could see his efficient secretary attending to paperwork before he passed it along for Arneth's signature. The chamber was one of many in the High Warden's domain, a huge, drafty, charmless building adjoined by various routes, some secret, to the king's palace. It was dead quiet, except for the rustle of paper in the next room. Arneth heard himself yawn, stifled the sound. He cracked a knuckle, stopped that as well. Slowly, with infinite care, he dipped pen in an ornate inkstand and affixed his name to the list of night wardens for the Twilight Quarter. He set it to one side on the vast, gleaming slab of polished wood he had been given for his official duties. He wondered what to do next.

He was a tall, muscular man with his mother's yellow hair and his father's green eyes, without their chilly sheen. His father, Murat Pyt, had worked his way with great energy and ambition from street warden to quarter warden of the Ports, and then of the Royal Quarter. He achieved his lifelong goal of High Warden about the time Arneth took to the streets himself. The rank of High Warden carried a title with it, which caused Murat Pyt much satisfaction with himself and sudden dissatisfaction with his son, who seemed content to be a street warden for the rest of his life. For several years he had badgered Arneth to take a more prestigious post that would reflect his father's glory. But Arneth liked his work. He was skilled in arms, intelligent, and he liked to challenge his muscles and his wits in the streets of Kelior. Frustrated, Lord Pyt put him in the Twilight Quarter, hoping that the strange hours and eccentric demands of that enclosed world would cause him to quit the streets and take up an occupation more appropriate to the High Warden's status. But Arneth found the quarter fascinating. Finally, Lord Pyt stumbled upon the only solution to his exasperating son. He promoted Arneth, rewarding his years of service with marble walls, a secretary to do his work, and the respectable title of quarter warden of the Twilight Quarter.

Arneth had never been so bored in his life.

He was pondering the question of what he would do with his life if he simply walked out of his position and kept walking, when his secretary passed along an urgent summons from the High Warden. Arneth wondered if his father had heard his thoughts. He went down several halls, up endless stairways to Lord Pyt's chambers, where he found his father pacing, under the opaque, honey-colored eyes of the king's newest counselor, Valoren Greye.

Arneth had met the young wizard once before and found him disconcerting. His father, Lord Tenenbros, had a craggy castle somewhere in the north country; the boggy hinterlands might explain his heir's damp temperament. He had spent much of his life refining his powers according to the exacting standards of the School of Magic; his reputation had preceded him to court and easily caught the interest of the king.

"My son, Arneth Pyt," Murat intoned, in case the wizard had forgotten. "Quarter warden of the quarter in question."

Valoren nodded, with no more expression than an owl. He was thin, slightly stooped; his light hair hung limply around his face. "I remember you," he said, giving Arneth an unsettling impression that he remembered everything he saw, and saw what everyone else missed.

"What's the question?" Arneth asked, settling onto a corner of Murat's desk. The High Warden glared; he removed himself hastily.

"The question," Valoren said in his quiet, even voice, "is the magician Tyramin, who entered the Twilight Quarter two nights ago."

"Tyramin." The name sounded familiar, but he could not remember why.

"He was rumored to be in south Numis last spring," Murat reminded him.

"And before that, in the west," Valoren added.

Arneth nodded, enlightened. "Rumors of Tyramin," he said. "I heard them several times on the streets of the Twilight Quarter. So, is he actually here? Or is it another rumor?"

"He was seen," the wizard said impassively, "entering Kelior. I have informed the king."

"What for? He's a trickster. A performer. He pulls paper flowers out of his sleeves. Doesn't he?"

The wizard fixed Arneth with an unblinking gaze. "Does he?"

"So I heard. When he was simply a rumor."

"What else have you heard?"

Arneth thought. "Not much. That he was born in a distant land. Also that he was born here."

"In Kelior?"

"In the Twilight Quarter."

Murat Pyt tapped his desk with the stone of his ring of office, as murkily green as his eyes. He was a hale, powerful man, utterly devoid of humor, whose hooked profile reminded Arneth of the paper crescent moons with painted faces on sticks sold in the Twilight Quarter. "Is that so?" he asked Arneth. "How could such magic be born in Kelior?"

"It's not real magic," Arneth suggested. "So I've heard. Just tricks, illusions. So they say."

"They," Valoren echoed softly, his eyes distant now, his thoughts indrawn. "I have been hearing about Tyramin for years. He is here, he is there, maybe working magic, maybe not. Maybe in Numis, maybe not. He attracts great, unruly crowds. Some say he teaches magic unlawfully and incites mischief. Others say he is simply a trickster, earning his living by creating illusions. He has come with his ambiguities into Kelior. The king is concerned. The High Warden says you know the streets of the Twilight Quarter as well as anyone and that he trusts your judgment. I want to know what it might take to arrest Tyramin if need arises: a single street warden or the entire School of Magic. Can you find out?"

"I don't know anything about magic," Arneth said simply. "I only know that in the Twilight Quarter everything can seem possible. Maybe a wizard would be a better judge of Tyramin."

"Perhaps. But Tyramin might possess the power to conceal from a wizard what he would not bother to hide from you. His first performance will be tonight. So rumor has it, at least. Go to it. Use your discretion. See what you can see. I want to know if Tyramin is any threat to the king, to Kelior, or to Kelior's wizards."

Arneth nodded, then looked at the High Warden, who seemed torn between annoyance at having to let Arneth loose again on the streets and pride that he alone had been chosen to do this secret task for the king. "I see I must release you from your duties as quarter warden," Lord Pyt said ponderously, and added with emphasis, "Temporarily."

"Yes, Father."

"Don't call me that here," his father said irritably.

"Sorry. Yes, sir."

He returned to his office, told his secretary to do without him for a while. He signed a few papers the secretary thrust hastily under his nose. After some thought, Arneth went home, changed his clothes, then rode alone into the oldest section of Kelior to pursue the rumor of magic.

The Twilight Quarter was so named because during the brightest hours of the day it barely stirred; it only came to life as the sun sank. Then doors were unlocked, windows opened; odd shops without names lit their lamps; people spilled into the streets. Smells of meat and onions sizzling on flames, freshly baked bread, kettles of hot soup mingled with the market scents of fruits and animals and exotic spices. Stalls as solitary as closed tents during the day rolled up a wall to show bolts of cloth, toys, tools, jewels. Jugglers tossed flames; fortune-tellers spread their bright scarves, their cards and crystals. Idlers threw dice and pitched knives; great puppets strode the streets on stilts, enacted stories for a coin. Oil lamps and torches cast an illusion of day. Light plunged too easily and without warning into shadow, where things disturbing in their vagueness might or might not happen.

Arneth could unravel that tangle of streets better than most, for during his years as a street warden he had ridden them many times. But he had not been there since he had risen to his new position; he had to scour memory as well as trust to instinct, for things changed constantly in that night world. Shops vanished; street signs disappeared; taverns turned into tanneries, houses into warehouses. Only the twisting labyrinth of the streets remained, demanding at every juncture: right or left? That night he had a truer guide than memory. Rumor traveled with him; he heard Tyramin's name at every turn.

He stopped at random to ask where Tyramin would appear. Everyone told him, with great certainty, something different. He followed a few people bound for Tyramin's Illusions and Enchantments, as the magician called it. He lost them at a noisy branch of streets; all went off in contrary directions. He found another group shrugging through the crowd and fell in with them easily, for he had met several of them at court events, which his father assiduously attended. They recognized him, hailed him cheerfully. They were the richly dressed scions of Galin's court, young men and women adventuring in the Twilight Quarter, like Arneth, following the rumors of magic.

He confessed to the same aim; he was elegantly dressed in dark silk and leather, nothing to mark him as a warden, make those he questioned wary of him. Everyone was used to the wealthy out for amusement, riding or wandering on foot through those streets. In high, shuttered rooms with ornate balconies overlooking the river, mischief happened; as a street warden, Arneth sometimes had to pay attention to it. That night, though, as he bantered with the idle rich, disguised as one of them, nothing about him suggested that he was looking for trouble.

Seeming only curious and vaguely bewildered, he demanded details. "Does the street we're looking for have a name?"

That caused gusts of amusement, both from acquaintances and passersby. A puppet on a pair of stilts, whose huge head with its mountainous cheekbones and nose hooked toward its chin reminded him of his father, turned precariously toward him, shouting, "Looking for Tyramin, are you?"

"How do you know?" Arneth asked, amazed, and repeated the question to the further amusement of the street. "How did he know that?"

"Everybody is, love," an old woman roasting beef on skewers called up to him. She waved a dripping skewer. "Go that way."

Laughing, they followed the direction of the skewer, found another eddy of streets, crowds around a pair of dancers wearing delicate, rigid porcelain masks and spinning voluminous satin skirts into perfect circles. Arneth guided his horse carefully, seemingly oblivious to the crowd while he continued his questions, pitching them to fall anywhere.

"But is he truly a sorcerer? I've heard it both ways."

"Yes and no," someone shouted back at him, and bowed deeply as Arneth's eye fell on him. "Your Lordship. There you have it, both ways."

"He does and he doesn't," one of the young courtiers said, holding Arneth's stirrup to keep himself upright. "Tyramin only pretends. Don't believe anything you see. This is the Twilight Quarter."

The dancers' skirts ignited suddenly, spinning wheels of colored fire. Arneth reined his horse, blinking. The courtier reeled against his leg, laughing again.

"Magic," he shouted. The dancers were suddenly motionless, skirts swirling, settling; sparks swarmed like iridescent insects up into the night and faded. "Not magic."

"But where," Arneth said, urging his horse forward and pulling the courtier off-balance again, "does he come from, this Tyramin?"

"Nowhere," his chorus chanted. "Everywhere."

"Everyone comes from somewhere. Even magicians. He wasn't hatched out of an egg in midair."

An egg flew into the air out of the crowd, snagging eyes. It broke apart; a crow flew out of it, fluttered above, scolding raucously, before it turned into a drift of smoke. For a moment the street was almost silent.

Then someone shouted, "Tyramin!"

The crowd broke apart, pursuing the hint of magic. Arneth tried to ride with it, but it went too many directions, dragging the courtiers with it down some side street or another. Stranded in the nearly empty juncture where several streets ended or began at random, he waited for noise, a sign, a sudden flash of colored lightning to indicate his way. A porcelain face caught his eye: one of the dancers, staring at him across the emptiness. She raised a graceful hand, removed the mask, revealed a white, rigid, delicate face beneath it exactly like the mask.

Arneth felt his own set face shift. The dancer smiled, revealing a broken tooth.

"Your eyes watch us," she called. "You forget to smile. That is the best disguise."

He smiled, and didn't even convince himself. "Where is Tyramin?" he asked.

She pointed at random, it seemed to him, but he went down that street anyway, and found himself at the ancient archway leading in and out of the quarter, the Twilight Gate.

He stopped there, rubbed his eyes, and sighed, wondering whether to turn around and lose himself again, or give up for the night and go back to work. Someone on foot passed quickly through the archway before Arneth could glimpse a face. But he recognized the dark, flowing robe, its sleeves and hood edged with silver. That robe was worn by students of the School of Magic, and it should have been seen nowhere near the forbidden quarter.

The student, he guessed, was also following the rumors of magic.

He rode back into the darkness within the arch, turned, and watched. Nothing moved in the square but shadows cast by lamps in bright rooms above, gesturing, drinking, laughing. He raised his eyes higher, saw the pale, delicate, rigid face of the moon watching him. For a moment, he stared back, challenging it to remove its mask, reveal its face.

The idea startled a genuine smile into his face. Something shifted against the wall near him; dark pulled itself from dark. While the silver-edged shadow hesitated, listening for a crowd's noises of wonder and delight, Arneth rode up to it.

He said, an instant before the tensed figure decided to run, "I am the warden of the Twilight Quarter. You should be in school studying, not sneaking around alone in these streets."

A face looked up at him, vague in the moonlight. The assurance in the student's voice surprised him; it was a young woman's and sounded more mocking than alarmed.

"If you are a quarter warden, I'm a princess. You're only a drunken idler with nothing better to do than accost women on the streets."

"You're a student of the School of Magic, and you're not allowed in this quarter."

"Leave me alone. If I scream, the Twilight Quarter will come to my rescue, and my father will let your bones molder in his foulest dungeon."

"If you scream," Arneth said calmly, "the entire quarter will know you are a student on forbidden streets, and you'll be expelled from the school. If you leave quietly, now, no one else will need to know you've been here. I'll escort you back."

She made an indecorous noise for a princess. "You will, will you? If you're a quarter warden, you're out of uniform."

"If you're a princess, so are you."

"That's my business."

"As a matter of fact, I am stone sober and working as we speak."

"You can't prove it."

Arneth shrugged, trying to see the young woman's face more clearly; the hood gave him little more than part of a nose, a chin, and a moving mouth. "I don't have to prove anything," he said. "I only have to whistle."

"And what will that prove?"

"That I can whistle up a street warden to escort you back to the school. He won't be discreet about it. He'll hand you to Wye herself. Take your pick."

Her mouth opened, closed again, pinched tight. She breathed something he couldn't hear. He guessed at it anyway.

"Tyramin? You came to see him, too?"

She peered up at him; he saw an eye then, catching a fleck of moonlight. "Is that why you're here?"

"Curiosity," he answered easily, not specifying whose.

She nodded. "Yes." She shifted slightly closer. "We could find him together, you and I. I'm not sure where I'm going, and they say these ancient streets are a maze."

"They are," Arneth agreed. "I'm not sure where to go, either. But I am absolutely certain that I'm not going anywhere in the Twilight Quarter in the company of a student of magic. I'd lose my position."

"Your position," she scoffed. "All right, then. I'll take the robe off."

"You do that, and I'll summon all the street wardens in the quarter to take you back."

She was silent; after a moment he heard her sigh. "Are you really," she asked dourly, "a quarter warden?"

"Yes. Are you really a princess?"

She stepped toward the gate without answering. He guided his horse beside her, breathing more easily once they passed through the archway, left the Twilight Quarter behind them. She walked mutely, her head lowered. The streets were quieter here, without the comfort of crowds or light except for the occasional smoking streetlamp. After a while, she raised her head; he heard her voice again.

"Whoever you are, I'm grateful for the escort."

"You can ride," he offered.

"No, thank you. I trust you only as long as both my feet are on the ground and yours are not."

"Suit yourself."

"After all, quarter wardens don't ride the streets like common street wardens when they work."

"I like street work. I meet the people of Kelior. They do far more unpredictable things than a piece of paper on a desk does."

He couldn't tell if she believed him; she only asked, "What's your name?"

"Arneth Pyt."

She said nothing to that, but her brisk steps missed half a beat. She cleared her throat. Arneth waited, but she had nothing to add to that, either. The great towers of school and palace were looming over them, high windows lit at random, making star-patterns of fire against the stars.

"I'll wait to see you safely in."

"Thank you," she said a trifle sourly.

"If I see you in the Twilight Quarter again, I'll escort you straight to Wye myself."

"You won't see me," she promised, crossing the street to the immense wrought-iron gates that led toward the main doors of the school. Arneth, on the other side, sat watching. At the gates she turned, seeming uncertain, to look back at him.

The streets and grounds were still; he saw no one, but he kept his voice low as he called, "Can you get in without trouble?"

She opened a small gate inset in the larger. "It's unlocked until midnight," she told him. "I'll be all right now."

She closed the gate, and the great moon shadows of trees swallowed her up. He rode to the corner of the iron fence, watched from there. She didn't come out again, but however it was she entered the school, it wasn't by the main doors; he never saw them open.

FOUR

Princess Sulys slipped through the trees down a side path around the school, unbuttoning the worthless robe as she walked. She hooked it over her shoulder with one finger, her straight brows drawn. Beneath it she wore a silk chemise and underskirt, both black mourning garments and not for public view. They wouldn't have caused comment in the Twilight Quarter; in that unpredictable place, the only garments that caught attention seemed to be the complete lack of them, and exactly what she had worn. She had been given the student's robe years earlier as a token of honor when she had paid her first royal visit to the school. She should have remembered the implacable rule about students venturing into that quarter. But she hadn't, and who would have guessed anyway that the High Warden's son would have spotted her before she had gotten farther than the Twilight Gate?

He would have recognized her if she had showed him her face. But she hadn't learned his name until they were nearly at the school. And he would have told someone, most certainly his father, how had had found the king's only daughter wandering alone in the dangerous, bewitching Twilight Quarter and rescued her. Lord Pyt, creature of ambition that he was, would have made certain that the tale reached her father's ear. Her father would have streamed fire from his nostrils and bellowed like a huckster; her brother would have imitated an icicle, dripping words like cold water; her aunt Fanerl would have suggested six eminently suitable young men for her to marry on the spot, all of them completely unbearable.

Her mother would have laughed.

But the king's consort had been born in a different country with, in Galin's view, a poor understanding of the complex link between power and magic. Sulys knew his speech by heart. The wizard Od had not started her school under a tree; she had stood under the roof of the King of Numis and asked permission to bring magic into Kelior. She had made her school, her knowledge, her power subject to the king. Both rulers and wizards craved power; to avoid contention and chaos one had to be bound by the other. Magic unbound was suspect, dangerous. Therefore, it was not permitted anywhere in Numis. The wizards of Numis, like its nobles, were subject to the laws of the land. All power in Numis, of magic, of law, of arms, ultimately belonged to the king.

Students were forbidden in the Twilight Quarter not because anyone seriously believed it harbored uncontrollable and suspect forms of magic unknown to the wizards of Kelior, but because rumors of such things floated constantly out of it, like seeds from a milkweed pod. An inexperienced student could get as confused as its streets by mistaking tricks for truth. It had happened several times during the school's history, most gravely during Flamin's rule, when a traveling magician and trouble monger nearly incited a students' rebellion against the king. Since then, the rule had been imposed rigorously: students of magic caught in the Twilight Quarter were expelled without appeal. Sulys was not a student and had every right to go where she wanted. But wanting to go alone and disguised into the Twilight Quarter suggested a dangerous lack of sense, as well as a puzzling desire to infuriate her father. To say nothing of the lack of decorum.

Why Arneth Pyt had not dragged her straight to Wye, she had no idea. Perhaps he showed mercy on her because she had gotten no farther than the gate. Being caught so easily, he must have felt, had made its point. She had been fortunate in that. But because their paths had crossed so inconveniently, she would have to pick another night, find another disguise, and pretend to be here and not able to be there to everyone all over again.

She had debated, as she went through the students' gate, about waiting until the quarter warden rode away and, then, sneaking back down to the Twilight Quarter. But she had no other disguise, and anyway, he showed every sign of sitting there on his horse all night, waiting for her to do just that.

She went from school grounds to royal gardens through a tiny gate nearly lost behind a cataract of vines. In the gardens white peacocks rustled their trailing plumes as she passed. She had left a sedate gown hanging on a hook inside a potting shed. She slipped it on in the dark and emerged for an innocent stroll among the rose trees. She picked one or two flowers, wandered into the palace. Because she had made it clear to everyone that she would be spending a tranquil evening with her great-grandmother, she decided to go up to the chambers high above the world and do just that.

Lady Dittany had last left her chambers a year before to bury her granddaughter. Since then she had seen no reason to leave. Indeed, she could see very little at all now with her fading eyes. The circumference of her visible world was measured by the distance that her teacup might travel around her. She spent her days in her bed or in a chair beside the fire. Sulys found her dressed in blue satin and yellowing lace, absently petting the mangy ball of fur on her lap as she chatted with her maid. They had grown old together, she and her lapdog and her faithful Beris; now they busied themselves with trying to find the most comfortable places possible in the luxurious rooms.

Dittany smiled as Sulys opened the door, though Sulys wondered how she could so quickly recognize the blur that came into the room.

"Sulys! My dear." She held up her frail hands; Sulys bent to kiss her.

"How do you know it's me, Grandmother?"

"I feel your mind like a fresh breeze. Sit down."

"I brought you —"

"Roses. You've been outside; I can smell it." She smelled the roses, then handed them to her ancient maid, who had risen to give Sulys a wobbly curtsy. "Beris and I have been reminiscing."

"I'll put these in water, my lady," Beris said, and withdrew to leave them in privacy. Sulys sat down. For a moment the ghost of her mother joined them, slight, golden-haired, and smiling on the hearth. She had taken nothing, not even the king, not even death, very seriously. Her dark-haired, dour daughter, with her weedy limbs and certain troublesome gifts felt that except for their blue eyes she had grown up to be completely unlike her mother.

Her great-grandmother said softly, as soon as she heard Beris shut a door behind her, "You didn't see him."

Sulys sat down on the plump, tapestry-covered stool beside Dittany's chair. Their heads, one dark, disheveled, the other capped with ivory braids and blue satin, inclined toward one another; they kept their voices hushed. "No. I stupidly went disguised as a student, thinking no one would notice me. I hardly took three steps beyond the gate before I was caught by a quarter warden."

"No." Her great-grandmother pushed a lace-enclosed palm against her mouth. "Were you recognized?"

"No. I pulled the hood close around my face and said I was a princess. Of course he didn't believe me."

"Who?"

"Arneth Pyt."

"Murat Pyt's son? How disagreeable."

"He escorted me back to the school, but he didn't take me to Wye. I suppose he had more important things on his mind. Like seeing Tyramin himself. I asked him to take me with him, but he refused to risk being seen with a student." She sighed, then added briskly, "Another night. Soon. I'll borrow some of Enys's clothes. Though it isn't easy trying to remember what lies I've told to whom so that nobody will come looking for me."

"They came looking tonight," Dittany told her. "Your ladies."

"Did they? What for?"

"They didn't say. I instructed Beris to say we were not to be disturbed. Beris does well at that; she pretends to be deaf until they go away."

Sulys smiled, wondering who had wanted her so urgently and why. Her father and Enys and Fanerl never bothered to climb the tower to visit the ancient Dittany; they seemed content to let Sulys see to her. Most of the time they seemed content to ignore Sulys as well, as long as she did nothing troublesome and remembered to show herself when expected. It made hiding the small mischiefs she and Dittany concocted much easier.

Little witcheries. Magic that didn't count; spells too small to be noticed by the wizards next door. So Sulys thought of those things that Dittany had been teaching her since she was small. How to summon a passing crow and give it a message, or ask it to keep an eye on something for you. How to see, in crystal or water, where someone was in the palace. How to bind a secret possession into stitchwork, so that it became invisible within the threads. How to find the odd missing ring; how to see in a candle flame what tomorrow might bring.

Sometimes they worked; sometimes they didn't. And they were all harmless, these things that Dittany had learned in the land where she was born. There, they were common as dreams, though not everyone had what Dittany called "the gift." Sulys's mother couldn't do such things; Dittany herself had half forgotten them until one day a very young Sulys had stared into a candle flame and seen great, white, plumed birds in it. They arrived the next day: white peacocks for the king's menagerie, a birthday gift from his father-in-law.

There were rumors that Tyramin had been born in her mother's country, that he, too, knew such small, secret magics. Sulys, who still missed her mother terribly, wondered if the traveling magician might have glimpsed her as he performed at her father's court. If, being of the same country, he might know how to laugh like she had, how to charm the heart.

It was a tenuous hope, but she was restless anyway, tired of her own grieving, and Dittany did not try to stop her.

"He'll be in Kelior for some time," Dittany predicted. "Magicians of such fame require a lot of baggage and travel slowly." She stroked the sleeping dog, her eyes growing filmy with memory. "I remember watching all those great wagons, all brightly painted and streaming ribbons, drawn by white oxen into my father's courtyard."

"Tyramin?"

"Long ago, on my sixteenth birthday. He picked roses out of my hair and told my fortune."

Sulys patted the fragile hand petting the dog. "Someone like him, maybe," she said gently. "Your Tyramin wouldn't still be alive and traveling now."

Dittany was silent; the cloudy eyes seemed to be trying to see through their mist. "You must be right. Someone like him. A traveling magician with his wonderful, endless bag of tricks: flowers, birds, fire, all kept in his hat or down his boot. He had a daughter, this magician, a lovely girl with ivory hair and sapphire eyes. He would turn her into fire, and then into a flock of doves . . ."

"What was your fortune?"

"That I would travel far and marry well, and have a long and interesting life."

"Magic," Sulys murmured dryly, and Dittany chuckled again.

"Of course I knew that already; what young woman doesn't see that as her fortune? And it all came true. I married the youngest son of the ruling family, and had your grandmother, who went off to marry in another country herself. When your great-grandfather died, a couple of years after your mother married Galin, she invited me to travel all the way to this country to live here with her. So." She patted the dog again, looking a little bewildered suddenly, as though wondering where her fortune had gone. "You see, he was right."

Sulys put her arms around Dittany, held her gently a moment. "It was a good fortune," she agreed.

"Well, look at me. I could be living on the streets in a—a wine barrel. I don't have my daughter or my granddaughter anymore," she added bravely. "But I have you."

"Yes. You have me." She loosed her great-grandmother. "Now what shall we do?" She looked around; her eyes were caught by melted wax rolling down a candle like a fiery tear. "Wax," she said softly, her attention tumbling down along with another tear. "Hot and cold, solid and liquid . . . a changeable thing. What spell can we make with that?"

"Nothing tonight." Dittany sighed. "Not with people wanting you. We might bumble into some wizard's magic coming up to search for you, and that would be trouble indeed. You should probably go down before they think you've gone off on your own and visiting me was just your excuse."

"I suppose you're right," Sulys said reluctantly.

"And maybe you shouldn't really wander the streets of Kelior by yourself, even dressed as your brother. Is there someone you could take with you next time?"

"I'll try to think of someone," Sulys promised, to make her great-grandmother feel better. She kissed Dittany, called Beris back, and left them with their white heads together, settling again for the evening's exchange of memories.

She got as far as the stairway. She would go down in a moment, show herself to the world again. But here it was peaceful, and no one made unpleasant demands. So she sat down on a step and thought who might accompany her to the Twilight Quarter. Not a wizard; they were all as shortsighted as her father. Not Enys, her brother, who had grown into a humorless, pompous prig since their mother had died. The quarter warden, she thought, hopeful for a moment. She would tell him the truth; he would guard her well, and he seemed to like the peculiar quarter. Then her hope slumped.

No. He would surely tell his father, and Murat Pyt would be eager to tell her father that Princess Sulys was chasing rumors of magic in the Twilight Quarter . . .

A boot intruded into her thoughts. It had stopped a couple of steps below her, black and very polished, just inside the periphery of her vision. She glowered at it; it refused to move. She gave a silent, mental sigh and raised her eyes.

"I thought I recognized that boot."

It was, as she expected, Galin's son and heir, her older brother Enys, with his first mustache creeping like a caterpillar across his upper lip. He had their mother's blue eyes, too, but his were more like chilly water than her warm sky-blue. Other than that, he looked presentable, with his father's vigorous figure and their mother's golden hair, which Sulys considered wasted on someone who had an entire kingdom to dangle in front of his suitors.

"What," he demanded peevishly, "are you doing sitting in the middle of the stairs?"

"Thinking," she answered coldly. "Sorry. Am I in your way? Surely you're not going up to pay a visit to your great-grandmother?"

"Surely not," he agreed. "At the moment I'm looking for you."

She gazed at him, baffled. "You? I mean, why you? You could have sent some—" She caught her breath then and rose, impelled by a confusing gust of memory. "Is anything wrong?"

"No," he said with annoying coolness. "Our father has chosen a husband for you. We thought you'd like to know."

Sulys sat down again, hard, on the marble step. The vague whoosh of sound that came out of her could have been interpreted as a question; so Enys heard it.

"You will be happy to know that you won't even have to leave Kelior. Our father has chosen among several suitable offers, including one or two from rulers of countries east and south of Numis. But, considering the extraordinary power at the king's command in Od's school, he decided that he did not have to marry you to another land for the sake of peace."

"Enys," she said between her teeth.

"Actually, you won't even have to leave the palace."

"Enys!"

"You can't guess?" he said with a little, pleased smile.

"No!"

"Our father's newest counselor, the wizard Valoren Greye." His smile broadened at her astonished silence. "He is young; his father, Lord Tenenbros, is very wealthy, with several large holdings in the north country. Valoren was recommended by the wizards to the king for his intelligence and skill; through the past year he has proved eminently worthy of his position here. Our father was very pleased that he asked to be considered as your suitor. Of course, neither of us wanted you to leave Kelior." He waited; she still could not speak. "Surely you must be pleased."

A memory rose in her head of a young, lean, secretive face, limp pale hair, eyes the color of honeycomb, at once direct and amazingly opaque. She felt her mouth move finally, heard her own voice. "We've scarcely spoken two words . . . How should I know?"

"Well—"

"I should have gone back to the Twilight Quarter," she whispered.

"What?"

A helpless despair rose in her, that she would never see past the walls the Kings of Numis had placed around magic;

she would never know how much more, if anything, there was to know. Not only must she marry one of her father's nobles, but a wizard as well, who would not expect her, the king's daughter, to have a thought of her own in her head. Any more than he did.

"Sulys."

At least, in another country, her mother's perhaps, she might have been able to think. She met Enys's eyes finally, found them shuttered, like windows in an empty room. "Does our father want me?"

"He's waiting for you, yes. With Valoren."

"Why didn't Valoren come? Why didn't he come to me himself?"

Her brother shrugged. "It's proper, this way. He hardly knows you."

"I don't know him!"

"No. But you do know our father."

"Do I have a choice?"

"I've seen your other choices," Enys said so dryly that she stared at him again in horror. "You'd be wise to accept with as much good grace as you can muster." He added as she stumbled past him down the stairs, "He really thought you would be pleased. And if there are reasons why you're not, you should forget about them before your foot hits the next step. What our father cannot guess, Valoren will, and his first loyalty will be to the king. So forget your dreams, brush the potting soil off your skirt, and smile."

FIVE

Brenden, walking into the roof garden in the morning, was seized by an exuberant gust that tried to whirl him over the wall along with the dried, golden leaves from the garden. He smelled the northern snow in the wind. He spent the rest of the day putting the greenhouse in order for the winter. It was a complex construct, running along one wall, of stone and wood and glass panels that slid open and shut against light and weather. He pulled dead, flowering vines out of the rafters, emptied withered plants and spent soil out of the pots and stacked them, put the plants that would survive the winter on one table to be watered, set his own tentative experiments, odd seedlings and cuttings that needed an eye kept on them, together on another table. He found a dilapidated broom and swept dust and dried petals out the door. He had upended the broom and was trying to untangle a stubborn vine from a shelf bracket, when he saw an odd growth in a crusty pot at his feet. He set aside the broom and hunkered down to examine it.

It had neither eyes nor mouth, it was stuck in dirt, and it was green. By which he assumed it was probably a plant. But whether edible, medicinal, or magic, he couldn't guess. It remained mute as he gazed at it. Perhaps it had nothing to say. Or it was simply dead. Or maybe it spoke a language of such profound magic that he couldn't begin to understand it. He tried, listening for a long time until it occurred to him that there were other gardeners on the roofs, who had been at the school far longer than he, and who might be able to put a name to the peculiarity. After another time, during which he lay flat on the floor with a finger against the cool, thick flesh, and his mind an open door to whatever might enter, he gave up, brushed himself off, and went to consult the others.

They came to gaze upon it: Sisal, who grew remedies for bruises and nightmares and indigestion, and Lemley, who grew vegetables for the table. Sisal, a tall, wiry woman with long straw-colored hair, rubbed her nose on her gardening glove and produced an opinion.

"That's the ugliest plant I've ever seen."

"Don't know what it is," Lemley murmured, puffing an old pipe as he studied it. His weathered face was wrinkled like parched, cracked earth. "But I know I wouldn't eat it." He sent a miniature cloud into the air, and ventured a guess. "A mushroom, maybe?"

"I've never seen a mushroom with thorns all over it like that."

Brenden prodded the bone-dry soil in the pot. "Do you think it's still alive?"

Sisal pulled off her glove, slid a finger between the thorns to touch the smooth, thick flesh. "Maybe it stores water in it-self. Some do. The last gardener here might have brought it from her own country. Or maybe found it in a stall in the Twilight Quarter. Odd things turn up there. But which is it?" she wondered, glancing at Brenden. "Edible or medicinal or magical?"

"Might be edible," Lemley said dubiously, "but only if you'd boiled your last boot."

He looked at Brenden, too, then, through a cloud. They were expecting something, he realized, waiting for him to do something. Sisal prodded him with a question.

"Did you ask it? What it had to say for itself?"

"Oh," he said, startled; no one had ever asked him that before. "Yes. It didn't say. Or I didn't understand."

Sisal's eyes curved in a little smile. "Try again. That's what you're here for."

Brenden pondered the mystery, trying to imagine in what strange world a plant might grow thorns like fishhooks all over itself and form thick, stumpy leaves to hoard what little water came its way. Green seeped into his eyes; his mind grew vague, cloudy as it had done for hours on end when he lay in the bracken watching a new bud unfurl. He envisioned the oddity in a forest, on a moor, on top of a mountain; it seemed to belong nowhere but in its pot. So he took that dry, crumbling soil into his head and spread it everywhere under a blazing, blue-white sky. The plant spoke unexpectedly, filling his arid earth with those thorny, stumpy shapes, the only green that came out of that ground. A jagged flash of lightning ripped through his thoughts; thunder broke like a bone in his head. The hot rain pounded down. Even through the sudden storm he felt the hot light everywhere, intense and constant, air like invisible fire, igniting itself now and then in a crimson flower that balanced crazily on the highest leaf, spread itself to take in more light, more heat . . .

He felt some disturbance in the air around him, and opened his eyes to glimpse the flower growing out of his own fingers, huge and bright and already fading away as he stared.

Sisal and Lemley were staring, too. Lemley's pipe had gone out.

He broke the silence after a moment, during which the wild rain in Brenden's head died away. "Never saw anyone go that far, before. Not in forty-seven years and six gardeners of things magical."

"What—" Brenden's voice caught. "How far did I go?"

"You were in bloom," Sisal said faintly.

He looked down at himself. "Did I grow thorns?"

"No. But you were turning green, there toward the end. Does it always happen to you that way?"

"No," he said, then amended that. "I don't know. Nobody ever watched me before."

Lemley scratched an eyebrow, regarding him quizzically. "I wonder if someone should know. You might belong elsewhere. Down there among the wizards and students, not up here talking to plants."

"I came to garden," Brenden said shortly, uninterested in the noisy, bewildering world he had glimpsed within the school. "It's peaceful up here. It's where I belong."

The doubt and speculation lingered in their eyes, but they didn't argue.

Sisal just said vaguely, "Things will sort themselves out; they usually do, here. What did the plant tell you?"

He told them as best he could, not knowing the words for all he saw. "It came from an empty, rocky land, very hot and dry except when storms crack open the sky. I've never seen anything like it. No grasses, no trees, just these, everywhere."

Lemley said, enlightened, "A desert, that would be. I've heard of them."

"Sounds like," Sisal agreed. "But do we know which of us should care for it?"

"It didn't tell me that."

"The librarian might," she suggested. "Maybe there's a picture of it somewhere. Some writing about it. I'd go down there and ask. Can you find your way?"

"I think so," he answered, remembering a huge barn of a room near the stairs, books on shelves from floor to a ceiling so lofty it seemed that only magic could reach them. He was reluctant to leave the comforting solitude of the rooftops. But the other gardeners were watching expectantly; it was, so it seemed, part of his job. He consigned the thorny riddle to memory and went to find an answer.

The hallways and stairs seemed as crowded as the city streets with students, all moving in the same direction with the single-mindedness of fish going upriver to spawn. Brenden, caught in their swarm, felt invisible. Most were richly dressed, highborn sons and daughters of powerful families. They spoke in low, dispassionate voices; their eyes no longer saw gardeners with dirt under their nails and boots that had walked across half a kingdom. He smelled what drew them: their supper, a portion of which would make its way eventually up to the gardeners. He saw a dark teacher's robe here and there, wizards keeping an eye on the elegant students who had shed their own robes at the end of the day.

Once the entire descending flow was brought to a halt when a prism in a chandelier caught fire and exploded in a hard, glittering shower of glass.

A deep voice, booming eerily off the walls, demanded, "Who did that?"

Out of the sudden silence, another voice rose, apologetic, but not, to Brenden's ear, remorseful. "Sorry, Master Balius. It was a bet. I was sure I couldn't do it."

"Who are you?"

"I'm Elver."

"Who?"

"Elver. I only just got here."

Master Balius, standing on the stairs near Brenden, raised his arm above the crowd. He was a tall, gray man with lines of perpetual severity etched deeply beside his mouth. "Well, Master Elver-who-only-just-got-here, walk with me while I teach you a few of the rules of this school, which, if you break as carelessly as you did that prism, will send you back out whatever door you came in."

There was a ripple through the bodies halted on the landing below. Movement began again, haltingly, after the ripple had climbed halfway up the stairs to join Master Balius. The teacher, declaiming rigorously through the clamor, was slowed by the weight of his words; Brenden, following, saw students flowing around the pair on both sides. After a moment or two, the students began bumping into the dark-haired young man being lectured. They would draw back in confusion, pat the air around him as though they couldn't see what obstructed them. Cautiously, their faces puzzled, they would give him a wide berth as they passed. The young man, seeming to listen gravely to Master Balius, paid no attention to the jostling and bumping.

Brenden, passing him, glanced at him curiously. He looked younger by a few years than most of the students; his clothes were plain and serviceable, neither patched nor ornate. He raised his head as Brenden went by, met his eyes; his own grew large, then flashed a smile at the gardener. Another student bumped him then, nearly sending him off the step. Master Balius broke off midlecture to gaze at him.

"Elver!" he snapped. "For very good reasons, such as this, only students at the highest level are permitted to use spells of invisibility."

"Sorry, Master Balius," Elver said meekly. "I didn't know."

"Don't just stand there invisible!"

"Sorry."

Brenden stood there, blinking a moment; someone jostled him from behind, and he moved again. On the main floor, he let the students stream one way while he went another, toward where he thought he remembered seeing the library. It wasn't there. The school quieted while he wandered, peering through doors at random. The halls emptied. Finally, he saw a likely pair of double doors, massive and ornate. He opened them. A great many faces glanced his direction, all busily chewing as he froze, startled, in the doorway.

Backing abruptly, he smacked into someone too close on his heels.

"Sorry," he stammered, appalled, and wondering if he would have to send the stranger to Sisal, for he had one hand against his nose, which had collided with the back of Brenden's head.

"What are you doing?" the man demanded stuffily through his fingers. He was tall and thin, with lank pale hair and eyes not much darker than his hair. Those eyes, the color of beeswax, pinned Brenden motionless with their strangeness.

"I was—I was looking for the library."

"Were you." The young man's voice sounded oddly remote, as though his thoughts had suddenly veered away from his pain. He dropped his hand; to his relief, Brenden saw no blood. He studied Brenden much as Brenden had studied the outlandish plant. "Who are you?"

"I'm a—I'm the new gardener."

"Which one?"

"Brenden. Brenden Vetch."

"I mean, are you turnips? Or foxglove?"

"Neither. I'm the third gardener."

"Indeed." He was a wizard, Brenden realized suddenly. He had a look in his eyes of standing guard over a closed door to a windowless room that might contain enormous treasure, or total chaos, or something completely unnameable that should never see the light of day. He came to a decision about Brenden; he seemed to take a step closer to him without moving. "Maybe you could help me. I need a gift. Something unusual. Perhaps with a touch of magic in it. Might you have something like that in your garden?"

"I might," Brenden answered, picking his words carefully under the disquieting gaze. "But I might not know it. I'm not used to recognizing magic when I see it. You'll have to look for yourself."

"You see it in me," the young man said softly. "You just told me so."

Brenden was silent, puzzled without knowing why by this lanky, dour young wizard. "Are you a teacher?" he asked finally.

"No. My name is Valoren Greye. I am one of King Galin's counselors. My father is Lord Tenenbros. You may recognize the name, being of the north country yourself, I would guess."

"The name blew through our village now and then. I never saw a face to put with it."

"Was this what brought you so far from home? You were drawn by the magic?"

"No. I didn't know this place existed. I was asked to come."

"Then you must be very skilled at what you do, for rumors of you to have reached as far as Kelior." He paused; a flush appeared along his sallow cheekbones, which he explained in the next breath. "I want a gift for Princess Sulys. We are to be married. The papers have been drawn up, and will be signed in a ceremony tomorrow morning. I want some small token to give her when we are formally bound. Something other than roses from her father's gardens."

Brenden nodded again, enlightened but at a loss. "You'd best come up with me and choose for yourself. If I can find my way back."

"I know the way."

He followed the wizard Valoren, watched him gaze curiously out of those light, secret eyes at everything he passed. Everyone else seemed to be at supper; they met no one Brenden recognized, only a student or two hurrying through the halls. Valoren scrutinized them as well, as though storing their faces somewhere behind his eyes for future reference.

In the hothouses and greenhouses, he applied his keen attention to the plants. Some were still in flower, cascading veils of tiny white and purple blossoms; others bloomed the vibrant colors of the season's dying leaves. The wizard sniffed them, asked a question now and then.

"What's this good for?"

"It helps you see in the dark."

"And these?"

"I watched for them when I made my way through the bogs. The ground around them was always solid."

The wizard grunted softly. "Have you any bog lilies? I remember them from home. The golden ones that smell like cinnamon."

"Only bulbs. None in flower."

"Of course, they always bloom in early spring. Pity. What magic is there in them?"

Brenden hesitated, shrugged slightly. "Nothing I know of. I just brought them to remind me of home."

"The magic of memory . . ." Valoren stopped in front of the nameless plant, snagged, it seemed, by the thorns. "Does this bloom?"

"Yes."

"Is the flower grotesque as well?"

"No. It's beautiful."

"What is it called?"

"I don't know. I only just noticed it today."

The wizard's eyes moved from the strange plant to focus on him. "Then how do you know it blooms?"

"I saw—I—" He stopped, under the wide, intent gaze, drew breath and began again. "It spoke. It showed me. That's how I know what plants might be good for. Or not."

"Who taught you to do that? See into plants?"

"No one."

"No one?" Valoren echoed incredulously.

"Well, no one ever told me that plants couldn't speak and that I couldn't see what they said. It was something I just did."

"What other things did you find you could just do?"

"Nothing. I'm just good with plants."

"And so someone from the school heard about you and came to invite you here." He ran his finger down a thorn, and then again, as though, Brenden thought, he were stroking it. "How strange this is. As though it grows thorns to protect itself against something. Or to catch something out of the wind. How do gardeners get found for this place? I never thought about it before. I remember the last gardener dealing with plants pertaining to magic. She was here for many years. Did she go searching for her replacement before she left?"

"I don't know."

"Well, who came to find you, so far away in the north country?"

"Od."

The wizard's hand snagged on the thorn, jerked. He stared at Brenden, shaking a drop of blood from his finger. "Od found you?"

"She came to me in my garden, asked me to work at her school in Kelior. You should take that cut to Sisal," he added uneasily. "The plant may be poisonous."

"When?"

"Last spring. I told her I would come down at summer's end."

"Through which door?"

"What?"

"Which door did you enter?"

"The door under the shoe. Why?" he asked, wary again under the impenetrable gaze. "Did I do something wrong?"

"I don't know." He made a visible effort, hid the power in his eyes away again, inside the windowless room. "It's like that plant," he said more easily. "An oddity. A riddle. Maybe useful, maybe not. We need to know more about it, to answer those questions. Much, much more."

"I was looking for the library to find out more when I bumped into you."

"The library is on another floor entirely."

"I got lost."

"Yet you found your way to the cobbler's door," the wizard murmured. "Strange." He turned abruptly. "I must go. I was on my way to speak to the teachers at supper when you brought yourself to my attention."

"Wait." The urgency in Brenden's voice caught the wizard as the thorn had, checked his precipitous movement. Brenden searched among his vials, found a salve for simple cuts, and applied it to the wounded finger as Valoren watched speechlessly. "Best to be safe," he said tersely. "I learned that the hard way. If it doesn't heal, take it to Sisal." He corked the vial, then picked up a pot half-hidden behind a mound of flowering vine. The flower that bloomed upon the single stalk was large, striped red and white, star-shaped. He offered it to Valoren. "The princess might like this lily. If it has magical properties, I can't see them yet. Its magic might lie only in its beauty."

"Thank you," said the wizard, settling it absently under one arm. His eyes never left Brenden, who wondered, when he had gone, if he had even looked at the gift he was bringing to his betrothed.

Brenden's supper came searching for him then, through two greenhouses and the hothouse before the servant found him. He ate it outside on the roof, so that he could watch the stars find their way out of the dark, reflecting the glimmering of the city's lights. They were all he had of home, those familiar patterns above his head. His eyes slipped away from them finally, into the streets, the torchlights and smoky lamps forming other patterns in the dark. Was Meryd down there among them? he wondered. When she had run away from him, had she run all the way to Kelior? He doubted it, but the idea comforted him: that among all those strangers might be one familiar face, eyes that recognized him, a voice that said his name before he spoke. And Jode. Was he behind one of those fire-washed windows, sitting silently over his ale, thinking of home?

The thought made Brenden edgy, that all three might be in Kelior, and none of them knowing the others were there. He would ask Wye or Yar if he might take some time to explore the city, during those golden autumn days before the winter bit at everyone's heels and whined at the closed doors. He couldn't get lost; the king's high towers overshadowed everything in the city.

He made another effort to find the library when he finished his supper. The halls were as quiet as before; the students all seemed to be shut away, studying or making magic, or whatever they did in the evenings. He tried to imagine making magic, got as far as a memory of Od with the lizard clinging to her ear, the one-legged raven perched on her shoulder. That had seemed more in the realm of kindness than magic. But there was Od's door beneath the shoe that appeared and disappeared . . . How could anyone possibly learn to do that?

He came across a young teacher, got precise directions, and found the library on the floor above his head. The thin, gray-haired man on a ladder putting books away on the endless shelves summoned the visitor with a crook of bony fingers. He leaned down, balancing adroitly on the rungs and listening carefully to the gardener's question.

"Plants, is it, you want? Magical? Medicinal? Edible? Poisonous?"

"I'm not sure."

"Tree? Herb? Wild? Cultivated?"

Brenden shook his head helplessly. The librarian held up his finger, finished shelving the last hefty tome, which exuded a puff of dry parchment and dust as it slid into place. Then he came all the way down to the last rung, stood there, angled as comfortably against the ladder as if he lived there.

"Can you describe it to me?' he asked, looking with his sharp nose and flyaway hair like a curious and friendly bird.

Brenden did the best he could. The librarian stepped onto the floor and vanished into the shadows of the great shelves looming all around them, some so high they obscured parts of the lovely colored panes inset along the back wall. Brenden waited; the librarian returned finally with an armload of books.

"Try these."

He put them on a table. Brenden sat for a long time, looking at page after page of sketches and paintings of plants, most from parts of the world he had never heard of. Fascinated by all that he didn't know, he scarcely noticed the students and teachers who came and left, the candles that melted into stubs and flickered out, the shadows that gathered around him. Finally, the librarian drew him out of distant forests, elaborate gardens, the bewildering jungles of beauty and knowledge that existed beyond his experience. He saw then how dim the library had grown: a brace of candles at his elbow, the taper in the librarian's hand all that was left of light.

"Did you find it?" the librarian asked.

"No."

"Well. I have no more books to show you. But." He leaned a bit closer, as though the shadows might be listening. "You're neither student nor teacher, so I can suggest this to you. Ask in the Twilight Quarter. Strange things from the trade ships find their way there constantly. The last gardener often brought back peculiar plants from the quarter. Perhaps that is one of them."

"The Twilight Quarter."

"Not far, just keep going downhill to the gate in the wall where the road curves to follow the river. The quarter sleeps by day and begins to wake at twilight. It's the place you go to see the things that don't quite meet the eye."

"Magic?" Brenden guessed.

The librarian shrugged. "Who knows?" he said, and handed Brenden a candle to find his way. "See for yourself."

SIX

In the Twilight Quarter, the magician's beautiful daughter threaded her needle with a filament the color of blood. She knotted it, picked up a length of silk so light it fluttered at a breath, and began to turn a hem in a dangling edge. Illumined by fire and enchantment when Tyramin amused the crowds with his tricks, her bones were long and delicate, her body without a graceless movement. Her hair, a cloud of rippling black, glittered with the star fire of jewels and its own sheen; her eyes hinted of visions, wonders trapped within the warm amber. Such beauty transformed easily into doves, colored fires, into air itself and never changed, not even in the curve of her smile, when she became herself again.

In less deceptive light, such as the oil lamps she had lit for sewing, she became transformed again. Short and slight, with reddened knuckles and calloused feet, her hair ruthlessly tied back and braided, shadows and faint lines under her eyes from nights turned into days, she could, and often did, go about her business unrecognized. Only the great, golden eyes, the lovely, oval face, hinted to the bleary-eyed patrons of her father's Illusions and Enchantments where they might have seen her before. But no, their wondering eyes would tell her, we are deceived: you are not she. And they would pass on.

She sat in a room in the back of an old warehouse near the river. She could hear sounds of hammering, heavy things being shoved along the worn, splintery floors, brooms plied vigorously against cobwebs and dust. Voices boomed in formless echoes in the cavern, sweepers sneezed, musicians tuned their strings. All around her on nails hung costumes of rich and airy fabric, colors rarely seen in the working day. Glass jewels, bright feathers, beads of onyx and mother-of-pearl gleamed on the sleeves, skirts, hems. Some costumes were very old; others she had made for herself and for Tyramin's dancers and the assistants who brought him scarves, swords, shoes, boxes, and great chests in which he found or made his magic. Tyramin's head lay beside her, staring at other masks across the room. He wore his massive, powerful, paper globe of a mask to make himself look larger than life: the broad face with its heavy brows and beard, the long dark hair that crackled fire during his magic, its painted cheeks and unchanging expression became the face of the sorcerer. Tyramin's voice boomed and weltered from inside it. Padding on his shoulders and in his great boots supported the illusion of the giant from an enchanted realm, revealing its secrets as he played with magic.

The door opened; a scent and a dancer wafted into the room. Mistral put her silk aside, shifted to a more comfortable lump on the heap of ancient quilts and rugs that protected the magician's gear when he traveled. The dancer, one of half a dozen who collected crowds for Tyramin to lure away with his tricks, knelt beside Mistral and handed her hot, spiced meat and vegetables wrapped in pastry from a stall.

"Thank you, Elide," Mistral said in her deep, cool voice.

"It's very hot."

"I'm very hungry." She blew, nibbled on a corner. The dancer, who worked her own magic in spinning skirts and a mask as mysterious as the moon, smiled, revealing tiny lines forming at the corners of her eyes.

"The streets are full tonight," she said. "So is the moon. Everyone is restless. Is that my skirt?"

Mistral nodded. "One of them. You tore the hem. I'm almost finished."

Elide pulled a few others off their hooks, began layering them on herself as Mistral ate. She said, her smile fading, "Sumic said there is a quarter warden looking for Tyramin. Be careful."

"A quarter warden." Mistral's eyes glinted toward her, amused. "We've only been here for a few days. Maybe he wants to see the magic."

"I'm sure he does. He wasn't dressed like a warden of any kind. But Sumic saw his eyes, watching for trouble. Someone told her he used to be a street warden here, and now he is quarter warden. His father is High Warden of Kelior. And you know how fiercely the king guards his magic."

"Like an old beggar woman guards her rags," Mistral said with her mouth full. She swallowed. "Let the quarter wardens come; we've got nothing to hide. Is that a rip in your shoe?" she asked, as Elide pulled a red satin slipper onto one foot. "What did you do to yourself last night?"

"I danced."

"Give it to me."

Elide tossed it near the froth of red silk. Mistral put the pastry aside, wiped her fingers, picked up the skirt again. They both looked up as the door opened abruptly. A wiry young assistant stuck his curly red head in.

"Ney," Mistral said emphatically. "Knock."

"Sorry. There is a brace of peacocks out here. They want to see Tyramin."

"Tell them to come back later."

"They want to see him now. They will pay to see him now."

"What do they want?" Mistral asked, running the needle in and out of the silk.

"They want a private showing for a handful of their friends. And real magic, if you please; none of the tricks he foists upon the slag-brained masses. What shall I tell them?"

"How sober are they?"

"Not very."

Mistral set a knot in the silk, snapped the thread with her teeth. "Tell them that the magician's daughter will speak to them after his performance tonight. Tell them that even she wouldn't dare disturb him when he is in seclusion beforehand."

"Don't we want money?" Ney asked wistfully. "Can't we pretend?" Mistral's eyes focused once more on his face, caught a sudden, cold reflection of fire. Ney rocked a step, his hand tightening audibly on the rickety door latch. "That would be no, I see."

"Not like that. Not here in Kelior, under the king's nose. Use your head."

He scratched it. "How do you do that? That thing with your eyes."

She tossed the skirt to Elide and picked up the slipper. "It's a trick my father taught me."

Ney's head disappeared. Elide pulled the flaming silk over frilly layers of voluminous skirts, which would spin a perfect circle around her as she danced. Over that, she settled a nearly invisible layer of what might have been cobweb strung with minute particles of something Tyramin had dreamed up. When ignited surreptitiously by someone in a crowd—Ney most often—the particles would dazzle briefly with their colored fires, then catch the air like cinders and swarm away, fading almost as soon as they were seen.

Such things Tyramin conjured in his solitary hours before a performance, when ideas shirred from his busy mind like sparks, and he turned them into magic. Mistral felt her own mind turning over such strange, brilliant evanescence as she pulled the rip in the satin slipper tight with her thread. How this might seem to change to that, and then change back so that nothing really became transformed except the expressions on the watching faces. There the magic lies, Tyramin said again and again. Not in me, but in the smiling eyes and enchanted hearts. It's they who do the work, not I.

She cast a glance at the great head, with the little holes concealed in the corners of the eyes where human eyes could see out. Lamplight washed over the dark, painted pupils; they seemed to flicker at her in recognition. Mistral felt her own heart smile at the illusion.

Finished with the slipper, she gave it to Elide, who was tying ribbons in her fair, rippling hair. Elide put the slipper on, picked up her mask, and went away to paint her face, and to find the other circle-dancer, who was late.

Time seemed a live thing in the Twilight Quarter. It was not measured in strict and predictable proportions. It could be told by the color of the sky, by smells in the air, by swirls and deepening pools of excitement in the gathering crowds, by their fading noise as they dispersed, by sunlit silence in the streets. Now Mistral felt the charged gatherings around her, as all through the quarter people tracked rumors of a name to its source. The pounding and massive shiftings as the makeshift stage was set in the warehouse had ceased; now she heard doors open and close, rushings through the back halls, boots turning into slippers, hammers into swords and goblets for juggling. Outside the dancers and tricksters would be bringing their followings to the open doors of the warehouse, which would be festooned with transparent veils that glittered, in the dancing weave of fire and shadow, with the suggestion of treasure. Excited by random magic in the streets, drunk on music, love, wine, or just the mysteries of the night, they would toss coins at the doorkeepers, jostle inside to see how Tyramin's magic might change their lives.

Mistral rose. Time, the noise and laughter said, for her to dress and for Tyramin to appear.

There was a knock at the door as she picked her own filmy skirt off a peg. She put it back again.

"Who?"

"A visitor." She recognized the smooth rumble of the dark-haired dancer Gamon. The little edge of amusement in his voice warned her to expect the unexpected. The peacocks probably, who would not take no for an answer. She sank back on the mound of coverings, cast about for her needle, pulled the nearest costume down, and drew the thread through cloth without knotting it.

"Come in."

The door opened and she blinked. This was no gaudy

drunken peacock demanding a glimpse of Tyramin. The man was far too sober and dressed to elude sight and memory: he could disguise himself as a shadow if he chose. Tall and fair-haired, in black silks and leather, he could easily be taken for a fop with taste, out for an evening's entertainment. But his eyes betrayed him. Mistral remembered Elide's warning: street warden's eyes, chilly and watchful above the affable smile on his lips. Behind him, Gamon raised his painted brows, which ascended giddily halfway to his hair, and opened an upturned palm. No stopping him, the palm said.

"Who are you?" Mistral asked curtly.

"I am curious," the visitor said, and stared a moment at the gigantic head on the floor.

"I found him wandering around back here," Gamon explained. "Peering into things. Doors and trunks and curtains."

"Is that Tyramin?" the man asked with awe.

"The magician spends his hours before his performances in absolute seclusion. Not even his daughter dares disturb him. Ever. For any reason. Is there something you want?"

"Just to see what magic looks like."

"Back here, it looks like nothing at all. An empty trunk, a boot, a gilded paper sword. All the magic begins with Tyramin's entrance. As you will see if you go out front and wait like everyone else."

"If I go out front, I will see only what everyone else sees."

Mistral took a stitch or two, weighing patience and anger. Both hung equally on her scale of possibilities. Summoning assistants to toss him out seemed imprudent if he were truly a street warden; on the other hand, he was taking up her time, and by the sound of it, the warehouse was filling.

She temporized. "If you wait where Gamon shows you,

I'll ask the magician's daughter to take you herself to the front of the hall, where, even if you see what everyone sees, you will at least see better than everyone else."

His smile broadened to touch his eyes. "That sounds fair," he said, and permitted Gamon to lead him out. When the door closed, she flung the costume down and hurried herself into her own, a confection of froth, and flame, and fool's gold, and feathers that could have fallen only from birds flying through a dream. In the crowded room where Tyramin's assistants disguised themselves, she painted her face the color of porcelain, her lips the color of blood. She unbound her hair, brushed it into a great dark cloud and filled it with glittering flecks of gold, jewels, paper rosebuds. In the mirror, the mask seemed flawless: the magician's daughter gazed back at her, amber eyes luminous, lips and fingertips glowing, her hair scented and filled with treasures.

Thus disguised, she found their visitor again, sitting atop an empty chest, looking innocent and expectant, like someone waiting for Tyramin to touch him with magic, turn him into a rabbit, or make him disappear entirely. The magician's daughter, trailing silk and gleaming, smiled her changeless, charming smile.

"My name is Mistral," she said in her deep, sultry voice, and he slid promptly to his feet. "I am Tyramin's daughter. You cannot speak to him now, but I will answer any questions as I take you to the hall. What is your name?"

"My name is Arneth."

"Come with me, Arneth."

He followed willingly as she led him through the maze of little rooms and hallways, magic scattered everywhere through them, but nothing recognizable as such. Like puppets of string, cloth, buttons, and paint, such things waited for Tyramin's hands, his voice, to reveal the magic in them. She watched Arneth's eyes collect them, put their words to memory: glove, cloak, mirror, jeweled staff, paper snakes, cages of cooing doves. His glance would return to her after he had stored away a word; she felt the little, brief touches of his eyes. She was used to that. Everyone fell in love, if only for a moment, with the magician's daughter.

He asked her, while his busy mind worked, "Will Tyramin let me see him after the performance?"

"He cannot see anyone tonight."

"When can I see him?"

"I will ask him that in a few days. It's never easy for him to come to a new place, especially a great city like Kelior, where so much is expected, and so much has already been seen. He will be in seclusion until he is satisfied that his illusions will enchant the hearts even of those who think they have seen through every illusion."

"Not an easy task," he conceded, then was silent for a turn or two, while the noises within the warehouse grew more restless and chaotic.

"Is there nothing else you would like to ask me?" she said, her own attention flicking ahead to an inconspicuous door that led into the streets. He must have come in that way, she realized. The door had been unlocked, and no one was there to stop him.

He laughed a little, softly, at the question. "Something foolish. I don't think you'll answer even that."

"Ask me."

"Why were you mending a black sleeve with red thread?"

She gazed at him a moment, feeling suddenly wary, for no

stranger had ever seen beneath her mask before. Then she laughed, too, giving him no other answer, and reached out to lock the door as they passed it.

She escorted him through the curtains, left him at the very front of the crowded hall; the rowdy watchers shook the rafters with their cries and applause as they caught sight of her. And then, for it was time, by the position of the stars, the smell of pitch from torches, the music weaving its own enchantment through the expectant gathering, she summoned Tyramin.

SEVEN

In some bleak, moonless hour of the night, Yar was wrenched out of a dream by a cry for help. He lurched to his feet, seeing the image of the labyrinth in his mind before he managed to open his eyes. The school was soundless around him; he heard no doors open, no startled voices in his head or in the halls. No one else seemed to have wakened. Or the teachers were all elsewhere dealing with other disturbances among the newcomers. So he went down alone into the depths of the school, moving quickly, half wizard, half shadow, and both halves wishing they were back in bed.

The labyrinth, which sat squarely under the library, had been built under Od's direction a century or so after the first time she disappeared from the school and everyone assumed she had died. It looked small; a strong arm could have pitched a stone across it from the outside. The walls were neatly cut marble blocks, laid upon one another, with a carved latticed opening here and there for those entirely lost to see out. It was a comforting idea, anyway. Yar had never heard of anyone actually seeing the latticework from inside the labyrinth. It was meant as a simple teaching device, Od wrote; she had added a map of it to her writings, so that the lost might be easily found.

What she did not mention was how the path of the labyrinth changed for everyone who entered it.

An oversight? Yar wondered dourly as always when he went to rescue someone. Or did Od truly not know her own powers, that she gave such a thing a mind of its own?

Usually by the time he reached the utter darkness beneath the school, he could feel the lost student's panic churning through him like high tide. This time, though he still heard the cries from within the walls, the student seemed fairly calm. He didn't seem to be running headlong down every opening; the voice was staying in one spot. Which meant either that he had more sense than most, or else that his light had burned out.

Yar didn't bother with the labyrinth opening, which tended to shift when someone entered it. He insinuated himself into stone, then into space, then again into stone, homing like a pigeon toward the voice he heard. A boy's thin voice, wavering a little with fear, called to his ears for help. His inner voice, wordless and silently fretting, pleaded just as clearly for help. Yar took the shortest path toward him.

He got lost.

The labyrinth tangled around him like a fistful of string. The center, which he should have reached easily, cutting a line as straight as a knife through a pie, eluded him. Walls kept rising in front of him. Some even showed him the latticework that should have been along the outside wall. He tried walking the path instead of passing through stone. He met more walls, rising up at every step, while the student's voice, which sometimes dipped low, sometimes squeaked as he called, kept changing position around Yar. Exasperated, the wizard stopped, stared, brooding at the endless, curving walls.

Where are you? he thought, and knew instantly that he had asked the question the labyrinth was asking him.

His mouth crooked. He felt stone and space untangle around him again. A moot point at best, he thought, crossing the final wall into the center. The labyrinth only raised questions; it never answered them.

The student was sitting on the center stone, a broad, flat circle with a map of the labyrinth carved into it. He was a slight, very young man, with tangled curly brown hair, a downy upper lip, and wide dark eyes. A stubby candle flickered beside his knee. He had just drawn breath to shout again; Yar's appearance out of stone made him loose it in a hiccup.

"You heard me—"

"You woke me," Yar said tartly, "out of a sound sleep. Who are you? I don't recognize you."

"I was late getting here."

"And have already found your way into trouble. You hardly look old enough to be a student."

"I'm considered highly intelligent," the young man said, his teeth chattering with nerves and early-morning chill. He rolled his eyes at the stones around him, and added before Yar could comment, "It was a bet. Sometimes I'm too impulsive."

"Do you have a name?"

"Elver."

"Elver. An elver is an eel."

The young man nodded. "And Od's name is odd. I know; I've heard all the jokes. Can you teach me how to walk through stone like that?"

"Yes. You will be taught—"

"I mean now."

"No."

"Oh. Well, then, how will we get back out?"

Yar was silent. The young man whose name was an eel had actually found his way to the center of the labyrinth. By accident? But nothing was accidental in that place. Yar regarded him with slightly more curiosity.

"Why don't you tell me?" he suggested. "How were you planning to find your way back out in the first place? And, having reached the center, what made you think you were lost?"

Elver looked around him uncertainly. "Is this the center?"

"Yes."

"I didn't—I didn't know." Then his thin face brightened. "I've won the bet!"

"Good. You've won. Now how are you going to get out and tell everyone before your candle burns out?" He paused, sighed. "Nobody ever thinks of that."

"You're here," Elver answered. "So I won't need a candle, will I?"

"Well, how am I supposed to get you out?"

"You know the way."

"No, I don't."

"Well, then. Well." He blinked down at the center stone, oblivious of the very precise and detailed map chiseled into the face of it. "What," he asked finally, "do you usually do when people get lost here?"

"Go back to bed and leave them until morning."

"No. Really."

Yar, debating with his curiosity, nearly relented. But curiosity got the upper hand. He melted away into air and dark, leaving the boy alone with his candle, his back to the map, looking everywhere for the wizard, who seemed to have done exactly what he said he would.

Elver made a small sound in his throat, the beginning of an argument perhaps. But there was no one to listen to him. He picked up the candle stub, which was about as high as his thumb. Circling the inner walls, he came to an opening and went through it, his steps very quiet, as though he were trying to find his way through a wild wood while not attracting the attention of its inhabitants.

Yar followed him.

Elver, clutching his candle, his eyes wide, his breathing soft, made one error, heading down a blind passage, which he corrected immediately. Whether the labyrinth had simply released the boy, or something in him was drawn by the continual flow of power and freedom, Yar could not guess. Elver heaved a great sigh when he slipped out and saw the stairs that led out of the depths to the taper-lit halls above. He blew out his candle and ran up. He had more problems finding his bed than he had finding his way out of the maze. But Yar did not have to intervene, and it was with an unaccustomed sense of interest that he finally made his way back to his own.

Everyone looked a trifle haggard that morning; it had been a rough night for more than one, and one was enough to awaken the entire school sometimes. Yar made the students tell their fears, their dreams. Some had been genuinely disturbed by others' dreams as they slept, which they recognized when such images were brought up into the light of day. Others, inspired by their surroundings, had tapped unexpected powers. They woke floating above their beds, or wondering if they had truly broken a library window with a thought, and if they should go and look. The students who had sent Elver into the labyrinth scoffed at his obstinate assertion that yes, he had won their wager, yes, he had reached the center. Yar cut short their derision.

"He found the center. And what's more, he found his way back by himself. I know. I watched him. And if anyone else thinks of trying to do the same, I warn you, I am not getting out of bed to rescue you."

Elver was staring at him. "I thought that's where you went when you left me."

"I wanted to see what you would do to rescue yourself. You will all have to do that many times in your lives, for power needs to be tested, as an edge needs to be honed, and we don't always choose wisely the predicaments we get ourselves into."

"You did," Elver said. "You rescued the entire city of Kelior on your way through the gates."

Yar was caught wordless. The boy's thin, heavy-eyed face was eager, hopeful; in spite of his mop of dark hair and his weariness he seemed to gleam a bit like the creature, Yar thought grumpily, after which he had been named.

"Yes," he said dampeningly. "That's a tale for another day."

"That's what you said last time," another student reminded him: a shy girl who rarely spoke. "Master Yar, this is another day."

They all pleaded, with words or without. They simply wanted a story, Yar realized, to take their minds off the harrowing night. Something that ended well, with a walk under the cobbler's shoe into the school as the reward for power used wisely. Something to remind them that despite their nightmares they, too, had chosen wisely in being there.

He sighed. "It was hardly my intention, when I woke up that morning, to do anything remotely heroic. For one thing,

I was sleeping in a haystack, and just moving out of the warm hay into the chilly air seemed like the most difficult thing anyone should be required to do. And then I had to find breakfast, which seemed even more difficult. I was hardly older than most of you. I had walked for days to get to Kelior because I had heard of the magic in it, and I hadn't a coin left to my name. In other words, I was poor and unknown and very hungry. I am sorry to have to admit to you that I stole my breakfast off a tree in a farmer's apple orchard."

He paused. Some looked at him with wonder, as though he must have walked out of a tale instead of an obscure village in western Numis. Others seemed skeptical, unable to imagine either hunger or a hero who had not been brought up to become one.

"I was so close to Kelior then that I could see the walls of the city across the river and the banner on the king's great tower as I walked along the road eating my purloined apples. You may wonder why someone with enough magic in him to save a city could not have conjured up a better breakfast. But that is exactly why I wanted to learn more magic. The powers I had were random, chaotic, and what control I had over them was very hard-won. I could see in the dark, but I had only learned that as an act of desperation, once when I was in such grave danger that if I did not see, I would die. Then, by dire necessity, I came to understand darkness, to make it a part of myself. I could use complex powers, but I didn't know rules for simple things. How to will an apple to descend from a tree, for example. I knew there must be a way, but in that case, my desperation was such that I used the easiest method, which had nothing to do with magic. I climbed the tree.

"Midway through my second apple, I saw something so terrible, so astonishing, above the city of Kelior that I sucked in a bite of apple and had to spend a precious moment or two settling it before I could wipe my streaming eyes and see if I had truly seen what I thought.

"It looked like some legendary, fabulous monster circling the air above the city. It was so huge that its shadow darkened part of the river and the entire heart of the city around the castle. It shone like a king's crown, like cloth of gold."

"Dragon," someone whispered.

"Maybe. To this day I'm uncertain. It made no fire. It had an extremely long neck, with a big, blunt head and a pair of wings that seemed to billow like sails. As I stood there, too stunned to take another step, it swooped around the highest tower, then angled down over the river, dipped its head down, and raised it again with what looked like a fishing boat between its teeth. This it carried back to the castle and dropped, for unfathomable reasons, into what I later learned was the royal rose garden.

"I saw an ephemeral glittering in the air above the tower, like cobweb makes in sunlight, and realized that the king's guards were shooting arrows at it. The arrows struck it and promptly fell again into the gardens. The monster finished its turn around the tower and headed back down toward the river.

"I started running.

"I had nothing much in mind at that point, except that I had made an arduous journey across Numis to get to Kelior, and I didn't want the monster to destroy the School of Magic before I could even set foot in the door. Assuming, of course, which I didn't, that anyone would let me in. I reached the river's edge just as the monster dropped its third boat into the king's yard. They fell from the height of the highest tower; it seemed doubtful to me that the fishers raining down among the roses would live to tell about it. Fragments of their boats are still unearthed by the gardeners, I'm told, as well as the stray fishhook.

"I hit the water running, swam to the nearest boat paddling hastily to shore, and pulled myself into it. Then I did something to attract the monster's attention. I shouted, or flashed some fire at it—some such. Whatever it was inspired the men in the boat to dive out of it promptly. The monster's head descended toward me. I threw myself flat among the fish, and its teeth, which were enormous, stubby, and stank ferociously, closed about the boat. It swung into the air; I stood up unsteadily in the dim cavern of the creature's mouth and tried to think what to do next."

Yar heard a click of teeth, a quick, loosed breath. He shrugged slightly. "As you see, we make our choices and must act upon them."

"What did you do?" Elver asked. His voice squeaked.

"Before I could come up with an idea, I felt my thoughts pulled into the furious and very powerful current of the monster's mind. I could see out of its eyes, suddenly, as well as out of my own. I could feel the rhythmic surge of its heart. I knew that it intended to batter the city of Kelior with anything it could drop—boats, stones from the walls, roof rafters, trees—without stopping, until either the city was a pile of rubble or else it got what it wanted.

"So I asked it what it wanted.

"It was so astonished it nearly swallowed me. I had to fling myself in the crevice between two teeth and hang on to the great splinter of boat stuck there to keep from washing down its long gullet into its belly. It did not understand words, of course. But it did seem to understand the unthreatening insertion of another's thoughts into its own. It dropped the boat immediately, which landed in the Twilight Quarter, I heard later, crushing a cloth merchant's shop and scattering fish and tackle all over the goods. The monster answered me without words. It slipped an image into my head that looked very much like itself chained by its neck and legs in a garden.

"I remembered the king's menagerie.

"The monster took me to the king's gardens, where I found the object of its desire chained to some enormous trees. It had been a gift, I learned later, and certainly an ambiguous one, from the ruler of a distant land upon the birth of the king's son and heir. King Galin had taken a liking to it, though its mournful twilight bellowing invariably caused the young prince to wail at the top of his lungs. Amid a cataract of arrows, the monster descended into the gardens, rested its head upon the ground, and I stepped out of its mouth. I broke the chains easily. Both monsters flew away together. I fled from the gardens before I got shot or arrested. I was walking down the street, looking for the entrance to Od's school and trying to brush fish scales off my shirt when some-one passing me said, "Look for the door under the shoe." Of course I looked for the owner of the voice instead, and glimpsed the back of a long-haired, barefoot giantess with what looked like a solid layer of pigeons clinging to her cloak.

Then I looked up and there was the cobbler's shoe. So I went in the door. To my surprise, the wizards had been look-ing for me. They gave me clean clothes and took me immedi-ately to the king, who, when he finished cursing the distant ruler and his intentions, questioned me closely. Finally, he asked me what I wanted as a reward. I told him why I had come to Kelior, and he handed me back to the wizards, who took me in."

Yar paused, felt the students' intent, expectant minds wanting something more, a moral to the story, the satisfaction of virtue rewarded. He gave them what he had.

"And here I have been ever since."

Later, with Ceta in her river house, he told her of Elver and the labyrinth, the disquieted students and their dreams, the broken pane in the library. She listened only absently, he thought, as she sat on the carpet and sorted obscure scrolls. But he was wrong. He cracked nuts, ate them with his wine, gazing out over the river, remembering the tale he had told. He realized that neither had spoken in some time. He turned, found her lovely blue-gray eyes upon him.

"Is something wrong?" she asked.

"I don't think so."

"Your voice sounds strange."

"How strange?"

"Sad."

"I'm just tired. It was a lively night."

"Maybe. What were you thinking of when I spoke?"

He was silent a moment, remembering, then felt bewilderment surface, like some great chunk of river bottom stirred afloat by the prodding of memory. "Shouldn't there have been something more?" he wondered. "Something more I should have asked for, something more I should have done?"

She sat back on her knees, holding a scroll open, bewildered herself. "When?"

"When the king asked me what I wanted as a reward for rescuing Kelior."

"But you did ask for what you wanted," Ceta reminded

him. "You wanted, more than anything else, to study magic at Od's school. That's why you put your own life in danger to rescue it. You wanted magic more than life."

"I wanted what I thought was magic." She shook her head, still perplexed; he tried again. "I had a dream of magic before I walked through the door beneath the shoe. Somehow, within the walls of Od's school, I lost sight of that dream."

"But you were taught everything the wizards know."

"I was taught everything the wizards are permitted to know."

He saw the sudden wariness in her eyes. "Then you must know everything that a wizard needs to know."

"In Numis," he said recklessly. "But what about in other lands where magic is as free as air, and you yourself make the path you travel?"

"Now I think you are dreaming," she said gently.

"No, I think I have been dreaming until now. I think I should have turned away from Kelior and run as far and as fast across the borders of Numis as I could go."

She was staring at him, astonished and troubled. "Yar, what makes you think another kingdom would be better? Numis has been at peace for decades; nobody has to fear dangerous or renegade magic—"

"Everyone fears it," he interrupted. "Every moment, in that school. Fear is the foundation stone of all our magic."

"It is the foundation of all our laws," she argued. "And so we are at peace." But he was not, and neither was she; he had shaken her. She added softly, "You don't say such things in your classes, do you? Yar, you would not give my cousin any reason to—to question you. Would you?"

"Valoren," he murmured, seeing the lean, sallow, humorless face as he spoke.

"Yar, you haven't—"

"I wonder what he would do." He saw her face then, and checked himself, his mouth crooked. "I'm sorry. I'm getting crotchety."

"You're getting restless," she said more accurately. "Are you tired of me?"

"In what realm of the imagination," he wondered, "would that be possible?"

"In any of several." But the tension had left her voice, and the glance she cast at him was wry. "Maybe it's the change of seasons. Winter on its way again, making you despondent."

"Maybe," he breathed. "Well. We do what we do, and that's the end of it." He watched her shift scrolls and papers on the floor. "What are you doing?"

"Trying to put Od's life in order. Your story about rescuing Kelior from the monster and seeing Od will be the last in my account of her life; all this must fit in before."

No, he almost said, thinking of the gardener, there is one more tale.

But he stopped himself, and was relieved when she veered away from Od, asking with a smile, "Have you heard about the princess and the wizard?"

"What?"

"Princess Sulys and Valoren—they are to be married. Perhaps one day a wizard-king will sit on the throne of Numis." She gazed at him in astonishment. "How can that make you look so bleak?"

He shook his head quickly. "I have no idea. I think my thoughts are still tangled in Od's labyrinth."

"The boy Elver sounds very gifted," she murmured, still looking bemused by Yar.

"At least, singularly clearheaded," he said, seizing the change of subject. "I don't know yet about his gifts. We will see. I was with you when he arrived, and the first glimpse I had of him was in the labyrinth. He's quick-witted and well-spoken, probably well educated. Some impoverished lord's son, I would guess, who could not have afforded to enter through the main gate without the king's favor." He stopped, for Ceta had stopped listening to him. He waited patiently for her eyes, fixed on some nebulous distance, to come back to him.

They did, finally. "What?"

"What were you thinking?" he asked.

"The labyrinth. Od's labyrinth, you said. I never connected it with her. I thought the wizards built it."

"No."

"Did she write about it?"

"Not a great deal, as far as I know. What we have is among her writings in the school's library."

She tapped a scroll meditatively against her lips, musing again. "Then I must pay a visit to the school . . . I'll ask Wye to take me to see the labyrinth, if you're busy. It sounds fascinating."

"Be careful," Yar said gravely. "It's more complicated than even Od understood." As is her school, he thought, but refrained from saying.

But again she wasn't listening; he could only guess at the labyrinth she was building within her imagination. "It must be like a mirror of your mind. No two ever alike . . ."

"So it becomes, to everyone who walks it. But I don't think that's what Od intended."

"What lies in the center of a labyrinth?" she intoned like a riddle.

"A map of how to get back out."

"Really? Is it accurate?"

"I have no idea. I always cut a straight path through the walls. Except last night," he remembered perplexedly.

"What happened last night?"

"I got a little lost." He rose then, joined her on the carpet among the scrolls to forestall questions. He did not want to talk about misplacing himself; it would only trouble her again. "Let me help you. Where does it begin, Od's life?"

"In Numis, with a kiss."

"Show me."

She unrolled a scroll, pointed to the tiny figures painted on it in the margin, and the caption underneath. "Thus begins the life of the great wizard Od . . ."

"Nobody," he protested, "can document a kiss with any accuracy."

She let the scroll flip shut and rapped his head with it. "I can. Why couldn't her mother?"

"She wrote that?"

"She was quite fond of her ungainly daughter. Od was extremely useful, from an early age, with the farm animals."

"Really." He thought of the new gardener again, with his plants, and wondered if that was truly when he had first felt the need to keep secrets from Ceta. Her eyes were so close to his, trying to read his mind, that they blurred. She flung her braid around his neck and pulled him neatly from the labyrinth of his confusion with as much skill as any wizard, and far less fuss.

He smiled. "Document this."

EIGHT

Sulys stood on a stool in her undergarments, surrounded by cooing ladies, bolts of cloth, seamstresses, and her aunt Fanerl, the king's sister, who seemed to be everywhere at once. She reminded Sulys of a spring, lean and coiled, bouncing at the slightest provocation. Even her graying chestnut curls, pinned like a bouquet atop her head, seemed to bob as she moved. She never stopped talking. Sulys tried to keep still while seamstresses unrolled great swaths of silk, dyed linen, satin and draped them over the princess for Fanerl to comment.

"No," was what she mostly said. "The princess is sallow enough as it is. That yellow gold leaches color out of her. Let's try this silk."

"What about the green?" Sulys asked, eyeing an interesting shade among the bolts.

"Dreadful. It reminds me of peas."

"Then the purple."

"You can't get married in purple."

"Why not?"

Fanerl drew out a monotonous length of silk the color of curdled cream, wrapped it around Sulys's shoulders. "Well," she said doubtfully. "At least it doesn't clash with anything."

"How could I clash? My eyes are blue, my hair is brown — what could possibly —"

"Chestnut. You have chestnut hair. Exactly as mine used to be when I was young. I looked my best in the palest of apricot silk. Or mauve. Do we — No, we don't. Why," she demanded of the room in general, "have we no mauve?"

"I will find mauve, my lady," a seamstress said, hurrying out to the hall, where merchants and their assistants waited behind a fortification of fabric. Mauve was brought in, while the princess was discreetly hidden behind a swath of something the color of deep red wine.

"This," Sulys suggested. "I like this."

"No." Her aunt watched while the mauve wound about Sulys's arms. "No," she said again, briskly. "What was I thinking? That's a color for your great-grandmother Dittany, not for a young woman on her wedding day. Try that."

There was a flutter of receding mauve and impending goldenrod. The princess sank within them, magically disappearing in silk. She reappeared, sitting on the stool beneath them and scowling.

"What does it matter?" she demanded. "If I get married in bog-mist gray or in raspberries and cream? Aren't there more important things to consider? Or am I imagining that?"

Her aunt's eyes, glittering like a bird's, almost seemed to see her for a moment. She drew a sharp breath. "That's it! Cream with tiny raspberry roses here and there and in your hair. It will be wonderful. Stand up." Sulys gritted her teeth, clambered up to stand on the stool again. Fanerl pointed. "That one. And that one."

"Aunt Fanerl—"

"Be quiet, child. The last thing anyone wants is that you should be forced to think on such a day. Valoren will be Lord Tenenbros someday, a power indeed in the king's court, both wizard and noble. And young and comely, too, still with all his hair and teeth. Your father chose well for you; I'm sure you are grateful. I suggest you practice smiling; you will need to do a great deal of it in the future." She paused to watch Sulys's effort. Then she closed her eyes tightly and pinched the bridge of her nose. "Your mother laughed at everything! Child, why can't you be more like your mother?"

An hour later, Sulys sat on the marble lip of a balustrade along the cages in her father's menagerie, her hand between the bars, stroking the ears of a little golden beast with enormous eyes and very long, spidery limbs. Its hands wrapped lightly around her hand as she petted and scratched; it shifted its round head to help her find the places where it most wanted her fingers. Sulys leaned her own face against the cold iron bars, smelling the familiar odors of the tidy cages: grains, rotting fruit, fur, the constant, underlying stench of wild animal.

The royal menagerie had been maintained for nearly a century. Some of the huge trees that shaded it were thrice as old; they formed a broad canopy of green and gold that Sulys found peaceful. In their enormous cage, birds from many lands darted and sang among flowering bushes and slender trees. Some birds were large, brilliant, and raucous; others like tiny flying jewels. Peacocks stalked the lawns beyond the cages; white owls slept among the trees. Other animals were fierce and quite dangerous. They ate raw meat and roared like thunder; they grew enormous sets of horns and frightening teeth. Sulys avoided them.

Od herself had brought back strange, magical animals from her journeys in earlier years for the wizards to study. But a noble's pampered son had gotten bitten, or burned, or something, and the king forbade them to be kept in the school. So out they went and into cages. They all languished. One or two died. Then one night they all simply disappeared behind the locked doors of their cages. Od, it was widely believed, had heard their distress and returned to free them. If so, no one saw her face except the animals. The animals themselves, great white cats that glowed in the dark, birds that sang fire, tiny flying dragons, creatures out of legend, were never again seen in Numis.

Sulys found the little golden creature magical in its own way: it recognized her, greeted her with little piping cries, and seemed to like the sound of her voice.

"Which," she told it darkly, "is more than I can say for my family. No one ever listens to me." The warm, furry head bent lower to get her fingers onto its neck. "You'd think the man who intends to marry you would want to know something about what he will be living with. But it doesn't seem so. Valoren at least pretends to listen to me when I tell him something. But I don't think he's really there behind his eyes. And he doesn't hear anything I say that my father would not want to hear. I mean that quite literally. He does not hear. Not that I would say very much of those things to him anyway. If he did hear them, he would go off immediately and tell my father. For example, do you think I would dare tell my betrothed about the small things my great-grandmother Dittany and I do when we are together? No. And do you think I would tell him about sneaking into the Twilight Quarter at night by myself? Never. And—" She tried to lean closer for emphasis, but only pushed harder against the bars. "Do you imagine that under any circumstances he might be persuaded to accompany me? Do you? If so, I wish you would tell me . . . I am about to marry a man with closed doors behind his eyes and Do Not Enter signs on his mind, and who knows what warnings attached to his heart. And does anyone care? Besides me? No."

The creature sighed under her hand, slumped into itself, shifting her scratching down its backbone. She contemplated it, smiling a little, ruefully, at the long, dry fingers clinging to her hand. "No," she whispered. "But you, at least, like my company."

She heard voices then, becoming clearer among the incomprehensible shrieks and mutterings of animals around her. She shifted, her captured arm outstretched against the bars, to peer around the side of the cage. She recognized the craggy, sour face of the High Warden, Lord Pyt, and jerked back. The man facing him, his back to Sulys, was her father.

He had come here among the cages to be private, she guessed. No one else was around but the caretakers; if anyone else saw them, it would not be considered unusual for the king to be out for a stroll to inspect his menagerie. Sulys peeked out again. The king drew something raw and bloody out of a sack and tossed it between the bars of the cage facing him. A low rumble acknowledged it. The long slender fingers around Sulys's tightened; the little creature squeaked nervously.

The king was very tall, his fair hair lightening now toward silver. He had the voice of something that preferred its meals raw and could outroar everyone else. Sulys had heard his laughter as well, many times as she grew up; it seemed to have ceased to exist since her mother had died. He and Enys had both grown grim and prickly without the wry, golden-haired queen to make them laugh.

So have I, Sulys thought, watching the back of her father's head. I wouldn't know how to make anyone laugh.

The two men watched the animal feed while they spoke, their voices traveling clearly to Sulys between the cages.

"My lord," said Murat Pyt, "he saw Tyramin's performance. But he was unable to talk to the magician himself. Only to the magician's daughter, who revealed very little about her father and certainly added nothing to what is commonly known."

"And what is commonly known?" Galin asked. To Sulys's amazement, he leaned forward, snapped his fingers, then slid his hand between the bars of the cage. She caught her breath. He did not instantly howl in agony; his hard face grew intent, curiously remote, as though it reflected the animal's expression. His forearm moved; he seemed to be stroking the beast who had just consumed the bloody offering.

Like me, Sulys thought, astonished again. He comes here to pet things. Only he pets things that might eat him.

"Not much," Lord Pyt answered him. "Ambiguities. Contradictions. Nothing seems certain. Tyramin was born in the remote backlands of Numis; he was born in a distant country; he was born here in Kelior. He is a trickster, he is a wizard. He wears a disguise when he performs; his face remains unseen. Arneth has his ways of finding things out. Reluctantly, at your counselor Valoren's request, I have given him leave from some of his duties as quarter warden to learn more about this vagrant magician who charms and enchants. The last time someone enchanted the Twilight Quarter the King of Numis nearly lost his city."

"My grandfather."

"Yes, my lord. The students of magic were seduced, incited into follies of power that became very dangerous. The guard and street wardens were able to stop them from turning their magic loose in the streets of Kelior. We were not forced to pit the wizards against their own students."

What kind of magic? Sulys wondered, trying to envision it, like her father's colorful and fierce menagerie, running amok through Kelior. What does magic do when it is freed?

She heard the faintest of snores; the creature gripping her hand had gone to sleep. So had her hand. She eased it loose gently, watched the little animal curl itself into a ball, its nose in its stomach, paws over its ears.

She heard an unexpected voice and shifted closer to the bars. Her betrothed had joined Lord Pyt and the king. Sulys regarded him glumly, wondering if he had ever laughed in his life. His face, while presentable enough, expressed itself rarely; everything in him seemed leashed, his thoughts, his words, his expressions. Young as he was, he bore a distinct resemblance to the older men; he might, Sulys thought, if he wasn't careful, find Lord Pyt's vinegary expression stuck on his face one day.

"My lord," he said to the king, then paused briefly, as though listening to something; in the pause, Sulys heard another snore. Valoren picked up the thread of his thoughts. "I asked to speak to you both in private because I'm not sure what to do. There seems to be another ambiguity in Kelior, within the school itself."

The king's face turned sharply up and away from the animal he contemplated. "In Od's school?"

"Yes, my lord. The new gardener."

"A gardener?" the king and the High Warden said at once. Lord Pyt cleared his throat, yielded to the king, who continued, "How could there be anything ambiguous about a gardener? They put seeds into pots, turn them into beans."

"This one works with the plants susceptible to power. Though he says he has little himself. I bumped into him in the school and asked him if he had a flower—something appropriate for me to give to the princess."

Lord Pyt nodded. "A proper thought," he said unctuously.

Valoren had given her a flower, Sulys remembered. An enormous, bold trumpet of a flower, striped a bit like the colors that her aunt had chosen for the wedding gown. But, she also remembered very clearly, Valoren's thoughts had been elsewhere when he had presented her with the unwieldy pot. It had nearly landed on her foot, an inauspicious place for a betrothal gift. She held her breath, listening carefully for a clue as to where his thoughts had actually been.

"The gardener—a young man from the north country—told me he had been hired by Od herself and that he had entered the school by way of the door beneath the shoe."

The king grunted, an abrupt and vigorous noise that jolted the little animal out of its nap. "Od is alive?"

"Nobody else can reveal the door beneath the shoe."

"Is she in Kelior?"

"My lord, I don't know. She comes and goes. The wizards haven't mentioned Od. Nor have they mentioned the gardener. That's what I found strange."

"Perhaps Od simply liked his gardening."

"My lord, I felt the power."

"Od's?" the king asked.

"The gardener's." He paused again; the two men watched him silently. "He seems oblivious of it. Indeed, it seems completely unformed as yet. He uses it to understand his plants, something which he taught himself. I don't know what else he might be capable of teaching himself, especially in the company of the best of Numis's wizards." The entire menagerie seemed to be listening, Sulys thought, even the birds were silent. The king neither moved nor spoke, only waited, his eyes on Valoren's face. "My questions are: do you want him given that freedom? And—"

"Why," the king finished softly, "the wizards themselves have not told me."

"Yes, my lord."

"I will ask them," Galin said. His voice had honed itself fine as a blade. "Thank you, Valoren."

Lord Pyt began to talk then, holding the king's ear with more about his son. Valoren bowed his head, let them move away without him. He turned; so did Sulys, giving one last scratch to the small head, bent now over a leftover scrap of fruit. She felt someone beside her and jumped.

It was her betrothed. His odd, pale honey eyes seemed to encompass all at once: the princess, the creature she petted, her solitude, her proximity to the king's recent conversation. His tall, slightly stooped frame, the unblinking intensity of his regard made her think of great, dark, crook-necked birds that gathered in the trees near the menagerie when one of the animals was sick.

They both spoke at once.

"I saw you—"

"How did you—"

Valoren stopped; so did the princess, looking at him warily, until he began again, "I sensed you when I joined the king and Lord Pyt. You were listening?"

"You sensed me?" she breathed, her skin prickling.

"I must always know who is near the king when I speak to him."

She gazed at him, appalled. "How—Do you go into my mind? Hear my thoughts?"

"That would be discourteous," he told her fastidiously; it sounded oddly like a rebuke. "I only do that when absolutely necessary or when I have asked permission. I don't expect it will be necessary between you and me. You are, after all, King Galin's daughter; he has brought you up to share his values, his beliefs." He paused. Her mouth opened, closed again; nothing came out. He repeated, "You were listening."

"Not on purpose," she assured him a trifle crossly. "I came out here to get away from people. My father and Lord Pyt chose to stop where they did; I couldn't help overhearing about Tyramin and the gardener. I don't—" She hesitated, continued carefully under those wide, watchful eyes. "I don't understand why you're disturbed about someone who only cares about his plants. If people do small, private magics that entertain others, or harm no one, why should you or my father care?"

"Why do you care?" he asked so astutely that again she was wordless. He waited for an answer; she found herself retreating hastily, hiding herself from him.

"I don't," she said, shortly. "Why would I care about matters—"

"It's what we don't know that matters."

"I know nothing about."

"Small things point the way to more complex things that could possibly be dangerous. The silence of the wizards about the matter of the gardener may also seem a small thing, but it is extremely disturbing as well."

"I see."

"Do you? I hope so. It is important to me that you and I understand one another. That's why I asked the king for permission to linger a moment with you."

"A moment," she echoed hollowly.

"As you heard, there are pressing matters to attend to."

"Yes. There always seem to be." She was stuck then, face-to-face with her betrothed, unable to think of anything else to say.

He seemed to have the same problem; a frown flitted across his pale brows. He reached into the cage, patted the little animal awkwardly, making it drop its meal. It chattered at him; Sulys wondered wistfully what it had found to say.

"You like this one?" the wizard asked tentatively.

"Yes," Sulys answered, making an effort. "I find it soothing to pet."

"It doesn't seem to like my petting."

"You startled it."

"You could keep a pet in the palace. Then you would have something to stroke when it rains."

"I don't mind the weather. The wizards keep it warm enough even in winter. It's more peaceful out here than in the palace."

He looked at her quizzically; she heard then, as though with his ears, the twitterings, mutterings, bellowings, and blasts all around them. Her mouth crooked; she told him impulsively, "My aunt Fanerl sounds exactly like this when she talks about the wedding."

But he seemed indifferent to the wedding, answering only, "Lady Fanerl has never said a word around me. She only smiles."

"She would."

"What do you mean?"

"That—" She faltered again, under his uncomprehending gaze. "Only that she is pleased with my father's choice."

"As you are, I hope."

"How can I be anything? You and I hardly know each other."

"We will have years for that."

"I see," she said, wondering bleakly if all that moved him was ambition. "You'll marry me anyway, whether we know each other or not."

"We know each other well enough, I think."

"It's my father you know, not me," she reminded him. "What if I have—habits, shall we say, of which you can't approve? What if—"

"You are the king's daughter. I'm sure you would do nothing he would not approve of, and what pleases him will please me."

"I am also my mother's daughter. You must take that into consideration. And there's my great-grandmother Dittany, who is from another country where small magics are as common as wildflowers."

He brushed aside those small magics with a gesture. "That's hardly your fault. None of us can mend the habits of our relatives. I had a great-uncle who ran off to live wild in the wood like an animal. The last anyone saw of him, he pretended to know only the language of owls and refused to say a human word. Does that make me crazed?"

"No," she said wistfully. "I can't imagine you indulging in any kind of wildness."

"There. You see. We do understand each other." He glanced toward the castle as though he heard a silent summons. "I must go." He made an awkward attempt at taking her hand, but missed, and gave it up. "I am good with magic," he admitted, "but not always with people. You might as well know that about me, though it hardly matters."

"No. I suppose it doesn't."

He hovered, then swooped at her, a bit like an owl. She started; his kiss landed somewhere near her nose. He smiled then, as though he had worked some successful magic between them, and left her there among the wild things while he returned to her father's side.

NINE

A rneth stood yet again in the midst of the rowdy, drunken, enchanted crowd in the warehouse by the river, watching the magician's beautiful daughter transformed into a flock of birds. The crowd gasped and laughed, flung comments into the air after the birds. The magician watched them through whatever eyeholes had been placed in the huge globe of a mask over his head. The mask's cheeks were apple red, its great beard and long hair the color of iron; its painted black eyes seemed glazed now and then with fire. Its lips parted in a perpetual half smile, it seemed always about to speak. The voice that came out of the dark opening was deep, powerful, confident. That voice summoned the birds abruptly, with a meaningless word and a blue-green flare of fire from the staff he raised. The fire flew free, surrounded the birds; they vanished within the glittering swirl. There was a sudden explosion; people jumped and laughed. The magician's daughter appeared again out of a puff of smoke, brushing feathers from her sleeve and favoring the crowd with her impervious smile.

She looked utterly unlike the woman Arneth had seen sitting on a pile of old quilts and mending a sleeve. He recognized her by her amber eyes, their color intensified by the ivory face paint. Jewels flashed in her coiled hair, on her earlobes, her fingers; even her brilliant smile seemed to catch light. She moved as though her every gesture flowed to music.

Tyramin pointed the staff at her again. It was a long gold shaft; fire erupted easily and often out of the top. Mistral picked up a small chest, opened it, turned it upside down and shook it. She closed it, held it out toward Tyramin. Yellow fire sprang from the staff, engulfed the chest. Mistral opened it. Huge indigo butterflies swarmed out of it. The crowd clapped. She closed the lid, almost put it aside, then held the box to her ear and opened it again. A cat leaped out, sprang after the butterflies. She closed the chest. There was a thumping from within. She opened it again quickly and a lapdog jumped out after the cat. The crowd laughed and cheered, made bets on the wild race across the stage. The stage darkened slowly. Dancers wearing the white porcelain masks and circling skirts spun across it. Their lovely, mysterious faces appeared and disappeared at every turn; there and then not there as the pale ovals vanished into night-dark hair. Tyramin's staff spat purple; their skirts swarmed with sudden stars, already fading as they flew away into the rafters.

Tricks, Arneth thought. Trickster's magic. Brilliant, skillful, unpredictable enough to hold a crowd in the fickle Twilight Quarter. But not true magic. Nothing dangerous nor threatening; the magician could probably not even light a candle with a thought, let alone ignite a city. Such was Arneth's unschooled opinion. But a word with Tyramin seemed appropriate; his father would expect at least that.

So he waited for the end of the performance. He was quite modestly dressed that night, no rank visible, nothing interesting to catch the eye or invite question. Perhaps the magician's daughter would not remember him when he asked her to let him speak to Tyramin. Even better, perhaps he could find the magician by himself in the relaxed chaos after the performance when everyone stripped off their masks and costumes to pursue what was left of the night.

At the end of the performance, Tyramin worked a series of wondrous and fiery illusions, impossible things appearing and disappearing, boats fishing in midair, winged horses, a dragon. His dancers, musicians, and assistants, moving among the illusions, became part of them. One by one they turned into wonders themselves, then vanished. Finally, only the magician's daughter remained with him. All the jewels she wore flashed suddenly, and she, too, was gone, nothing left but air and a lovely porcelain mask floating in the smoky air, lingering for a moment longer than she.

Tyramin's staff blazed one last time, a bolt of lightning, a heart-stopping bellow of thunder. Then he, too, was gone. Only an empty stage was left for the dazed crowd to blink at, no sign, not a paper rose nor a pigeon dropping, of the marvels that had been there.

Arneth moved more quickly than the crowd, while it was still catching its breath and wondering whether to applaud. It decided; he heard the cheers and whistles as he disappeared behind the moth-eaten curtain strung on sagging rope covering the back wall of the stage.

He found a door there, as he had hoped, went through it quietly. He heard voices up and down the dusty halls, saw a dancer loosen her hair as she turned a corner and disappeared from view. Doors opened, banged shut. Arneth went the opposite direction from the dancer, listening for Tyramin's voice.

He reached the door behind which, the previous night, he had found the magician's daughter. He listened, heard nothing. On impulse, he opened the door. He found himself face-to-face with Tyramin.

The great head, lying on the floor, gazed at him out of enigmatic eyes. He glanced around. No sign of the magician himself, just a long gilded staff leaning against a wall. Arneth stepped across the room to examine it. It seemed only a rounded length of wood, sanded smooth and painted gold. He inspected both ends of it, weighed it in his hand, tried to pull it apart. Not a trick anywhere in it that he could see, and, from the feel of it, solid as a broomstick.

Where did the fire come from?

The door opened abruptly. The magician's daughter stood looking at him quizzically. He saw both her faces, then: one side of her face moon white, the other cleaned, revealing its faint lines; one side of her elaborate hair had been dismantled. Her mouth was still painted crimson, but she was not smiling.

"You again," she said.

"Where is your father?"

She glanced at the mask as though the magician might be under it. "My father is resting after his arduous performance."

"May I speak with him?"

"Who are you? What right have you to come prowling through our private quarters without asking?"

"My name is Arneth Pyt. I am the warden of the Twilight Quarter. My father, Lord Pyt, the High Warden of Kelior, sent me here at the king's wishes to investigate rumors of magic."

"What rumors?"

"That Tyramin's magic may be truly magic. And therefore unlawful in the Kingdom of Numis without the king's permission."

She was silent a moment, studying him. She settled herself in a fluid movement against the doorpost, folded her arms, frowning at him, but not, he thought, truly angry. An illusion of anger. Perhaps she truly had nothing to fear.

"What would a quarter warden know about magic?"

"Not a thing," he admitted. "But my father trusts my judgment."

Her frown eased a little. "So my father must only convince you."

"Yes. May I see him?"

She shook her head. "No. Not tonight. He asked me to let no one disturb him. Each performance exhausts him, but even then, he sometimes doesn't rest. If a trick goes wrong, even if only in his eyes, he must pick it apart like stitchwork and redo it until he gets it right." Arneth opened his mouth; Mistral held up her hand. "But. If you will be patient, I will ask him to speak with you tomorrow night for a few minutes before the performance. Will that content you? And the king?"

He bowed his head. "Me, at least. The king will let you know."

He told Lord Pyt, the next day when one of their working hours crossed, what the magician's daughter had promised. The High Warden gazed at him morosely.

"You are a quarter warden on the king's business, and you must wait upon this magician's leisure?"

"He hasn't broken any laws," Arneth pointed out.

"So? Bring him here; I'll question him myself."

"I'll question him," Arneth answered mildly. "Tonight. If he raises my suspicious, I'll bring him to you."

"And I will bring him to face Valoren Greye; that should satisfy even the king." He stirred edgily, fussed a paper straight on his desk. "If this were not mystery enough, now we have a gardener."

"A gardener."

"Who may or may not be a formidable wizard. No one seems to know, not even the gardener."

"Do you want me to question him, too?" Arneth asked, baffled.

"You haven't questioned anybody yet," his father said peevishly.

"I have spoken to the magician's daughter. And I explored a little of her world when she wasn't looking. I saw only the tools of the trade of any competent trickster, things that, seen by the light of day, would never be recognized as magical."

Lord Pyt grunted, unconvinced. "I want a full explanation of him. Where he was born, where he has traveled, where he learned his tricks."

"You will have it."

"You can't even tell me what he looks like."

This was true, so Arneth ignored it. "I should go," he said, feeling the restless rhythms of the Twilight Quarter pulling at him, as daylight withdrew from the streets, and night spilled behind it over the cobblestones.

"If you suspect him," Lord Pyt said as he left, "come to me at once. I will have him put out of Kelior at dawn tomorrow while the Twilight Quarter sleeps."

Arneth, instead of sneaking in the back door of the warehouse, took a place early in front of the stage where anyone, taking a peep between the threadbare curtains, could see him. Someone did. Before the warehouse began to fill, the dancer came out to him. He recognized her smile, with its broken front tooth, and smiled back at her.

"You see, I was right," she told him cheerfully, "about you. You have a street warden's eyes."

"I must remember to wear someone else's eyes when I come here."

"You'll have to wear someone else's heart, too, then, for that is where you begin to see. Mistral sent me to bring you in; she is with Tyramin, helping him dress. You must promise to turn a blind eye at all he wears, though, because he carries many of his tricks up his sleeves."

She led him through the little maze of corridors and rooms behind their stage, where once, Arneth assumed, merchants locked away their most precious goods and tallied their wares. At the end of a long hallway, where grimy panes overlooked the dark river, she opened the last door. Arneth saw Tyramin again, this time with arms and legs, looking oddly undersized for the great head that turned away from its reflection in the mirror toward him.

"Father," said the magician's daughter, "this is Arneth Pyt, warden of the Twilight Quarter. I promised him that he could ask you some questions."

The head gave a deep, hollow chuckle. "So I have unnerved the king himself with my great powers."

"You've caused speculation," Arneth said. "May I see your face?"

The head consulted his daughter and sighed. "Must you?

It takes us an hour to attach the mask properly. You see the hooks and loops."

"We have no time to put it on again," Mistral explained, showing Arneth the edge of silk at the neck that was attached, by means of what looked like a hundred tiny hooks, to the neck of Tyramin's shirt. "And I have to pad his shoulders, and his legs, get his boots on, and fill his sleeves with everything he uses."

"Like what?" Arneth asked curiously. She showed him two boxes, one for each dark, voluminous sleeve, of fake birds, paper flowers, gold coins minted out of tin, silk butterflies, other assorted oddments for making noise, Arneth guessed, and spitting fire.

"And then," she added, "I must dress myself."

Indeed, she wore her plainest face, Arneth saw, with its tired shadows and her hair pulled severely back. But she could not disguise those eyes, he thought, nor that deep, charming voice. Even her least remarkable face held a calm, graceful strength, and the promise of what, under the magician's fires, it could become.

He found himself smiling at it and composed his own face, wondering at himself. For a moment he felt the magician's attention; the flat darkness of the painted eyes seemed to study him. Then the great head turned back to the mirror, and Mistral began to tie stuffed pads of silk along his shoulders.

"Ask away," Tyramin said. "What does the king want to know?"

"Where were you born?"

"I was born in a village in western Numis. The magician Tyramin came to life in a desert kingdom far south of Numis, one blazing summer when I had a wife, a tiny daughter, and no money whatsoever. I borrowed a mask, slipped a few odd things into my pockets, and became Tyramin, Master of Illusions and Enchantments."

"You invented all your tricks?"

"Every one of them. They are my art, my toys, the delights of my heart's conception. In other words, I enjoy what I do, and strive unceasingly to outdo myself with wonders always more wonderful than the last."

"You did not study with mages or wizards in other lands?"

"No one with true power would take me seriously."

"The king does."

Tyramin shrugged. "He has no power. He fears illusions." He gestured, opening his arm, and then his hand. A butterfly rested in his palm, its wings gently moving to his breath.

"Father, you have no time," Mistral murmured. She coaxed one foot into a huge boot. Tyramin closed his hand, opened it again; the butterfly was gone.

"A trick. Something to charm the eye, bring a smile. Nothing more." He settled himself into the other boot, then balanced himself and grew until the great mask loomed suddenly over Arneth. Mistral dropped oddments into the inner pockets of a long, black silk cloak and held it up to him. He tied it at his neck, settled the darkness around him. Arneth blinked at the burly giant with his secret face, fire up his sleeves, his pockets full of mysteries. Looking down at him, Tyramin laughed, a huge, buffeting sound that seemed to echo through the corridors and continue into the streets to become the night laughter of the Twilight Quarter.

"Illusion," the magician said.

Mistral opened the door. Arneth felt the questions in his head, scattered like a swarm of indigo butterflies, suddenly transformed by the magician's enchantment into one. He followed the magician's daughter and the echo of the laughter down the hallways to the stage, where as he passed through the curtain it spilled over him again from the crowd overflowing the warehouse.

Who, he asked the illusion on its way to entertain them, is behind your mask?

TEN

Walking toward the tower steps in the early afternoon on his way to teach, Yar caught an unexpected glimpse of Ceta through the open doors of the library. He did not hesitate; his waiting students could wait another moment. He slipped into the chair next to her at the long table; she brought her attention out of the faded lines of what he recognized as Od's handwriting, blinked at him, and smiled.

"What are you doing here?" he asked softly.

"I'm reading what Od wrote about her labyrinth." She showed him her notes; he saw her copy of the little thumbnail sketch that Od had made of it. "Which is not much at all; she scarcely does more than mention it in passing, here. Is there a piece of writing I've missed?"

"That's all we have. The royal library might have something more."

"I looked there," she said. "I only found something that I wasn't looking for. But nothing more about the labyrinth. Will you have time to take me through it this afternoon?"

"Are you sure you want to go, in view of its peculiarities? Who knows where you'll find yourself?"

"Yar, I can't believe that Od didn't know it undergoes such changes." She tapped the little map. "This is what she says it looks like."

"The changes are well documented; the librarian will show you all the complaints about it."

"I want to see it for myself."

"Then I'll take you," he promised, "if you want to wait for me." He rose. "I'd better go."

"Wait." Her fingers brushed his wrist, and he stood still. "Just let me show you something. I found it in a cobwebby corner of the royal library. I think I understand it, but I don't know what it means or how important it is." He sank down into the chair again, watching the play of her dark brown hair against the light blue and gold of her flowing silks as she took a scroll out of her notecase and opened it. Several students at another table were watching her raptly as well, Yar noticed.

He leaned close, read over her shoulder as she whispered to him: "'I went again to Skrygard Mountain. The sun does not go there, so you would never notice that they cast no shadows on the snow. Unless you shed a light and looked for shadow. Something drove them into hiding. Into waiting. To this place. I do not know yet if they are of Numis or of other lands. Maybe I can make a path for them back into the world if we can begin to understand each other.'"

Ceta stopped, gazed at Yar with raised brows. "What is she talking about?"

He was silent, grappling with various strange images. "It's like a riddle," he breathed. "What is it that casts no shadow?"

"Well, what does? Or doesn't?"

He shrugged slightly, baffled. "Something that doesn't wish to be seen."

"But what are they?"

"I don't know. In my world, it takes magic not to cast a shadow."

"Skrygard Mountain is in the north country. It's a cold, craggy, bleak place, uninhabited except by mountain goats and eagles. I've never heard anything more mysterious about it than that."

"When was this written?"

"Several centuries ago, I would guess, from references she makes in it of other journeys, lands she visits for the first time. Yar, could the path she wants to make for them have anything to do with the labyrinth?"

"I don't know," he said again. "It seems unlikely. Maybe, in another scroll, she rescues those strange beings."

"Maybe in yet another, she explains them." Ceta rolled the scroll carefully; still she left a trail of fragments like bread crumbs on the table. "I'll keep looking."

He rose, kissed her cheek swiftly, ignoring the intake of breath across the room. "I must go. I'll come back as soon as I can."

The odd image she had put into his head, of power and age and great fear, accompanied him up the tower steps, and even through his classes, lingering at the edge of his thoughts as the mysterious beings themselves waited endlessly at the edge of shadow.

He dismissed his students at the end of the afternoon, and his thoughts turned again to Ceta. As usual, Elver lingered after class with a question, a comment, a passage in a book he didn't understand. Yar, packing up books and papers in his leather case to take with him to Ceta's, found Elver underfoot everywhere he turned. He seemed determined to be annoying, his thin face alight, intent, as he worried a point of argument like a bone.

"But how does the king keep his power over the wizards if he himself has no power?"

"The king chooses wizards as counselors and protectors; they guard his power for him."

"But what if they rebel against him?"

"They are trained in this school; those of such conniving or restless temperament rarely finish a year here, if they even make it through the gates. And they are closely watched throughout their lives."

"But—" Elver, close as a shadow, dodged out of Yar's way as he turned abruptly to reach for a book. The students had been discussing the history and methods of magic earlier that day. Most, having followed fathers, siblings, cousins, through the gates, were familiar with the close connection between king and school, the power of state and the power of magic. Nobody bothered to question it but Elver, who seemed to have followed his nose through the gates. "But if the wizards in other lands learn different ways of magic that are forbidden here, they could attack the king, and no one could stop them."

"Magic itself is not forbidden; methods of learning it are forbidden. You may not study magic outside of this school, for instance, without the permission of the king, or without the advice and guidance of someone who has studied here and passed through the wizards' gates into the world again. Elver, these are all good questions—"

"So—"

"And I wish you would—"

"But what if—"

"I wish you would save them for discussion when we are with the other students."

"They don't care," Elver said with such offhanded accuracy that Yar stopped to gaze at him. Elver, pursuing his thought, nearly bumped into him. "They only want to know what the rules are so they can follow them. That's what the king wants, isn't it? Wizards who follow his rules?"

"Yes."

"What if they change their minds after they are trained?"

Yar looked at him silently, wondering if the boy had been catching at the drift of his own thoughts. "Then," he answered grimly, "they face the very formidable powers of king and school together."

"But why—"

"Elver—"

"But why do wizards become subject to the king in the first place? Od was far more powerful than King Isham. She rescued the king from his enemies; she saved the king's realm for him. She could have taken Numis from Isham and ruled it herself. Why didn't she?"

"Because she was—still is—a very great wizard. Great wizards pursue knowledge and magic, not power. They are never content with what they know, what they possess. They search constantly for the farthest boundaries of magic, moving at whim across the world and pushing those borders farther if they can. They are not confined by the boundaries of a king's power, nor by any law except the laws of magic, which are exacting and as compelling as any king's."

He stopped. Elver, eyeing him curiously, commented, "You don't say such things in class."

Yar sighed. "Of course not. The students are trained only to work for the king." He tied the fastenings on his case, slung it over one shoulder. "I must go. Someone is waiting for me in the library. Raise the question in class if you want," he added recklessly. "It might be interesting to hear what your fellow students say."

"I know what they'll say. I've already asked them. They say things are the way they are because that's the way they are."

Yar chuckled, shepherding Elver toward the open door, and found, as they reached it, Valoren taking shape suddenly and noiselessly on the the threshold in front of them.

Elver backed up, startled, stepping on Yar, who took one look into Valoren's eyes and slid the case off his shoulder. He gave Elver a gentle nudge. "Go," he said, and Valoren, without taking his eyes off Yar, stepped aside to let him out.

"Master Balius suggested that I keep an eye on Elver," he told Yar when the boy had vanished. "I found him with you when I got here, so I decided to listen to what he had to say for himself."

"The boy has a flexible and inquisitive mind."

"Master Balius suggested that he might have a dangerous mind. He knows more than he should, and he is unruly. You," he added, "seem to encourage him."

"He asks," Yar said tersely. "I answer. That's what I do here. Give him some time; he'll lose his flexibility and conform like everyone else."

"Perhaps," Valoren murmured. "But why put ideas into his head that will never be possible except for Od?"

"It was an ideal I had once. A glimpse of possibilities." He saw no dawn of comprehension in the younger wizard's eyes, only the stubborn refusal to admit that there was anything to see. "You, I take it, were never troubled by such dreams."

"I have all I dreamed of having," Valoren said simply. "My

place in King Galin's court, his confidence and trust, and his daughter. I don't need to dream." He paused, asked Yar curiously, "Do you, still? You have your reputation, a life of respected work and comfort here, your place in my cousin's affections. Do you still dream of more?"

"What more could I dream of," Yar asked him with no irony whatsoever, "in Numis?"

"I'm not sure," Valoren answered slowly. "It occurred to me to wonder."

"Why? Why are you wondering about my life?"

"I'll let King Galin tell you," Valoren said without a flicker of expression. "He is waiting for you in Wye's chambers."

The king's own expressive face resembled a mottled seething pot of something about to boil over. Wye stood behind her vast worktable, her face drained of color and covered with a delicate lacework of lines. Gazing helplessly at Yar, she started to speak.

But the king, staring at Yar himself, said abruptly, "I know you."

"Yes, my lord," Yar said, for the king knew everyone who taught in his school. "Yar Ayrwood."

"No." The ire was banked; the colorful mottling in Galin's face lessened a little. "I remember. You were that young man out of nowhere who rescued Kelior from the monster."

"Yes, my lord. I was that young man, once."

"Yar also entered the door beneath the cobbler's shoe," Valoren reminded the king, and Yar blinked. He met Wye's eyes very briefly, saw the apology in them.

"I take it," he said ruefully, "this is about the gardener."

"Wye told us that you met him first when he came in," the king said. He was controlling his temper because of Yar's legendary act and his blameless reputation. But it still bubbled, Yar sensed, and would spill if Galin was not happy with the answers he received.

Wye spoke quickly. "My lord, I am responsible for his silence and your ignorance."

"No, you're not," Yar said. "I am responsible for my own silence."

"It was at my request," Wye said stubbornly, and succeeded only in fanning the flames.

"He has a mouth," Galin said pithily. "He should have opened it. Who exactly is this gardener of remarkable, untrained power who was sent under the cobbler's shoe by Od?"

"My lord, we do not know," Wye said. "He was sent here to garden. He—we saw no need to trouble you every time we change gardeners."

Valoren gazed at her speculatively; Yar closed his eyes. Galin made a sound like the cobbler's wooden shoe hitting the cobblestones. "You saw no need to tell me that a stranger with such secret powers has taken up residence under my roof?"

"My lord," Yar said, "Od sent him to us; why would we assume the gardener would be any kind of danger to you? We were simply waiting for him to reveal why Od sent him, other than that he seems an excellent gardener. He doesn't seem interested in anything else, not even in his own power. He has only been here a short while. He came from a remote village in the north country; we decided to let him settle himself here before—" He hesitated, wondering: before what? Fortunately, the king did not wait while he groped for an explanation.

"You decided. How dared you decide? If I hadn't known you so long, Wye, or your reputation so well, Yar, I would wonder what exactly you intended this powerful and untutored gardener to do for you." They both opened their mouths; the king held up his hand. "Enough. Let the gardener speak for himself. Bring him here."

Yar went, since Valoren showed no inclination to leave the king alone with the seditious and dangerous Wye. There was no sign of Brenden around his greenhouses or among his rooftop pots. Yar consulted the other gardeners; they only shrugged. He was always there, they told him. He never went anywhere. Yar glanced over the roof, saw no sign of a fallen gardener. He went back down, checked the dining hall, where the students were beginning to gather for the evening meal. No gardener there. He found a quiet stretch of hallway, opened his mind to search, feeling down corridors and up stairways for the shadow of secret and chaotic power he had sensed in Brenden. He found nothing. Puzzled, he wandered at random, glancing here and there into likely and unlikely places. With an inner start, he remembered Ceta, whom he had left in the library to wait for him. He went there swiftly to suggest that she wait for him at home until he had gotten himself out of trouble.

She was not there. Neither was the gardener. Perplexed, he questioned the librarian, who was gathering an armload of abandoned books from the tables.

"Did Lady Thiel leave a message for me?"

"She simply left, Master Ayrwood. I don't know where she went."

"Thank you." On impulse, he paused to ask, "Have you seen a gardener?"

"Today? No."

"Recently?" Yar guessed.

"That young man with the pale hair and the solitary eyes?"

"He did come here, then."

The librarian set his pile of books down. "He had a plant up there he couldn't name. He searched my books for it."

"Did he find it?"

"No." He paused, holding in some thought; Yar waited. "He looked," the librarian said finally, "as though he could use a breath of air."

"He works on the roof," Yar reminded him mildly. "Where did you send him?"

"Some color, then. A little life beyond his plants. A smile, maybe."

Yar touched his eyes, felt an unaccustomed chill in his fingertips. Now, of all times, he thought.

"Where—"

"To the Twilight Quarter."

Yar dropped his hand, stared at the librarian, whose silvery brows peaked worriedly. "You didn't."

"He's not a student. All he wants is the name of a plant, and they know strange things in the—"

"Don't," Yar said thinly, remembering Valoren, "keep saying that."

"I don't understand. He's just a gardener trying to do his job. Why should anyone be concerned? He'll be back. Can't it wait?"

Yar shook his head wordlessly, trying to think. If he went back to the king with news that the mysterious gardener had probably vanished into the Twilight Quarter, the lid would blow off Galin's wrath, and there would be an army at the Twilight Gate before midnight. The bewildered young man looking for a plant would be hauled in front of the king, and Valoren Greye would expose his mind as ruthlessly as a street warden searching a stall. No telling what might happen then. Yar, hovering on the threshold of the library, still had a choice.

He made it, turning abruptly toward the doors of the school. "If you see him, send him up to Wye."

"Where shall I say you've gone?" the librarian called after him softly. "If Lady Thiel comes back and asks?"

"If you see her again, please tell her I don't know when I'll be back. If anyone else asks—" He paused, seeing Valoren's watchful eyes. "Just tell what you know. You'll have no choice."

He paused at the doors only to throw a cloak over his teaching robe before he went through the wizards' gates into the streets of Kelior. He decided to walk; if Brenden took the shortest way to the quarter, down the gentle slope from the school toward the river, perhaps Yar would see him. The dusk was windless, chilly, redolent with scents of burning wood and pitch. Beneath the smoke of autumn fires, the moon drifted, beginning its arc across the darkening river. Most city folk had found their shelter from the coming night, at home or in taverns, eating their suppers. Yar searched each passing face on his way to the river; none was familiar. He moved more quickly, a blur to the casual glance, a shadow dimly perceived through smoke and the clammy river mist wandering ghostlike through the streets.

He reached the Twilight Gate without catching sight of Brenden Vetch. Standing on the other side, he cast a call like a fishing line into the wakening streets, baited with what little he knew of the gardener's mind. Around him torch fire sprang alive. Stalls opened their shutters and curtains. A drum thumped nearby; acrobats leaped nimbly onto one another's shoulders, lumbered like a gangling giant through the gathering crowds. Yar moved again, randomly, through the labyrinth of the quarter, trawling patiently through all the quicksilver thoughts around him. Finally, at some juncture of unfamiliar streets, he touched a massive, unwieldy dark he recognized. He hauled in his thoughts so he could see, and found the ubiquitous, exasperating eel again under his nose.

"Elver!"

The boy had had the forethought to take off his robe before he followed Yar. He was shivering, though, hunched against himself in the night air. Yar heard his teeth chatter as he tried to smile. "I f—f—f—"

"You followed me," Yar said. "Yes." He let his voice rise, a muffled bellow in the noisy streets. "You have expelled yourself from the school! Do you realize that?"

The dark head bobbed. "You said that true wizards have no b—b—boundaries."

"You aren't a wizard! You're a student, subject to the rules of Od's school until you have proved your powers, which is highly unlikely since that assumes an intelligence of which you don't seem to possess enough to occupy the brain of an earthworm—" He gave up, flung a corner of his cloak over the shaking shoulders. Suddenly suspicious, he demanded, "How much did you hear?"

"Wye's door was open."

Yar found the head buried within his cloak, grasped a handful of hair, and drew the boy's face up. "You listened?"

Elver nodded as best he could. "I thought of something else I wanted to ask you. I was just going to wait for you outside the classroom. I heard where you and the other wizard were going, so I went there. Then, while I waited for you outside of Wye's door, I heard the king shouting—I guessed it was the king—"

"The other wizard is the king's counselor, Valoren Greye," Yar said grimly, gazing into the wide, dark eyes. "He should have known you were listening. He should have sensed you. That's his duty, when he is with the king."

"I suppose he doesn't pay attention to eels."

Yar's mouth tightened. He let go of Elver's hair, clamped a hand on his shoulder instead. "I have no time to take you back to the school now, and I don't imagine for an instant that you would go if I sent you. I have work to do."

"I know—"

"Be quiet. I don't want to hear your voice again. If you say another word, I will turn you into an eel and leave you in the nearest fish market." He waited; the boy was unexpectedly silent. His attention moved beyond Elver to encompass the sounds of the street again, the speech and thought and feeling running strongly as river currents all around them. His thoughts caught at them, flowed with the exuberance of the quarter, until he found again the wild, unending deeps he had recognized.

He let that current seize him.

ELEVEN

Earlier, Sulys had made a determined effort to find her betrothed. She had not seen him since his cursory attempt in the menagerie to know her better. He seemed content with her; she foresaw disaster with him. She had not been honest, and for the first time in her life she realized that she could not keep her magic hidden up in Dittany's tower for the rest of her life. She debated telling her father, but he was, if anything, even less interested in her life than Valoren. The only person who took an interest, those days, was her aunt Fanerl. And Sulys preferred the racket in the menagerie to Fanerl's endless ruminations about the wedding. The details seemed tiny and exacting, like stitches in a tapestry, and Fanerl seemed determined to examine, pick apart, and expound upon, at length, every single stitch. And then change her mind completely. Sulys's wedding dress was now endless layers of delicate rose and gold.

I can at least console myself, she told herself morosely, with the thought that with Fanerl changing her mind every time she makes it up, one of us will die before I ever get married.

She caught a glimpse of her father striding toward her down the hall. But no Valoren. Well, the king would know where to find him. She quickened her pace to meet him.

"Father—"

To her dismay, he stalked past her, forcing her to turn and hurry to catch up with him. Behind him, a flurry of councilors and nobles were attempting to do the same thing. As though, Sulys saw with wonder, they were all racing the king down the hall.

"What is it, girl?" her father growled.

"I was looking for Valoren, Father. It seemed to me that we should—"

"I need him at the school, on urgent business. You'll have to wait."

"Are you going there now? Could I come and talk to you a little, along the way?"

He was silent a moment, his gaze distant, fixed on something she couldn't see. Then he said, "What?"

"I just wanted—"

"Is it important?"

"Well—"

"I'll send him to you when we are finished at the school."

"No, you won't." She sighed. "You will forget."

But his thoughts had already strayed. He barked again, "What?" and as she slowed, he turned. She held a breath of hope. But he only gestured his following away; they slowed, discouraged, and began to scatter. Sulys stood gazing after the king. Guards opened the doors for him between palace and school; he disappeared.

Another door opened near her; brisk steps came to a halt beside her.

"What are you doing," her brother Enys asked, "loitering like a ghost by yourself in the hallway? Surely you have things to do, a wedding to plan."

"I was looking for Valoren."

"He's busy with the king. Aunt Fanerl is looking for you. Something about the color of your dress."

"Not again!"

"Well, you should make up your mind. You'll have to marry in bed linens at this rate."

"It's Aunt Fanerl," she protested, "who keeps changing her mind."

"You decide. You tell her what you want."

"She never listens to me."

"She would if you cared," he said, so shrewdly that she blinked. Once, she remembered, a long time ago, they had liked one another; they had talked.

"Enys," she said impulsively, "did our father know our mother well before they married?"

Whatever in him had opened to understand her closed up tight at the mention of their mother. "What a strange question," he said stiffly. "I have no idea. I'm sure Valoren will find you himself when he has time. You should go to Aunt Fanerl. It you have doubts or questions, she'll . . ." His voice trailed away; even he couldn't finish that thought.

"Never mind," Sulys said coldly, and turned. "I'm sorry I bothered you. I'm sure you're busy, too."

Enys's voice followed her unexpectedly down the hall. "She used to laugh," he reminded her gruffly, "at Aunt Fanerl."

Sulys turned quickly, but he was already away on his own

business. Sulys watched him a moment, wondering under what layers of change and sorrow her true brother hid himself, and if there was any way to find him again. She heard her aunt's voice then and looked wildly for escape. The stairs to her great-grandmother's chambers seemed likeliest; she started up them just as Fanerl, making noises to rival the entire menagerie, rounded a corner to the empty hallway.

As always, Dittany was happy to see her great-granddaughter. She poured Sulys half a cup of very hot, watery tea; Sulys sat on the broad velvet stool beside her chair, held the cup in both hands, soothed by the warmth.

"Did you," she asked Dittany, "know your husband at all before you married?"

Dittany's sparse white brows wrinkled as she thought. "I don't remember," she said finally. "I get my marriage confused now with so many others . . . I barely remember his face." She paused; her face smoothed slowly as she traveled back into past. "Oh, yes. That was him. I hated him, at first."

"Really?" Sulys breathed hopefully. "Did you begin to like him later?"

"Oh, no, dear. He was always unbearable. But I had my children and my place in the world, and my good friends . . . at least until he enticed them away from me. Not many could say no to a prince. And he had such charming ways."

Sulys put her cup down; it trembled against the saucer. "So you weren't happy."

"I managed to find my own happiness, after I realized I could wait forever without getting it from him." Her cloudy eyes seemed to search Sulys's face. "But every marriage is different. Your mother and father, for instance."

"Did they know each other before? Were they friends?"

"I don't know, child, I wasn't there. But they certainly became friends. Your father roared; your mother—"

"Laughed." Sulys sighed. "Didn't she ever want to cry? Or run away?"

"Well, she did throw a teapot at him once."

"What did he do?"

"He laughed."

Sulys shook her head. "I don't understand any of this. Enys thinks I need to care, but Valoren doesn't seem to care if I care, nor does anyone else, and the only thing anyone seems to expect of me is to be quiet and fill up my wedding dress on the appropriate day."

Dittany leaned forward, patted her hand. "You're having anxieties," she said. "That's normal."

Sulys thought of the wizard's unreadable eyes, more like the eyes of a menagerie animal than anything human. "I think," she whispered, "it's more than anxieties."

"But, child, you must just accept such things. What else can you do? Your father has made up his mind." She paused, listening to the quality of Sulys's silence; she added fretfully, "I do wish you still had your mother. That's who you need now, most of all."

"No, I don't," Sulys said hollowly. "I need a friend. But you can't make friends with someone who doesn't even see you when you're under his nose talking to him. You'd think a wizard would be more observant."

Dittany patted her hand, then patted her lapdog, as though she couldn't remember which needed her.

"Have more tea, child," she said, nearly missing Sulys's cup entirely as she poured it. "I can understand why your father would want you to marry Lord Tenenbros's heir. But why he wants you to marry a wizard I don't know. My sister married one, in the country where we were born, and she was never the same afterward. They live in several different worlds at once, as far as I can tell, she told me. Oh, they might look in on you now and then, but most of the time they can't remember which world you're in." She paused, blinking. "Oh, did I just tell you that?"

"Yes."

"I only meant to think it . . . Valoren may be quite different, of course."

"Of course." She straightened her shoulders, then, at her great-grandmother's worried expression, and took note of the game board on a little table. The oversized pieces, in the middle of their battle, had not moved since the last time she had come up, except for the dragon-queen, who had fallen over. It was an ancient set, carved of red and white jade; Dittany had brought it with her when she came to live in Kelior. "It's peaceful up here. I want to stay a while. Shall we play Dragons and Swans?"

"What about your aunt?"

"She'll find me if she needs me. Can you still see the pieces well enough?"

"Oh, yes," Dittany said with alacrity. She added, lowering her voice, as Sulys carried the table over and set it between them, "Beris and I play, but she always loses; I don't think she takes naturally to the game."

"Do you want dragons or swans?"

"Oh, dragons. They were always my favorite."

They were in the midst of the game, the armies of dragon and swan dealing ruthlessly with one another, when a pair of Sulys's attendants begged entry to speak to the princess. She must come down, they pleaded, panting from their run up the stairs. Lady Fanerl had ribbons for her to look at, and she must choose her shoes, and whether she wanted pearls or cloth of gold on them, and about the colors of her dress —"

"All right," Sulys said wearily, "all right. I'll come."

She went to kiss Dittany, who had just taken Sulys's last swan-knight off the board. "You're in trouble," her great-grandmother told her cheerfully.

"Yes, I am. But I intend to fight until the end, so don't claim victory yet. I'll come up and finish it soon."

She bore as much as she could in a windowless chamber Fanerl had chosen as her battlefield for the event. The room was too warm, the air cloyed with the scents of dried petals in bowls mingling with lamp oil. Sulys, surrounded by seam-stresses, shoemakers, ribbons and fabric and laces, her ladies cooing, Fanerl draping her with this and that until she felt like an elaborate cake in the royal kitchens, wanted, after an hour or so, to burst into tears or scream.

She did neither. She ran instead, when Fanerl left the room in the company of three maids who kept bringing her the wrong shade of silk hanging they were purloining from the windows in adjoining chambers. Sulys looked around. Everyone was talking, examining fabric and ribbons, trying on jeweled buckles the shoemakers had brought. Nobody no-ticed when she walked out the door in a pair of shoes with jewels like great gaudy beetles all over them. She fled down the nearest passage into the gardens, thinking morosely of Aunt Fanerl chattering away and never hearing the alarmed silence around her. If one of Sulys's ladies had the sense to throw a veil over her own face and stand in the princess's place, Fanerl would never even know she had gone.

It was twilight by then, and chilly. She had only a forgot-ten swath of butter-colored satin draped over her shoulders.

The cool air in the gardens smelled of earth and rain, and late apples still hanging on the trees. She walked swiftly, taking deep breaths of it, trying to clear her head. The still, secretive face of her betrothed kept intruding into her thoughts. As it would intrude into her life, soon enough. It doesn't matter, she told herself fiercely. It doesn't matter. I will find my own happiness, like Dittany. Somehow.

But it did matter. She stopped near the edge of the royal gardens, stared up at the massive, graceful towers, the broad walls with their lovely, colored casements opening to the students' chambers, all brightly lit as though behind them, the budding wizards were deep in their studies, absorbing words and transforming them into magic. Also behind one of them was her honey-eyed betrothed, his rigid, powerful mind the crowning achievement of the School of Magic that had begun, centuries before, in the abandoned cobbler's shop.

She began to walk again, with some idea now of where she was going. She would not marry masked chance and find out what face it wore for good or ill after the event. Nor would she go masked to her own wedding. She would show Valoren her true thoughts and let him make his own choice then. If he and her father grew scales and breathed fire at her, so be it.

She went through the small gate in the wall between school and the castle, and then along the path that led to a side door into the school. She had no idea where Valoren might be, and she saw no one who might be able to tell her, just the occasional tardy student hurrying, by the smells and sounds coming out of the dining hall, to supper. She wandered a little, came to the main hallway with its broad marble stairways on both sides leading upward, both empty except for the sound of some slow steps coming down.

A woman rounded the graceful curve in one stairway. She was willowy and dark-haired, dressed in fine silks that mingled sky-blue and palest gold as they drifted around her long limbs. They struck Sulys in that moment as being the perfect colors for a wedding dress. Her eyes rose to the face above the clothes and she recognized Ceta Thiel, Valoren's cousin, who might possibly know where to find him.

Ceta had stopped, midstairs, at the sight of her.

"Lady Sulys?" she said wonderingly, and Sulys remembered the raw length of satin over her bare shoulders and the hideous shoes on her feet.

"I'm a fugitive," she confessed to Ceta, who was hurrying down the rest of the stairs, "from the wedding preparations." Ceta's eyes, kinder and more perceptive than her cousin's, actually smiled.

"Is that the chosen color?"

"I hope not. I look terrible in butter."

"You need a shade with some fire in it."

"Aunt Fanerl does not believe in fire. Have you seen Valoren?"

"I've seen nobody." Ceta sighed. "I've been up in the tower, waiting for Yar Ayrwood to take me through the labyrinth. He seems to have vanished."

"Have you heard my father shouting? Valoren would be with him."

"Why would the king be shouting at his wizards?"

"I don't know. He was disturbed and heading this way when last I saw him."

Ceta's dark brows crumpled; she glanced up the silent stairway, looking disturbed herself by the news. "That may explain Yar's disappearance," she breathed. "Oh, I hope not. I hope he hasn't done something reckless."

"Yar?" Sulys said surprisedly. "Wasn't he the one—"

"Yes."

"He has never give my father a moment's—"

"I know."

Sulys eyed her. "Do you really think he is capable?"

"I don't know." Ceta folded her arms and brooded up the stairwell as though wishing might produce the wizard. Her voice grew very soft. "He has been worrying me lately; I can believe he might have done something ill considered enough to inspire the royal wrath."

"Really?" Sulys asked hopefully. "For instance, what?"

"I can't imagine."

"Oh."

Ceta seemed to hear the disappointment in Sulys's voice; she glanced bewilderedly at the princess and was distracted again by her apparel. "You must be cold, my lady. Perhaps you should wait for a more peaceful moment to discuss things with my cousin."

"No. I have made up my mind. I am going to speak to him tonight while I have the courage. Even if he only wants to marry for ambition's sake—and I can't see any other indication at this point—there are things I must tell him. We have hardly spoken. I thought we should get a few matters clear between us before we marry."

"Oh, without a doubt you should," Ceta said firmly. "I had the same trouble with my husband, Lord Thiel. Before we married, he rarely spoke; afterwards, he never listened. I might as well have been a bird singing in a bush."

"What did you do about it?"

"Nothing helped, until he solved the problem by dying."

"Oh," said Sulys. "Oh, yes."

"I take it my cousin is not easy to talk to."

"He would like to be, I think," Sulys answered carefully. "But he doesn't hear me when I speak, and I don't think he would like what I have to say if he began to listen to me."

Ceta gazed at her, amazed. "What could you possibly have to say to him that—" She stopped herself. "What a question. I'm sorry, my lady. It's Valoren you need to tell, not me."

"No." Sulys hesitated, continued impulsively, "I would—I would like—I have no one to give me advice except my great-grandmother."

"Ah."

"And Aunt Fanerl, of course."

"Of course," Ceta said with sympathy. "We all have them. Mine was my grandmother, who told me endlessly that reading was bad for the skin and would wash the color out of my eyes."

Sulys laughed. The unexpected sound surprised her; she had forgotten that she could. She took a step closer to Ceta. "Do you—can you stay for a little and talk to me? I desperately need advice."

"Of course," Ceta answered quickly. "Of course I can. But where—" She glanced around them doubtfully. "We can't talk privately in the library, the students will be roaming the halls when they've finished supper, the gardens will be dark and cold, and I don't know how long we would be private in Yar's chambers . . ."

"You mentioned a labyrinth," Sulys suggested. "I've heard it's a very small thing, down in the cellar. That would be private and warm enough, I would think. We could take plenty of candles in case we get lost. No one would interrupt us there."

Ceta hesitated for a breath. Then she cast away doubt and shrugged lightly. "Well, as you said, it's a small place, and I wanted to go there anyway to see if the tales of it are true."

"What tales?"

"That it takes a different shape for everyone who goes into it."

Sulys was already plucking tapers from their sconces along the walls, blowing them out and filling her makeshift shawl with them. "That may be so," she said absently, "but as far as I've heard, everyone makes their way back out eventually."

"I suppose if we get truly lost, someone will find us," Ceta said, and began to pick her own bouquet of tapers. "They haven't lost even a beginning student down there yet."

She handed a final taper, still burning, to the princess, who followed her to the cellar stairs and into the dark.

TWELVE

Brenden recognized the Twilight Quarter easily. It was the only place waking up just as the rest of the city began closing itself away from the night. He passed through the Twilight Gate when it was still just light enough to see the stalls lining the square beyond, pushing back shutters and curtains like insects opening their wings to reveal the hidden color. Streets ran without pattern away from the square, curved between high, narrow buildings beginning to part their hangings, open their doors to cast a crosshatch of light over the dusky street below. The city behind Brenden seemed to vanish; he stood at the boundary of a secret world that appeared by night and disappeared by day. Entranced by colors, smells, sounds, he watched it thoughtlessly until a pair of horses snorted impatiently behind him, and he was jostled by others crossing the borders of the night world.

He wandered, astonished by dancers' glittering, whirling skirts, by giants with painted faces stalking through the crowds. Wye had given him some money for his work; he spent a coin on mutton rolled around cloves of garlic and roasted on a skewer, another on a cup of ale. He ate watching a knife-thrower extinguish candles with his blades. After a while, as the streets filled and the line between torchlight and night grew more intense, he remembered why he had come there.

He looked for plants. It seemed an implausible thing to find in that upside-down day, in that season. But he found stalls that carried potted herbs he recognized and other oddments that he didn't. He stopped to study one with long, green swords for leaves, each blade serrated along the edges. It had healing properties, the old woman within the stall told him. It soothed burned flesh, kept small wounds clean, and made rough hands smooth. She bent her head closer, the fringe of brass beads on her veil catching firelight, and added softly, "It has its magic, too, young master, if you put it out at nights to take in moonlight. The moon pulls a pure white flower out of it that you give to the girl of your choice when the moon is full. One whiff of it, and she will love you until the moon sets again."

"And after?"

She cackled. "After that you're on your own. From the north, are you?"

"How do you know?"

"I know. Everyone in the world passes through the Twilight Quarter once. Pay me now, and I'll keep the plant for you until you're ready to leave."

Brenden shook his head, unable to conceive of anyone who might compel a magic flower out of him. "Another time. But I have a strange plant myself; maybe you could tell me the name of it."

He described it. She didn't know, she said, but Grovlin might, two streets that way; he sold squash and rutabagas at that time of the year, but in spring his stall was full of peculiarities. Brenden thanked her and turned away and saw Meryd.

He felt his heart twist painfully in his chest; stones of grief shifted precariously, threatened to fall. He tried to call her. His voice would not come. He watched her move away from him, lithe and graceful, her long, heavy hair feathering out of the dark bundle at her neck, the pearly skin of her cheek and jaw and eyelid briefly flushed with the hot light from coals under a grill. He tried again to say her name; sound stuck in his throat as though he had forgotten how to speak. The angle of her head shifted; he only saw the back of her now, moving inexorably away, leaving him again. Before the crowds closed around her, he broke what seemed a spell over his limbs and found he could move.

He ran after her, his hand outstretched, caught her shoulder finally. She turned. Words pushing at last into his throat died again. Some trick of the quarter had transformed her into a stranger, he thought bewilderedly. Or else the illusion he had named Meryd had never been there at all.

"Sor—sorry," he stammered, releasing her hastily. She gazed at him expressionlessly a moment. Her eyes, a lovely, glittering amber, were nothing like Meryd's, he saw. Meryd's were sky-blue, and they knew him. "I thought—you were someone—"

"Someone else," she said. Her voice, unexpectedly deep, sweet, made him want to hear more of it. She smiled as though she read his mind. Then the smile faded a little; her eyes widened, became remote again, stranger's eyes, but gazing at him as though they recognized him.

"Who are you?" she asked abruptly.

"No one. Brenden Vetch. Just a gardener at the school."
He added, at her silence, "I came down from the north country, this past season. I knew someone with your dark hair,
who might have found her way to Kelior."

"You're a gardener."

"I'm looking for a plant." He backed a step. "I won't trouble you. I just thought—"

"You thought you knew someone," she finished softly,
"among all these strangers."

He swallowed, mute again, feeling the stones he carried
with him everywhere, the terrible weight of his solitude. He
shifted them mentally, settled them as though they were a
sack of boulders over his shoulder. Her eyes flickered oddly,
reflecting light, he realized bewilderedly, like an animal
across a night fire. Such things must be common, he guessed,
in the Twilight Quarter.

"I hope you find her," she said, and turned away, lost from
sight in a step as a giant who was twirling firebrands crossed
her path, trailing a wake of onlookers down the street.

Brenden stood staring at where she had been, seeing
nothing now, not even memory, for nothing was all he had, he
knew then. Nothing and stones. Nothing and the stones of
sorrow he had been living with for so long he couldn't remember how to live without. They weighed in him again,
great massive things he nearly could not balance, could not
settle. His grief, his loneliness, his anger at being left again
and again, seemed impossible to quiet. They threatened to
roll, threatened to thunder, despite all his efforts to calm
them. Like legendary beasts in a menagerie, agitated by
storm, they paced, cracking flagstones with their gigantic
feet; they strained against their bars, distorting their cages,

while he, the helpless mortal, barefoot and drenched in the furious storm, ran desperately from one to the next to placate them.

But they would not be still. Aware, for the first time, of something in himself that was stronger than the strength he knew, he came close to panic. What would happen if it broke free? If the boulders roared and rolled, if the beasts snapped the bars of their cages and burst into the world?

"What is it?" he heard himself ask breathlessly, and when someone screamed in answer, he thought that the enormity inside of him had finally taken shape on the streets of the Twilight Quarter.

He looked for it frantically, seeing outside of himself again. Everyone was staring upward, including the giant juggler. The only monster Brenden saw was fire. One of the giant's burning brands, he realized, must have flown far too high. It had been caught on a tiny balcony at the top of a house and was busily eating the hangings on both sides of the window. Still hungry, it swarmed up toward the roof. Glass shattered suddenly; what looked like a bucket flew out the broken window and over the balcony railing. Someone followed it. There were sharp, scattered screams from the crowd around Brenden. The figure did not fall like the bucket. She stopped at the balcony's edge, careened over it, caught herself with a movement so precariously balanced it did not seem human. Her dark, rippling hair flowed free; Brenden could not see the color of her eyes.

She cried out. Meryd? he thought confusedly. But there was no time to wonder. The fire eating her roof would jump to the houses beside it like an acrobat-magician, scaling heights, making things disappear, transforming the old houses into cinder. He looked around desperately, saw a dancer with a golden sash around her waist. Her fists jammed over her mouth, she squeaked rhythmically in horror. When Brenden grabbed the end of her sash and pulled, she tucked in her arms and whirled as though she were in the middle of her dance. Brenden spun her off-balance into the giant. He teetered, broke into three parts that tumbled into the crowd, one of them catching the dancer as she fell.

The sash had no weight to carry it. Brenden carried weight; he carried so much weight it was overwhelming him, so much that a heart's worth of weight was nothing to him. He attached his heart to the end of the sash and flung it upward toward the balcony. It was not long enough to reach. So he made it longer, letting the end he held trail through him into the wild dark he carried always. Weighted with sorrow, fed endless hungers and chaos, the sash flung itself around the balcony, elongated into a narrow bridge of gold between the gardener and the fire.

The crowd gasped. The woman leaped to meet it, caught it midfall, and breaths stopped. The sash held. She slid jerkily down it, limp as a rag doll but for her hands that shifted and clung, shifted and clung. She was barely halfway down when the roof caught fire. The balcony railing, a scrollwork of iron attached to the wooden beams of the house, was beginning to wobble. A corner sprang loose. The sash bounced; the woman swung, still a floor or two above the crowd. The giant, who had reassembled itself without its painted head into young men standing on one another, was still too short to catch hold of her. Her hair fanned through the air as she turned her head to look fearfully at the balcony. Brenden, remembering such a long, lovely dark that shielded him at night from thought, pulled more out of himself, an implacable strength to match his wish. It hammered the railing back into place against the burning wall; the flame he felt licking at it as futilely as words could not free it again.

The woman descended. The giant, swaying and hovering, was poised to catch her as she neared. The crowd closed around the giant, keeping it upright as the woman made her way toward it. Brenden still could not see her face clearly. The crowd murmured anxiously. Someone had caught the fallen bucket; it was passing from hand to hand on its way to the little fountain in the middle of the street. Someone near the house threw the water at the fire. It arched upward a little way, then splashed down again, drenching the upturned faces.

Without thinking, Brenden reached for the water in the fountain. He guided it as he had guided the golden sash, through the same enormity of darkness, where it became something he could mold with his desires, transform to his implacable need. He tracked the water splashing into the stone basin to its underground source, and felt a power there to match his need. The river, cold, strong, deep, flowed with its own will. His need was stronger; his had no boundaries, it seemed, knew no end. He shaped the river flowing out of the fountain to his wish.

The basin cracked in two; water shot out of it, spilling all over the street. Brenden raised his hands, coaxed it upward into a column, higher and higher, not seeing the startled faces staring at him now instead of the fire. Tears he held, a deep welling of grief, and something else, more powerful than either, that he had mistaken for sorrow. It had no name, this power, no name he had ever learned, and no face but his own.

He touched the fire then, let it come into his mind. That, too, he recognized: the glowing, dangerous beast that ate and ate and was never satisfied, never finished until there was nothing left. It gave life and death without knowing either word; it was of a piece, always itself whether as big as a thumbnail or as big as a house. Brenden found, in the great, grinding shift of stones within him, the spark they made that blazed to life within him, fueled only by the nameless dark.

Fire and water leaped toward one another within him, and outside of him. Great, awkward, unwieldy beasts, they staggered together and clashed above the heads of the crowd. There was a huge hiss; a cloud smelling of river and smoke roiled over the street; for a moment no one could see. It dispersed, leaving half the street in darkness, for the water had put out all the nearest lamps and torches.

Fire sprang to life all around them, this time in tidy, controlled patches clinging to burning brands, to hanging lamps. As the crowd began to see again, it became suddenly vociferous, laughing, shouting, applauding. Brenden, still holding the sash taut as the woman descended finally into the giant's waiting arms, found his eyes drawn beyond her to the house she had fled. He blinked. The sash, loosed from the balcony, rippled down in little rivulets of gold. The woman caught it and stood, as gracefully as the acrobats who formed it, on the shoulders of the giant.

The house stood unharmed. Not a single splinter burned in a beam; not a shadow of ash marred its painted face. Even the hangings hung whole. The water had stopped shooting out of the cobblestones; the fountain was again in one piece and singing softly to itself. Nothing, Brenden's stunned brain told him, even looked damp.

Someone shouted, "Tyramin!"

The crowd echoed the word with one voice, like a roar of water. Brenden felt hands seize him, lift him off the ground. The crowd chanted now, rhythmically, as it raised him limb by limb and balanced him somewhere between earth and air.

"Tyramin!" they shouted to him. "Tyramin! Tyramin!"

He looked around bewilderedly, not knowing what the word meant. A fire had burned; he had put it out; now he was riding the wave of a crowd through the streets, a stranger to himself, but not to the crowd, who seemed to know exactly who he was.

"Tyramin!"

He twisted to find the dark-haired woman, whom he thought he had rescued. Maybe, he hoped wildly, it was Meryd and she would recognize him.

She looked down at him from the giant's shoulders, close enough for him to see the glittering amber catching fire in her eyes. She did not smile, nor did she call that name. She seemed, as her wide eyes held his in that instant, as surprised as he. Then the giant strode ahead, the top figure catching hold of its painted head as the crowd tossed it up. Brenden shifted again, trying to drop. But the crowd would not let him go without magic, and magic, he finally understood, was what had gotten him into that predicament in the first place.

Unexpectedly, he recognized a face. It belonged to the tall, darkly cloaked man who gazed at him under a torchlight on the edge of the street. Brenden stretched a hand toward him.

"Yar! Yar Ayrwood!"

His voice did not carry through the din. But he felt the riveted attention of the wizard in the shadows, and he pleaded silently, with all his strength, as though a stone within him cracked open and spoke:

Help me.

A figure rode between them then, a man wearing some kind of uniform, buttons and sword hilt glittering, his short hair as red as fire, his eyes narrowed as Brenden swept past him, caught like a spar in the night currents of the Twilight

Quarter. He turned his mount to ride with the crowd, keeping abreast of Brenden, who didn't like what rode with him, but didn't know why.

He glanced back desperately, but could not find the wizard again. The crowd bore him down toward the river, still shouting his incomprehensible name.

THIRTEEN

News of the flamboyant and mysterious doings in the Twilight Quarter made its way swiftly out of the Twilight Gate, up the streets to the office of the quarter warden, who for once was actually in his office. He was trying to decipher a bill of lading for a ship docked in waters under his watch. Lord Pyt seemed to think it suspicious; Arneth found it nearly unreadable. The few words he understood seemed to have to do with exotic varieties of fish. Or was it trees? He couldn't say with certainty. He opened his mouth to summon his secretary, a knowledgeable young man; the secretary put his head in the door before Arneth produced a sound.

"One of your street wardens is here," he said. "Paquin Bel. He says it's urgent."

Arneth closed his mouth. Perhaps it was urgent, perhaps not; Paquin Bel had an exalted sense of duty. He nodded; the door opened wider, emitting the brawny, red-haired man.

"Sir," he said briskly.

"Yes."

"In the matter of the magician Tyramin, we have finally found a face."

Arneth raised his brows. "Really?"

"Yes, sir." Expression came into Paquin's eyes then; he leaned impulsively over Arneth's desk. "There was magic tonight in the streets of the Twilight Quarter." He found his hands on Arneth's desk and straightened hastily. "True magic." He stopped, then added, "I think."

Arneth grappled with that. "What form," he asked finally, "did this magic take?"

"Fire."

"Fire? Fire as in what? Tyramin uses fire in his tricks like a cook uses pepper."

"A house on fire. As in, Tyramin put it out." He paused, added again before Arneth could speak, "I think."

"What do you mean you think?" Arneth demanded. "A house on fire anywhere in the city is an extremely dangerous matter. Don't tell me what you think, tell me what you know."

"Yes, sir," Paquin said, his face wooden again. He fixed his eyes somewhere on the wall above Arneth's shoulder, and continued without thinking, "A giant juggling fire tossed a brand too high; it fell onto the top balcony of one of the houses. The house caught fire. A woman was trapped on the balcony. A young man in the crowd below rescued her by means of a dancer's sash, which he caused by magic to elongate itself to reach the balcony and remain stiffly in the air while she made her way down it by means of her hands. While she did that, the young man broke open a fountain nearby, pulled the water out of it with his hands, and directed it toward the fire, which had spread by then to the roof and was threatening the buildings next to it. There was a puff of smoke. Or steam. Or both. When it cleared, the fire was out, the woman on the ground, and the"—he hesitated, continued doggedly—"and the house and fountain as they had been before the fire broke out."

"What?"

"Unchanged, sir. Not a mark on them. The streets were bone-dry. The crowd chose to see it as a trick of Tyramin's. They bore the young man away, down to the warehouse where the magician performs, shouting his name along the way. Magic or not magic, I don't know. That's what happened."

Arneth closed his eyes, opened them again. He rose abruptly. "Come with me."

He took the street warden to Lord Pyt, who listened silently as Paquin Bel repeated himself, word for word, Arneth noted with wonder. Lord Pyt's craggy face turned from the color of suet at the threat of fire to the hue of undercooked liver at the threat of magic.

He glared at Arneth as though he were somehow responsible. "Magic or no magic, this Tyramin might have set the Twilight Quarter on fire!"

"He put it out," Arneth said. "Very handily, it seems."

"If it was truly a fire," Paquin reminded them.

"Fire is fire," Lord Pyt snapped.

"Tyramin might say it was an illusion of fire," Arneth said. "Another trick."

"His tricks are becoming very disturbing." Lord Pyt thought a moment, calculating various aspects, and added portentously, as Arneth expected, "The king should hear of this immediately. Then you, Arneth, must find Tyramin and arrest him yourself."

"Yes, Father."

"Don't call me that."

"Yes, Fath—Yes."

"You will take the royal guard with you. And wizards from the school in case he is dangerous."

Arneth hesitated, but only briefly; his father did not notice. "Yes, sir."

"Both of you, come with me."

Lord Pyt led them through the endless hallways and the drafty marble tunnel that connected the High Warden's offices to the palace. In an antechamber at the end of the tunnel, he sent word to the king of the strange events. They waited for an unusual amount of time for word to come back to them. So much time, Arneth thought, that the king must have sent someone else—Valoren Greye perhaps—to investigate the fiery incident in the Twilight Quarter.

But Valoren came to them himself.

"The king has been at the school with Wye," he told them. "He sent me ahead to question you. There is also a mystery at the school. It may be related."

"What mystery?" Lord Pyt demanded officiously.

The inexpressive eyes considered him a moment before the wizard answered. "The gardener, Lord Pyt."

"Ah," the High Warden intoned mysteriously as Paquin Bel echoed bewilderedly, "Gardener?"

"The new gardener," Valoren answered, "who may indeed be a powerful wizard, has vanished from the school. The king had taken me with him earlier to question the wizards about him. They seem to know very little. And now the gardener cannot be found. There was some suggestion that he might have gone to the Twilight Quarter. Tell me," he added, at their baffled silence, "what has disturbed the quarter."

"In brief," Lord Pyt said, "magic. My son the quarter warden will tell you."

"Paquin Bel will tell you," Arneth amended. "I wasn't there."

Paquin Bel had dutifully begun, "A giant juggling fire tossed a brand too high—" when the king entered. Paquin stopped, swallowing audibly. Galin's face was flushed beneath his white-gold hair as though he had been fanned by the flames from the Twilight Quarter.

"What is going on?" he demanded. "I'm hearing rumors of fire in Kelior."

"From whom, my lord?" Valoren asked instantly.

The king gestured incoherently at the question. "Guards on the walls—What does it matter? Is there, or is there not—"

"Yes, my lord," the High Warden answered.

"Yes, which?"

"Both, as far as we can ascertain. Yes and no—" The king's color deepened alarmingly; Lord Pyt finished hastily. "As the street warden Paquin Bel was about to describe to us."

The king looked explosively at Paquin, who swallowed again. Then his eyes crossed slightly in concentration; he drew breath and started over courageously under that fixed glare. The glare did not dim by a flicker when Paquin finished, but the king turned it upon Valoren.

He consulted the wizard silently a moment before he spoke. "The gardener?"

"It may be, my lord," Valoren said slowly. "The gardener and the magician appeared in Kelior about the same time. And no one sees Tyramin's face."

"We haven't seen the gardener's face, either," Galin said testily. "Nor the wizard Yar's, since we sent him to find the gardener."

"If it was truly magic," Valoren guessed, "Yar would have been drawn to the Twilight Quarter. Do you trust him?"

"Yar? He saved my city before he even passed through the doors of the school."

"By means of unsanctioned magic."

"He didn't know any better," the king said impatiently. "And he has remained at the school ever since; his reputation—if not his good sense—is impeccable."

"Then we will trust him to find the one who worked the magic," Valoren said simply. "If he needs help, he can summon any of us. With such a faceless force loose in Kelior, I will not leave you unprotected."

Lord Pyt cleared his throat. "My son will take armed men from the royal guard to the quarter. I have given him orders to arrest this man called Tyramin."

"And if he uses magic against the guard?" the king queried.

"I'll instruct the wizards to keep their minds open for the unexpected use of power," Valoren told him. "They are finished with their teaching for the day; they can put their full attention to this. Most of them can be in the Twilight Quarter in a breath if there is need. And, if Yar is already there, he can protect the quarter until he has help." He paused, added to Arneth, "It would be best if Tyramin is arrested as quietly as possible. If he is really a harmless trickster, then it will be the crowds he draws that pose the greater danger. Can you manage that?"

"I'll do my best," Arneth said, relieved that there was some measure of common sense behind the unsettling eyes.

"Then go," the king said brusquely. "And don't come back without him."

Lord Pyt went to assemble the guard in their quarters below the palace; Arneth armed himself and called for his horse. He sent Paquin Bel back to the Twilight Quarter to see what he could see with orders to meet Arneth at the Twilight Gate if he saw anything amiss. The royal guard was armed and mounted without delay; Arneth rode to meet the lines of men in the yard, two dozen guards armed from helmet to metal bootheel, waiting for his order.

He surveyed them a moment, thinking. Against a very clever and annoying yet harmless trickster, they were overpowering: the king's mailed fist hammering down to crush an ephemeral pleasure. Set against great magical power, they would be helpless; they would be destroyed. Either way, as a threat or a weapon, they were useless.

So he left them outside the Twilight Gate to wait for his summons and rode alone to find Tyramin.

FOURTEEN

Mistral rescued the astonishing young man when the exuberant flow of people reached the warehouse by the river. They carried him inside. Somehow, between doors and stage, they lost sight of him; they misplaced him; he disappeared. Still they called his name, certain that Tyramin would rejoin them to work his magic. They settled themselves to wait. Some climbed up into the rafters, or opened windows and perched on the sills. Even from the rafters they could not see over the curtain behind Tyramin's stage; Mistral made sure of that as she guided the stupefied young man into the tiny, untidy room where she did her sewing.

He gazed bewilderedly at the vivid costumes hanging on their hooks, the swaths of airy, glittering fabric strewn on the floor, the empty-eyed masks. Riveted by the gigantic head, he caught his breath.

"Who is that?" he whispered.

Mistral picked up the head, a finger through one eye-hole. "Tyramin."

He struggled over that, trying to understand. "What happened out there? The house was on fire. Meryd—it looked like Meryd up there on the highest floor. But it was you again, wasn't it? I put—I put—"

"You put the fire out."

"I put the fire out," he said, summoning courage to say it. "I did that. I didn't know how, but I had to. That was magic."

"Yes. Very powerful magic you worked, in front of the entire Twilight Quarter, street wardens and all."

He stared at her without seeing her, remembering something. "There was other magic. Someone else."

"Listen. You must stay here, hide so that—"

"Someone else put the fountain back together. Mended the house. I didn't do that."

"Didn't you? I must go and help Tyramin dress, so that he can appear before the crowd grows too restless." She paused briefly; he was seeing her again, too clearly, she felt, more clearly than she permitted any stranger. "Wait here," she said, backing toward the door. "Stay hidden. The street wardens will be searching for you."

He started to speak, say what he saw. She reached him in a step, put a finger to his lips, and then to hers. So close to him, she sensed the bulky enormity he carried, that he had barely begun to shape and define as his own. It was the shadow, the footprint, the wordless voice of his power. He stood silent again; she pulled the huge head into a firmer grip, watching him grapple with his own cumbersome burden.

He loosed the soft breath of an empty laugh. "I just came here looking for a plant."

"Please," she said softly. "Wait here until we have finished the performance. The crowd has followed you here thinking that you are Tyramin. They want more magic. Tyramin will give it to them. By morning they will barely remember what you look like. They will only remember this face." She patted the painted paper in her arms. "You'll be safe in the streets, then. The night wardens will have gone to bed; nobody will remember anything, except that Tyramin played one of his wonderful tricks again and filled the warehouse for his performance."

"And then what?"

"What?"

He gazed at her, hearing very clearly, she saw, all she did not say. "I don't even recognize myself," he said simply. "Where do I go to forget?"

She hesitated, not knowing what to tell him, for she had no experience of such things beyond Tyramin's world. "We'll talk," she promised, "when I come back. Don't go outside for any reason. Wait."

She turned; he said, as she opened the door, "I don't know your name."

She looked back at him, producing the smile she must wear for the next hour or two, no matter what. "My name is Mistral."

He nodded. And that, he standing there surrounded by silk shirts and satin skirts, eddies of finery and feathers on the floor, masks staring at him, tricks of her trade, illusions, was the last she saw of the bewildered gardener.

Tyramin's performance was breathtaking, legendary. He painted darkness with such fires, such dazzling apparitions, such brilliant colors that held the crowd motionless at the sight, their upraised faces turning all the various shades of magic. As though he wanted to overshadow his own stunning illusions in the street, he worked complex and elaborate tricks, each more wondrous, more unbelievable than the last.

Mistral, her smile so immutably charming that it seemed a piece of the magic, barely had time to notice Arneth's face among the crowd. He came late, she saw; beyond that she had not a thought to spare for him, nor for any other of the wardens disguised among the crowd. Tyramin ended his performance with a great, colorful fountain of stars, which showered over the upturned faces but never touched them. The last star fell; Tyramin faded away like a dream, left them all in the dark.

Mistral moved quickly; Arneth was almost as fast. She had turned the key in the door where Tyramin sequestered himself, and was carrying his mask away when she saw the quarter warden edging through the dancers and assistants going this way and that to change out of their costumes, put the props away. She turned instantly, felt his eyes on her back. Good, she thought. Follow me. She led him away from her costume room and the bewildered young man within it. Arneth caught up with her in a turn or three down the hallways, as far as she could get from either Tyramin, and the only one she would permit him to see in her arms.

Arneth didn't bother looking at the mask. "Where is he?"

"Where he always is," she answered evenly, "after a performance. In solitude. Not to be disturbed."

"I have," he said as evenly, "two dozen armed guards waiting outside the warehouse. They will tear this place apart at a word. Where is the young man who worked the magic tonight?"

"There is no magic. Only illusion."

"Where is he?"

"I don't know. He was a stranger, someone caught up in one of Tyramin's tricks. Not one of us. He escaped from the crowd as soon as he could."

Arneth was silent, still gazing at her as if he were trying to see beneath the paint and glitter on her face to find the true, tired lines beneath. He said, his voice unexpectedly soft, "A street warden saw the entire incident. The dangerous fire that vanished as if by magic, leaving no trace. The king and Lord Pyt are ready to place a guard around the quarter, isolate it from the city, and drag Tyramin out by force if I give them word. There are street wardens waiting outside. If they don't see me very soon, they will call in the guard. Tyramin has disturbed the king, the High Warden, and the wizards of Kelior, both in the palace and in the school. Which should I call in first to force Tyramin out of his seclusion? Might? Or magic?"

Mistral looked back at him; behind her golden, unblinking eyes, her thoughts, busy as mice swarming through a maze, bumped into wall after wall. She felt a line seam the paint above her brows.

"It was never our intention to disturb," she said helplessly. "Only to entertain."

"Then convince me," he begged her. "Let me speak to Tyramin. Let me see his face."

She was silent again; one hand dropped from the mask, felt at the solid wood of the doorway behind her, gripped it. He waited, while she studied his face, the angles of bone, the shape of his mouth, trying to tell her fortune from the lines in it, her future. She had to clear her throat before she spoke again.

"You have seen it."

He blinked, startled. "Who—"

"You are looking at Tyramin's face."

He stared at her, his lips parting. Then she saw the blood flush into his face and knew his mind had leaped to the only conclusion. "Magic," he said without sound.

She brushed her lips with her forefinger, whispered, "We mean no harm. We'll be out of Kelior by dawn, and out of Numis as soon as—"

"The fire," he interrupted. "Was it real? Or—"

"It was real. An accident; a juggler threw a torch too high."

"And you put it out."

"Yes."

He was silent then, studying her face as she had studied his, searching in it for both their fates. "That's not what the street warden told me," he said steadily. "He said that the young stranger worked magic with fire, with water, with a dancer's sash. What can you expect of me if you lie to me? How can I help you, then?"

"How can I trust you?" she asked despairingly. "You're a quarter warden of Kelior; you belong to the king, who fears any magic beyond his control, even the most frivolous and innocent. I shape air into paper flowers; how can that threaten him? Please. Just let us go."

Around them, the chambers and hallways were suddenly very quiet, as though all motion had ceased; everyone, frozen in place by a spell, could only listen.

"How do you do it?" Arneth asked. He had shifted his weight to lean against the other side of the doorway; his voice was very quiet. "While you work the magic, who wears the mask?"

"No one. Tyramin is my puppet. I am his breath and motion, his voice." She paused, added, for it might help, "He used to be real. He was my father. A true magician, a master of illusions. Not a bone of magic anywhere in his body. But he could make you see magic, feel it, be charmed, enchanted by it. He loved his work. I grew up assisting him. He taught me many things. One day he realized that our definitions of magic were entirely different. He made paper flowers grow out of his sleeve. I made them out of my thoughts. He tried to learn, but he couldn't. So he used me to enhance his own illusions. I loved the work, creating the illusions, even the illusions of costumes, traveling to strange lands, sharing wonder everywhere we went. When my father died, I simply kept his name and his mask and continued his performances.

"Those who knew him gradually left me or died; I continued the illusion of his life because of his name, which became well-known. There was always speculation; I couldn't make a seamless transition from his death to his seeming agelessness. Too many had known him. Rumors about him blew on the wind: that he was truly a sorcerer, that he was ancient, that his wild powers were dangerous, subversive. None of that was ever true. Nor is it true of me. But rumors, like unhappy children and hungry dogs, follow us from land to land."

"Why did you come here?" Arneth asked. "With all those rumors of magic haunting you, how did you dare come to Kelior?"

She sighed, lines under her eyes hinting of a rueful smile. "They always loved Tyramin in the Twilight Quarter. I have grown tired of traveling. I thought that if we could convince the king that our illusions were simply tricks to charm away an hour, he would ignore us. We would become just one more bit of color in the quarter. But rumor, apparently, played its trick on us."

Arneth nodded. "It did precede you." He hesitated, running fingers through his hair, then added slowly, "I might persuade Lord Pyt that I have spoken to Tyramin and found no harm in him. But there is still the matter of the young man implicated in the magic that put the fire out. Where is he?"

"I don't—"

"Please," he interrupted wearily. "Where will we get to if you keep lying to me? How can I let you go then? The young man is suspected of being a wizard disguised as a gardener at the School of Magic. Lord Pyt and the king think he might also be Tyramin. Most of the Twilight Quarter certainly thought so tonight. Let me question him. I must give the the king something."

"The gardener?" she answered dryly. But she knew that the young man's power, undefined and unpredictable, would not stay secret long, now that he himself had wakened it. Still, she was reluctant to give him up in exchange for her safety. She had brought him there for his protection; she had made herself responsible. He was the unknown, the wild, lawless magic the kings of Numis forbade within their realm. Must she trade him for herself?

The answer, she found, was very simple. She was a magician, master of illusions; she would create another one.

She turned without a word, thinking as she walked, the great head in her arms, her other self, staring down the night before her. Arneth followed. She made things disappear all the time. In a room full of costumes, masks, she could make a young man old, a dancer into a marionette, a gardener disappear. As long as he was clever enough not to give himself away . . .

She stopped at the costume room, let Arneth open the closed door for her. Her thoughts slipped in first, busied themselves with fabric and masks, before she realized, stepping across the threshold, that the room was empty.

Her thoughts groped, came up empty as well. He had not just hidden himself; he had gone. She put the head down, blinking, relieved yet disturbed. What would he do with himself now? she wondered. Where in Kelior would he go for help?

"Where is he?" Arneth asked.

She shook her head, not knowing if he would believe anything she said now. "I left him here while Tyramin performed. I have no idea where he went." She added uneasily at his silence, "Please. He has nothing to do with us at all. Shouldn't you go out and tell your street wardens outside that you have nothing to fear from us before they bring the king's guard in here to search for you?"

"My—Oh." His mouth crooked. "Them. You're not the only one who can lie. There's nobody waiting for me but the guard outside the Twilight Gate, and they won't come until I summon them. Either you or that gardener must come with me to the king. I suggest you help me look for him." He seemed to see through the flash of speculation in her eyes, their sudden flick at the door. "If you lock me in here, I wouldn't blame you," he said steadily. "But my father, the High Warden, would be furious with both of us. Don't make things more tangled than they already are. Help me."

It was, she realized, not a demand but a plea. Wordlessly, she waved him out the door, where he waited outside while she changed the illusion she had made of herself into a more mundane mask suitable for the night streets of Kelior.

FIFTEEN

Yar, on the track of power, found Brenden Vetch and lost him and found him again. Or thought he had. Since Elver was with him, as cumbersome as a third foot, he couldn't move as quickly as he wanted. At least the boy was quiet while Yar dragged him ruthlessly along, his eyes always on the hapless, pale-haired figure cresting the roiling current of the crowd. Brenden could not rescue himself, Yar guessed, because he had no idea what he could or could not do, or what terrifying chaos might result from anything he did. Why the raucous crowd had decided he was Tyramin, Yar had no idea.

He was enlightened later when he saw the enormous painted mask, the bulky costume that concealed the magician within it. He stood at the edge of the throng, casting about for Brenden and wondering what mind possessed that head. The crowd had lost sight of Brenden, but not of Tyramin; it mistook the young man who had put out the fire for the one who wore that mask. But Yar, briefly aware of the mind

within the great painted head, swarming with colorful transformations, did not recognize it. The magician's daughter,
with her delicate, painted oval of a face, her amber eyes glittering with fire, he remembered seeing some nights ago as
she rode with Tyramin's company through the Twilight Gate.
Again she took on mystery with her serene face that seemed
kin to the moon, her endlessly graceful movements, her
changeless smile. He had to tear his attention away from that
illusion. And then he had to pull the enraptured Elver away,
too. It almost required sorcery to break free of the crowd,
which had grown behind him in a few brief minutes to spill
through the doors and windows of the old warehouse, and
out onto the cobbles.

On the street again, Yar resumed his search. Brenden
must have escaped when the real Tyramin caught the crowd's
attention. Beyond the warehouse, the quarter seemed calm,
no disturbances, no curiosities, just people going about their
business under the chilly stare of the moon.

Elver spoke. "May I speak now?"

"No."

"I could wait for you in the warehouse. It's warm in there,
and you could do what you want more easily without me."

Yar hesitated. The boy was shivering in spite of Yar's
cloak. He couldn't get into worse trouble watching the magician and his beautiful daughter than he was already in. Yar
fixed him with a grim eye.

"Promise me that you will be there when I come back for
you. That you will not follow whatever will-o'-the-wisp beck-
ons you out the door. I won't look for you."

"I promise," Elver answered meekly. Yar watched him
slither back through the crowd as easily as a fish through fingers, toward the music and the thunder of magic. Yar consid-

ered the perplexing question of Elver for a moment, then let it go. Finding a way to wriggle Elver out of trouble was moot, considering the trouble he himself was likely to be in if he didn't return to school and king with Brenden Vetch.

If nothing else, the gardener had learned how to disappear quickly enough. He was probably hiding from himself, fiercely blocking any hint of magic from his thoughts with whatever was in front of his nose: a stone wall, a solid slab of locked door, the impenetrable dark at the end of an alley. If that was how he looked at himself, that was all Yar could see of him as he made his way through the streets, casting thought everywhere. He moved a little more slowly than his thoughts, only barely visible, searching faces and shadows as well as minds for the errant gardener. The moon, a drooping eye that night, was moving to meet the river mist, the crowds from the warehouse had scattered through the streets again, exclaiming vividly and hoarsely about marvels Tyramin had shown them, when Yar finally stopped his search, stood staring blankly at a stall full of gaudy puppets.

Maybe, he thought, Brenden had simply gone back to the school. Frightened by the crowds, bewildered by his powers, he had gone where he would be safe and where such mysteries could be explained. Yar could sense him nowhere in the quarter. Wye could tell him then and there if Brenden had returned. But no, he amended quickly, pulling thought away from her. If Valoren was still waiting with her, and Brenden was not, the king's wizard would join Yar in a breath to help him search. Brenden's first glimpse of the true face of power in Kelior might well be disastrous, considering his own incomprehensible state of mind.

Yar took a step toward the Twilight Gate, remembered Elver, and turned back toward the river. In that moment, as though something had leaped out of the dark water into the silvery light of the moon, he glimpsed the flow of an unusual power. It drew him, this vague glittering that might be Brenden's mind. He moved more quickly than he had all night, through the labyrinth of streets, until he felt the complex and lovely flow of power quite close to him. He stopped, seeing its source. But it was not the face he had expected.

Two people stood in a torchlit conjunction of streets. He recognized the quarter warden, Lord Pyt's son Arneth. The woman, slight, dark-haired, plainly dressed, he didn't know at all until she turned her face for a glance into the dark, as though she sensed someone's attention. The amber eyes, fire melting through them, made Yar blink. In an instant, as though Tyramin had struck the cobbles with his staff and spoken, she was transformed. This was Yar's smiling vision, the daughter of the moon, who juggled bits of colored fire and turned herself amiably into doves or butterflies at her father's command. She wasn't smiling now, nor was she trailing swaths of silk; her hair was bundled at her neck, all the stars fallen out of it.

Her mind, Yar realized, was a firestorm of magic. Was she the force behind Tyramin's powers? he wondered. Or was she simply heir to it? Either way, such true magic made them both dangerous and endangered on the streets of Kelior.

The golden eyes searched the dark in which he hid himself, trying to see him, failing. Yar stood very quietly, listening while she spoke to the quarter warden.

"I can't find him. He must have gone back to his plants. He was terrified by the crowd."

Arneth Pyt looked at her narrowly, not trusting that. "Are you sure?"

The quarter warden was also searching for Brenden, Yar realized with a touch of apprehension. The ambiguities of the fire and the missing gardener must have been brought to Murat Pyt's attention.

The magician's daughter cast a glance across the dark again. "I don't know where to look. He could be anywhere in Kelior."

"He didn't tell you—"

"I asked him to wait for me. He didn't know where to go anymore, what to do with himself. I think he must have gone to whatever place he thought he would be safe. The school, maybe."

The last place he will be safe, Yar thought grimly.

Arneth refused to yield Brenden to the night. "Nothing won't satisfy the king," he warned. "Or the king's wizard Valoren. If I go back to the school and the gardener isn't there, I'll be forced to come back here, and I will be in the company of wizards."

She inclined her head. "I understand."

"Nor will I take the guard from the Twilight Gate if I go back now."

"I understand," she answered again, in her low, silky murmur.

"So. It would be better for everyone if we found him now. I would be justified then in taking the guard from the quarter in order to escort him back to the school. Do you understand that?"

Yar did, suddenly illuminated. The gate will be unguarded, Arneth Pyt was telling her; all attention will be on the gardener. It will be safe for Tyramin to leave then.

Magic, the wizard marveled. She has enchanted the quarter warden.

She bowed her head again. "Then we must keep looking."

They moved down the street. Yar went the opposite direction to retrieve the abandoned Elver.

He found the boy in one of the little back rooms where the performers were wandering restively, most still in odd pieces of costume, jewels in their hair, flecks of glitter in smudged paint on their faces. They clustered around Yar eagerly as he entered.

"You've come for the boy, haven't you?" a curly-haired young man asked. "He says you're a wizard. Did you chance across Mistral out there?"

"Mistral?"

"Tyramin's daughter. There's some kind of trouble in the quarter. We heard a rumor of royal guards at the Twilight Gate, and she's not here to tell us what to do."

Yar shook Elver, who was drowsing on a pile of moth-eaten skins and old packing blankets. The boy got to his feet, yawning.

"Yes, I saw her. I believe she was negotiating a route out of trouble with the quarter warden."

Some smiled; other faces grew tight, hard as fears were confirmed.

"Tyramin's magic came too close to real tonight," someone breathed.

"Where is Tyramin?" Yar asked curiously. "Why isn't he here to tell you what to do?"

They gazed at him, as though puzzled that he would ask. "We never see him after a performance. He rests, he invents new tricks—"

"Even when you might be in danger?"

"Mistral will know what to do," they told him. "Tyramin dreams and performs. The master magician must hone his art; he thinks of nothing else. It's Mistral who handles the world outside his head."

Yar grunted, wondering, "Who is he? This Tyramin?"

They only looked at one another, shaking their heads and smiling; no one offered to give him any other name, much less explain him. His mystery was part of his disguise, Yar guessed. He tugged at Elver, who seemed spellbound by the shadowy curves within a dancer's glittering bodice.

"Thank you for letting him stay. If I see Mistral again, I'll tell her that you're waiting."

The streets beyond the warehouse were growing quiet; the moon had vanished. It was that dark, chilly, timeless hour, the dregs of night. Even the Twilight Quarter sensed the dawn beyond its farthest border. Elver, swaying with weariness, yawned hugely and tripped over the cobbles. Time, Yar thought, to return to the school, face whatever waited there.

Elver stopped. He stood like a post in the middle of the street, refusing to take another step; Yar wondered if he had fallen asleep on his feet. Then his head turned slowly. He stared at a solid wall of black between two buildings whose front windows were still lit.

"What is it?" Yar asked softly. And then the boy was gone, swallowed up so quickly into the darkness that he startled Yar. The wizard cast his own light into the alley, a pale fire ignited quickly and with little thought by his alarm. The flash, brief and cold as moonlight, illumined two figures. Then the alley went dark again. Yar, sighing with relief, stepped into the dark, stopping the two at the edge of light.

"Brenden," he whispered. "They're searching for you."

"I know," the gardener said bleakly.

Yar's hand closed on Elver's thin shoulder. "How did you see him?" he asked. "I didn't."

Elver scratched his head. "I think I was dreaming," he answered vaguely. "I saw the stones in the wall move."

"In the dark?"

He shrugged. "In my head."

Yar eyed him narrowly. Magic, it seemed, was revealing itself everywhere he looked in the Twilight Quarter that night. Unruly, unpredictable, and liable to cause them all a great deal of trouble before the long night was over.

He looked at Brenden questioningly. The young man nodded. "I've been here in the dark for hours, I think. I remember when the stones seemed to crowd around me, into my mind. It seemed the safest thing to be. A stone wall. Nobody ever looks at a wall."

"We followed you down to the warehouse, then lost you. I've been searching for you since then."

Brenden nodded jerkily. "I thought I'd wait until dawn, then go on back home."

"Home."

"North. It's quieter there."

"You're frightened," Yar told him. "You terrified yourself, and then we did. It's not easy to think clearly when you're afraid."

"No," Brenden agreed starkly. "I don't know what's happening in my own head. I don't know how I'm doing the things I do. What if I do something wrong?"

"But you didn't," Elver said eagerly, his tired eyes alight. "You saved the Twilight Quarter from burning up. You rescued that woman with the golden eyes."

"She rescued me." Brenden hesitated, his eyes on Yar; his voice grew very soft. "I put the fire out. But she made the burned house look like itself again; she sent the water back into the river and put the fountain back together. She turned my magic into Tyramin's trick."

"Did she," Yar breathed.

"She understood that I didn't know what I was doing, or what I am. She wanted to talk, to explain things to me. But I ran away from her. I decided just to get away from everyone. It's best that way."

"Not for the school. The wizard Valoren told the king about your powers, and now Wye is in trouble. And so am I, if I go back there without you."

"Valoren!" Brenden exclaimed. He cast a glance at the silent street as though the wizard might suddenly appear at the sound of his name. "How would he know what kind of powers I have? All we talked about was flowers."

"It's his duty to be aware of these things. Wye saw the power in you. So did I. You don't know how to conceal it. So now the king also knows, and with half the Twilight Quarter calling you Tyramin, even the street wardens know. There was a fire in the quarter that you put out by magic. Fire isn't something anyone ignores in an ancient city. Nor does anyone easily forget the man who puts it out by summoning a river up out of the cobblestones."

Brenden slumped back against the wall but stopped himself somehow from vanishing back into it.

"What should I do, then?" he pleaded. "To get us all out of trouble?"

"He's not Tyramin," Elver protested. "And he's done nothing wrong. He rescued the Twilight Quarter. The king should reward him the way he rewarded you for rescuing Kelior from the flying monsters."

"By keeping me under his eye and training me to teach only what he wanted me to know?" Yar asked sharply, startling himself as well as Elver. The boy stared back at him, wordless for once. "Where else did you think all your questions would lead?"

"What flying monsters?" Brenden asked.

"Never mind them now." Yar sighed, pulling his thoughts together. "Elver has a point. You have done nothing wrong, and the king should be grateful to you. If you go home, Valoren will think you have something to hide, and he will come looking for you. He will find you, and he will bring you back to Kelior, one way or another. It would be better, I think, if you go back to the school by your own choice. The quarter warden is looking for you as well—"

"For what?" Brenden asked incredulously. "Putting out a fire?"

"For being associated with Tyramin, and with magic that is suspect, beyond the king's control."

Brenden closed his eyes, opened them again. "I didn't—I never said—I didn't even know Tyramin's name until they shouted it at me."

"We'll go back and explain. May it be that simple. The Twilight Gate is just up the street. Keep to the shadows. And," he added to the strangely mute Elver, "no talking."

They made it within sight of the gate without mishap. But the line of armed guards across it, men and horses raising a mist with their cold breaths, armor picking up stray gleams from the last stubborn lights still burning in the city, made them all duck back around a corner.

"What should we do?" Brenden whispered.

"I'm thinking." For no reason at all, he thought of the strange, shadowless shapes Od had written about, who had hidden themselves and their power in a place not even the sun could find. Skrygard Mountain. That might be just far enough, he thought wearily, from the king's justice and Valoren's cold, relentless, shortsighted eyes.

"We could all turn invisible," Elver ventured. "I taught myself how."

"Why am I not surprised?" Yar murmured. A horse flicked an ear their direction, and he drew them farther back behind a food stall where dying coals still pulsed within the brickwork of the fire pit. But why should I? he argued with himself. Why should I? Impulses and submerged angers chose that inconvenient moment to surface; he fought them, trying to think what would be best for Brenden, for Mistral and Tyramin, even for Elver, who seemed to have made his own impulsive decision.

"Skrygard Mountain," Brenden whispered, and Yar started. He looked at the gardener, who seemed surprised as well. "It just came into my head."

"It was in mine," Yar told him. "You heard it. What do you know about Skrygard Mountain?"

"Nothing much. I found myself there early last spring. In a quiet, cold, shadowy place. There were odd shapes in the snow. I don't know anything about them."

"Still there," Yar said wonderingly. "After all these centuries. What did you think when you saw them?"

"They seemed alive. I don't know why. I waited for them to speak. I listened. But I didn't hear. So I turned around and went back down. Have you seen them?"

Yar shook his head. "Od wrote about them."

"We could hide there."

"We could hide," Yar repeated slowly, "like they did . . . But from what, I wonder."

Brenden nodded toward the guarded gate. "That," he suggested simply. "And the likes of Valoren." He shrugged a little at Yar's quizzical gaze. "It's just a thought. I'd rather be there, now, than here, that's all."

Yar was silent, his thoughts straying from Skrygard Mountain to Ceta, who had first shown him the name. Elver huddled against the fire pit bricks, tugging a corner of Yar's cloak over him. "At least it's warm," he mumbled, his eyes closing. "Tell me when you make up your mind."

Brenden drew breath, held it, then shifted to get up. "I should just go with the guard. You won't have to explain anything to anyone then."

"Oh, I'll have some explaining to do," Yar said thinly. "Anyway, why should you? Why should you go back under guard?"

"Because that's the way the world is?"

"Why should it be?"

"Then we'll go invisible. We can get back to the school without anyone noticing." He added, at Yar's stubborn silence, "You just told us what you thought would be best."

"I'm having second thoughts."

"Now?"

"I don't want to go back," Yar said, and felt, as the words left his mouth, an enormous relief that all his despair and restlessness had finally found their way into words. "I know exactly what and how Valoren has been taught, and I know a few things he doesn't. I am not allowed to say what I know. To become anything more than what I have been trained to be. I don't teach lies, but I do not teach all I know is true, and I am not allowed the dangers of curiosity and wonder. If you go back, the king will reward you for rescuing Kelior, and at the same time he will put walls around you, so that the only power you will master will be under his command. I don't know what to do for you, or even for myself. I only know that I don't want to go back to what I have been."

"I don't like the sound of where you've been, either," Brenden said tersely. "Do we have a choice?"

"No." He was silent a little, thinking again for them all. Brenden waited, watching him. Yar heard a snore from Elver. He sighed. "Not at the moment, anyway. I'll find Arneth Pyt and tell him that I'm taking you back to the school with me. He'll be able to take the guard from the gate then, and let the magician and his daughter leave the quarter. That much we can do."

"I just came to Kelior to garden," Brenden said helplessly. "Od said I could go home when I wanted."

"You could try telling Valoren that. It might help." He put his hand on the young man's shoulder, rendering him and the dreaming Elver as unremarkable as the brickwork. "No one will notice you if you don't move. I'll be back quickly."

Brenden nodded. Yar, scarcely more visible, cast about the emptying streets for the quarter warden. He found him easily, and, to his surprise, very close. Yar stepped around the corner and saw Arneth standing at the Twilight Gate, speaking to someone who had just ridden through it.

The messenger's voice did not carry, but the wizard's ear picked it out like a thread in a weave across the air.

"Lord Pyt sent me to tell you that absolutely no one is to be permitted to enter or leave the Twilight Quarter, and the gate will remain under guard until the king himself sends word."

"Now what?" Arneth demanded tightly, echoing the words in Yar's head. The messenger leaned down toward him, nearly whispering, but Yar heard him.

"Princess Sulys has vanished. She hasn't been seen since before sunset. No one can find her. The king and Valoren fear that either Tyramin or the missing gardener—or both—may have something to do with her disappearance."

Arneth made a noise that sounded like a muffled curse. Yar raised his eyes to the vacuous sky and swallowed his own comments. He returned in a single step to his spell and found it broken.

The brickwork that was Elver gave a snore and was still again. The brickwork that Brenden had been was nothing but bricks.

SIXTEEN

The missing princess sat with Ceta on the center stone of the labyrinth. They had been talking for many melted candles; there was no other way in that windowless, magical place to measure the passing of time. They had lost sight of one another immediately upon entering the stonework. Sulys had heard Ceta's astonished comment very clearly. Then their voices, calling back and forth, sounded with bewildering randomness, one moment separated by a single wall, it seemed, and the next by the entire labyrinth. Sulys, wending her way alone through the shadowy place, blocked time and again by walls that seemed to rise up out of nowhere, took comfort from Ceta's unperturbed voice.

"But what's the point of it?" Sulys demanded once, exasperated by the endless fits and starts of the path. "Going around and around and getting nowhere?" Ceta answered something; the words, oddly faint, bounced off stone, frayed beyond recognition. "What?" Sulys shouted back, alarmed.

"I think it's meant to imitate your life," Ceta called back, abruptly very close and startlingly loud.

"Well," Sulys answered after some thought, "it does remind me of Aunt Fanerl and my wedding."

Ceta laughed, far away again. Sulys smiled wryly, struck by a skewed vision of the topsy-turvy preparations, which had resulted in her escape in a pair of dreadful shoes and a length of fabric to run in circles through a labyrinth. It shouldn't be that difficult, she thought. I should just tell Aunt Fanerl what I want. But that, she realized instantly, was not the problem. She could not want anything unless she wanted Valoren.

She nearly tumbled over a broad stone in her way. Its sides had been carved into a perfect circle; the top was flat. Tired and footsore, she sat down, deciding to wait and see if Ceta might wander along. She called; Ceta answered from some distance. Sulys lifted her taper, looking for the nearest opening in the wall. The marble made a ring around her, she realized; there was no place left to go.

"Oh, I'm here," she whispered. Her little circle of light illumined other half-burned candles and blackened ends dropped by previous questers. She picked up a few, lit them with her candle, and fastened them in their hardening wax onto the stone around her. She called out Ceta's name, telling her excitedly, "I'm here!"

"Do you see a round stone with a map on it?" Ceta asked, sounding very close again.

Sulys looked around, then got up and studied the stone she had been sitting on. There were carvings in it, a neat spiral through what looked like a very simple maze, nothing that resembled the elaborate, obstacle-riddled path that had impeded her. "Yes," she called back, adding dourly, "a map of something anyway. Nowhere I've been."

"Then you have reached the center."

"Where are you?"

"I don't know," Ceta answered.

And suddenly there she was, stepping through the ring and blinking.

"How strange," she breathed, joining the princess to gaze down at the center stone. "I kept thinking of Yar and coming up against walls. As though the maze had refashioned itself around my thoughts. But this little map looks like nowhere I've been, either."

"Maybe it's the way out?"

"I hope so. I hope it's that simple." She lingered, frowning down at it, still thinking of the wizard, Sulys guessed. Ceta said slowly, "It was when I told you I didn't know where I was that I found myself here. As if this is not the end of the maze but the beginning. The place where you finally realize you are lost."

"What do you mean?"

"That I finally understood that I have no idea where Yar is, these days. What he's thinking, what's troubling him. That he might have gone somewhere I'm afraid to follow. I didn't want to admit that anything might be wrong between us."

Sulys nodded, comprehending the gist if not the details. "I was thinking of Valoren, and I kept stumbling into our wedding. My brother Enys saw it: that I can't care about it unless I care about him, and so far I've found no reason at all to care about anything."

Ceta sat down on the center stone, folding up her long legs in a fashion that would have caused Aunt Fanerl's curls to uncoil. Sulys relighted a candle that had sputtered beneath Ceta's silks, and sat beside her, sliding her feet with relief out of their shoes.

"Yes," Ceta said simply. "I felt much the same about my marriage."

"Do you know your cousin well?"

"I knew him better when we were growing up than I do now. He borrowed my books. He liked studying peculiar insects, I remember, and he kept a pet raven. He used to know how to laugh."

"Really?"

"And then he went to Kelior to become a wizard, and I got married . . . I didn't see much of him for years. When the king introduced him at court as his counselor, I almost didn't recognize him. My sweet young cousin had grown so distant, so watchful. So—"

"Suspicious," Sulys said succinctly. "As though he's waiting for you to do something wrong. How can anyone marry a man like that?"

"But is he really like that?"

"I don't know! We tried to talk, but we might as well have been speaking different languages, and he didn't give me time to find the courage to tell him things he has to know."

"What things?"

"Things." She held her breath, looking for words, loosed it helplessly. "Little things."

"Like what? You sing in your sleep? You hate being touched?"

"Worse."

"Worse," Ceta repeated blankly. "All right. You would rather be bound to a stake and burned to a crisp by a dragon than be married to anyone."

"I wouldn't go that far."

"You love someone else."

Sulys shook her head, swallowing. "I wish I did," she whispered. "I wish I loved someone. My great-grandmother married without love, and found a way to be happy. Is love always a matter of chance when you marry?"

"Often enough. Not always." She paused, gazing questioningly at Sulys. "What exactly are you afraid of? That you can never love Valoren, and you will be miserable for the rest of your life?"

"That, of course."

"But that's not all."

"No," Sulys answered hollowly. Ceta waited wordlessly. Sulys bent finally, pulled one of her shoes off. She held it so that the jewels of red and blue and green reflected fire. Then she picked up a taper, blew it out. Smoking wick drew close to fire burning deep within a jewel. Fire filled Sulys's eyes, flowed from jewel to princess, then to the candle wick. The fire flicked alive upon the wick, as green as emerald.

Ceta's gasp nearly blew it out. "Touch it," Sulys said, staring into the jewel.

Ceta drew a finger through it. "It's cold," she whispered.

"It's not real. Just a reflection. Illusion." She blinked her eyes; the little green flame on the wick disappeared. "It's just a game my great-grandmother taught me. Play magic, she calls it. Magic too unimportant to notice." She moved her eyes from the wick to Ceta. "Do you think it will be too unimportant for Valoren to notice?"

"I don't—I have—" She paused, said more coherently, "I think I'm beginning to understand the problem. Where did the magic come from?"

"My great-grandmother's country. They permit such small things there."

"What else can you do?"

Sulys glanced upward toward the shadowy vault above the labyrinth, half-expecting to see Valoren's eyes searching the source of the power through the ceiling. "If I had some water, I might be able to see where Valoren is."

"Or Yar?"

"Perhaps. Though my great-grandmother can see such things far more easily than I. Sometimes we find missing things that way. She can't see well, and she's always mislaying something. She also taught me to hide little secrets—a letter, or a ring, a flower—by sewing a certain pattern of stitchwork around it. Sometimes, when I look into a candle flame I can see what will happen."

"You can?"

"She didn't teach me that; I was born with it. But I'm sure I inherited it from her."

"Could your mother do these small things also?"

"No. And she made my great-grandmother promise to keep such things secret. So I never told my mother what I can do; that way she wouldn't have to keep secrets from my father. You see, that's the other difficulty. I won't be able to keep anything secret from Valoren. He'll make me tell my father, and my father will—he'll—I have no idea what he'll do with a daughter working forbidden magic under his roof."

"And you won't like Valoren any better for having forced you to confess."

"No," she said starkly. "I won't. So you see why I must talk to him before we do something that will force us to hate each other."

"Get married, you mean."

"Yes."

Ceta thought, long, jeweled fingers tapping at her lips. "Well," she said finally, "this would be one way for you to get Valoren's attention. He'll either find out before you're married, or after, and you're right: far better for him to find out before. You could work some of your small magics now, and see if it brings him down here. I can fetch whatever you need. Are you hungry? I know where the kitchens are; it's something I learned while working for long hours in the library."

"Oh, yes." Sulys sighed. "I forgot about supper when I ran away. But how will you find your way back here?"

Ceta's mouth crooked. "The same way I did before, I suppose. Sooner or later I will reach the point that the labyrinth is trying to make. Maybe it will be easier the second time. Now tell me what you need."

Sulys stood up, paced a moment in her bare feet, thinking. "Paper. Scissors, if you can find them. Water. A cup. Buttons. Well, never mind buttons. I can pull them off my sleeves. Ink, or something like it. I have cloth. We have plenty of candle wax; we can shape things out of that."

"I'd better bring more candles. And I have buttons, too." Ceta revealed a long row of them down the front of her underskirt. "Anything else?"

"Whatever looks magical in the kitchen."

"Everything looks magical in a kitchen when you're hungry." She hesitated. "Won't they wonder where you are if you're not at supper?"

"No. They'll just think I'm with my great-grandmother. They never really wonder unless they need me. Anyway, my father is still with the wizards, as far as I know. So I might as well be here as anywhere."

She rose to let Ceta study the map of the labyrinth again. Even in the flickering light the path back to the beginning seemed simple: a turn here, there, here again, then there, and there, and there you were, stepping into time and the world again.

"I'll let you know," Ceta said dubiously. She paused before she left, gazing quizzically at Sulys. "Are you sure you want this here and now? Would you rather come back up with me?"

"No, I wouldn't. I don't see any point to waiting."

"All right. I'll hurry."

Left to her own devices, Sulys sat quietly for a few minutes, wondering about Valoren, and what the odds were that he might rather not wed himself to her suspect powers, and she could go live in disgrace and in perfect contentment in the tower with Dittany. A candle sputtered out. She lit another, made idle hand shadows on the wall. An idea sidled into her mind. She glanced at it, then gave it a second look. She thought: Why not? I have thread, I have fire, I have jewels on my shoes. Let's see what it takes to get a wizard's attention . . .

She picked threads out of the rough edge of the satin around her shoulders. As Dittany showed her, she spread them on the face of the stone, in the shape of the first letter of Valoren's name. She melted drops of wax on the tops and bottom of each V to hold them in place. Then she moved the light slowly back and forth across the transfixed letters.

"Valoren," she murmured. "Where are you? Valoren. Show me where you are. Where are you?"

Light caught in carvings, spilled through circling stones. Shadow followed, clouding the passages. Light illumined them again, like a tiny sunrise, night following always behind it. After a while, during which absolutely nothing happened, not even Ceta, Sulys noticed how the letters intercepted passageways on the face of the map, made walls through openings, V getting in the way everywhere through the spirals of the labyrinth.

She sucked in breath, wondering if Ceta were bumping into them. She put the candle hastily into a pool of its own wax and pulled the threads back off the map. She was picking away the thumbnail chips of wax that had held them down when Ceta finally appeared.

She put baskets and other paraphernalia down on the stones, looking flushed and slightly askew.

"It took forever to get back! As though the labyrinth were trying to keep me out."

"I think that was my fault," Sulys confessed. "I was trying to lure Valoren down here. I accidentally laid my spell on top of the map."

"More likely it was my own tangled thoughts," Ceta murmured as she unpacked a basket. "I heard some strange news from the librarian, who gave me paper and scissors and ink. String and candles I got from the kitchen, along with bread, cheese, cold roast chicken, cups, a crock of water, and pears. And a knife."

"What news?"

"Some trouble in the Twilight Quarter. A mysterious fire attributed to Tyramin, a missing gardener, a missing wizard . . . The king and Valoren are still here, so they tell me, waiting with the wizards to see if their power is needed."

"A missing wizard? How can you tell if a wizard is missing, or if he just went off to do something magical? Who is he?"

"Yar." Ceta applied the knife vigorously to the bread a moment, then stopped midslice to gaze pleadingly at Sulys. "Will you look for him? I brought you water. He went to the Twilight Quarter sometime ago to bring the school's new gardener back, and hasn't returned. The wizards are all in seclusion in Wye's chambers, along with Valoren and the king. I can't ask if they have found him, and no one else has any idea where he is."

"Of course I'll try." She reached hungrily for bread and cheese, relieved that it was nothing more complex than a lost gardener and Tyramin's tricks disturbing Kelior that night. Ceta balanced backward on the edge of the stone in her cross-legged fashion, picking at chicken with her fingers and studying the map as she ate.

"You'd think that Od, who designed this labyrinth, would have written more clearly about its eccentricities, especially since she meant it to teach the students."

"Maybe she never got lost," Sulys suggested. "She always knew where she was."

"Maybe. Yar thinks she didn't fully understand her own powers. Or her own intentions, which is ultimately how the power of the wizards came under the control of the rulers."

"She traveled, didn't she?" Sulys asked, vaguely remembering that her father had asked Ceta to write a book about Od and the rulers of Numis.

"Yes, a great deal, to many distant lands."

"She might have gone to my great-grandmother's country."

"Which is?" Ceta asked, licking her thumb.

"Hestria, I think. Or was that the name of the royal city?"

"Navar, in Hestria."

"Yes, that's where she was born."

"Od visited Hestria, yes. So," Ceta added, easily picking up the path of Sulys's thought, "she might well have learned those small magics, too. Since nothing Od learned was forbidden in her own school, the magic you and Lady Dittany practice may well be lawful here."

"Except that I didn't learn it from a wizard. And I kept it secret."

"Well, we'll just see what the wizards have to say about that."

They finished their makeshift supper, put the scraps back into the basket. Ceta, who seemed oddly fascinated by the untrustworthy map, brushed crumbs off it, her fingertips lingering over the spirals. "That's strange," she murmured, bending over it suddenly. "Look. The center stone on the map is completely different."

Sulys, who was pouring water into an extremely ornate goblet that must have wandered into the school kitchen from the palace, set the crock down to see. On the map, the round center stone of the labyrinth, which they had just used as a supper table, had been carved as a pyramid.

"It's hard to carve a circle?" she guessed.

"Whoever chiseled this managed perfectly well with the rest of the labyrinth." Ceta crouched beside it, propped her chin on her hands at the edge of the map, her eyes narrowed. "I love maps; they have always fascinated me. Especially the very old ones, with pictures on them of sea monsters and the faces of the winds. Suppose . . . just suppose this is not the way into or out of the labyrinth, but a map of something entirely different. That would explain why it's all but useless."

"A map of what?" Sulys asked bewilderedly.

Ceta pondered, then tapped the tiny pyramid. "A map showing the way to that."

"But what is it? And where is it?"

"I'm not sure. A fortress, maybe, or a mountain. Someplace that Od wanted hidden and yet at the same time wanted it to be found."

"I think the chisel just slipped."

"Perhaps." Ceta's voice had grown very soft. She was seeing something in the pattern, her eyes luminous in the candlelight, intent. "Oh, I wonder," she whispered. "I wonder . . . We have to find Yar. It's Od's secret, and it would be safe with him."

"What secret?" Sulys asked, her skin prickling at the notion that even Od kept things hidden from the wizards.

"A mountain. Not even Yar knew about it until I showed him the name in Od's writings. I wonder if this is how you get there from here, if you are a wizard."

"Where?"

"North. Far north." She straightened, her eyes still full of whatever mystery the stone had shown her. "I wonder if we could follow this map to go there, see what she's writing about."

"Now?"

Ceta shook map and mountain out of her eyes, seeing Sulys again and why they had come down there in the first place. "No, of course not. I'm sorry. One problem at a time. Where were we?"

"Finding Yar."

"Oh, good." She sat down firmly on the map so that it wouldn't distract her, and watched Sulys finish filling the cup. "How does your spell work?"

"It may very well not," Sulys warned her. "My greatgrandmother thinks it has something to do with the weather, but I doubt it."

"There is no weather down here."

"She says reflections get windblown, traveling from place to place. I think it has more to do with how clearly you are able to see, which is better some days than others."

"Internal weather."

"Yes." She picked up a candle, tipped it to melt the wax onto stone. "Breath, wax, and fire . . ." Liquid wax made a Y on the stone. She used the bread knife to lift it gently when it hardened, float it on the water. She bent over the cup, breathed Yar's name into it, then spelled it with the reflection of fire across the water. "Yar," she whispered again. "Yar." The name echoed in her head, rippled out across her thoughts. She had only a vague memory of meeting the wizard, but she formed the image of a teacher's somber robe in her head, hoping that would keep the faces of any number of Yars throughout Kelior out of her cup. "Yar . . ."

She found a man in her thoughts, like a waking dream, as she balanced between the thin boundary between water and air, fire and dark, name and image. She heard Ceta's quick breath, and knew she was seeing the vision in the cup.

"Is that Yar?" Sulys asked, trying not to wake herself.

"Yes. But what on earth is he doing?"

There was a flash of green and purple through the water. Stars glittered across the wizard. And then doves. And then a pair of human eyes, lucent amber and very beautiful, floated like a memory across his face.

Sulys blinked. The image vanished. She looked questioningly at Ceta, who was still staring into the cup, her brows raised as high as they could go.

"I thought that he went to the Twilight Quarter to look for a gardener."

"I know what that was!" Sulys exclaimed. "He's watching Tyramin perform. Those were the Illusions and Enchantments."

"Evidently," Ceta murmured a trifle dryly, still staring into the water as though Yar might be lingering in the bottom of the cup. She straightened finally, studied the air in front of her, frowning at it. "But why, I wonder? Is he so tired of his life that he's going to run off to join the magician's company?"

"Valoren," Sulys said suddenly, and Ceta's eyes moved to her.

"My cousin is responsible for this, too?"

"Valoren and my father are suspicious of Tyramin's power. I heard them talking about it. They must have told Yar to watch him."

"A trickster?"

"Small magics," Sulys said darkly, pacing again, "may point the way to more complex dangers. So Valoren told me." She stopped abruptly, remembering the small magic she had just done within a school full of wizards.

They both stared upward a moment without breathing. Nothing happened. Wizards did not rain out of nowhere to investigate. No one came.

"You'd think," Ceta said tartly, "that someone practicing magic in the middle of the labyrinth in the middle of the night would attract more attention than this. Show me what else you can do."

"Everything?"

Ceta pinched a guttering candle and lit another to take its place. "Why not? If Tyramin can get the attention of the entire school of wizards by pulling paper flowers out of his sleeves, why shouldn't you?"

"Maybe my power is too quiet."

"That's the kind of power Valoren should fear most. If he's worth the king's trust, he'll hear you, and if he's worth your love, he'll start listening to you. Keep trying."

SEVENTEEN

Mistral, waiting for Arneth in a shadowy corner as he spoke to the guard, heard his stifled imprecation most clearly and drew her own conclusions. She shifted farther into the shadows and emptied her mind of all magic, as she did when she went about her business in the quarter, presenting her least remarkable face to the world. She waited. Arneth spoke a little longer to the guard, then turned away, his quick footsteps echoing through the empty streets, the drowsing, shuttered houses.

He found her in the dark, told her softly, "Now Princess Sulys has disappeared. Of course they suspect Tyramin. The quarter will remain under guard."

"Why? Why Tyramin?"

"Why not? The princess has vanished; the magician or the gardener must be to blame. That's what my father would pounce on, anyway. Where else could they imagine a young woman might be at this hour of night?"

Mistral remembered the ancient, creaking docks beyond the warehouse where the odd ship still moored itself, full of strange spices and plants and exotic fabrics of interest to the eccentric quarter. "What about the river? Is it under guard?"

"Not that I know," Arneth said. "Somebody will remember to do that soon enough. But maybe they'll expect me to think of it."

"You are the quarter warden, after all."

"Yes. Let's go and see."

She touched his arm, checked his impulsive step. "You'll get into trouble if we escape now."

He shrugged slightly. "Only for being careless." He stood a breath longer, looking at her; she saw his jaw tighten against something he might have said. He turned abruptly. "We should hurry. How fast can you pack, if you can get out that way?"

"We can leave the wagons and heavy gear, pack what we can on the horses and go. Tyramin has been very successful here; we can afford to leave things behind."

His face turned away; he said something she didn't hear.

"What?"

"Where will you go?"

"South. It's the quickest way out of Numis. And there are fewer towns to remember us; those we can pass through at night."

He looked at her again, his eyes catching some still-burning lamplight from an open shutter. "I'm sorry."

She nodded wordlessly, then turned her own face firmly toward the river, black now and nearly invisible since the moon had set. They walked swiftly, as quietly as possible. A few torches burned along the water for night fishers, sailors, and wanderers wringing the last measure of amusement out of the hour before dawn. The dock was quiet, a single small vessel tied along it, sails furled, seemingly empty.

"No guard," Arneth said tersely, as they neared. He sounded surprised. Mistral could see the huge old warehouse on the next street towering over the river houses. She wondered if the performers had picked up gossip of the night's events and had already begun to pack. They crossed the sunken cobbles of the ancient street meandering along the bank of the river.

She sensed it before she touched it: a wall of power that rose between the quarter and the river, indistinguishable from shadow and air, but as adamant as stone. She had a brief, incoherent impression of many minds weaving their wills together and stepped back hastily before her own power became tangled in it. Arneth walked blindly into it before she could warn him. The invisible structure flung him away from it like a bull flicking a bird off its horns. He struck the cobbles hard, rolled over groggily, looking astonished.

"Wizards," he muttered, and got to his feet, rubbing an elbow. "Valoren's idea, most likely. He has a mind for detail."

"Are you hurt?"

He shook his head, still trying to see what had attacked him. "Can you—I mean can Tyramin—"

"Hush," she breathed. "They may be listening."

He took her arm, walked a few paces up the street, and whispered, "Can you make an opening through that?"

"Maybe, if I had nothing better to do and no one else to worry about. It would be like unraveling a weave by following threads and picking them loose. Only these threads are thoughts, and they would be aware of me the moment I touched them."

"Not a good way out then."

"No."

He stared at nothingness again, scratched a brow, then turned to stare as bewilderedly at her. "Then how? How can I—"

"Let's go to the warehouse," she said softly, before he let loose something that made the wall grow an ear. "We can talk there."

In the warehouse, they found the company of performers waiting anxiously. They had removed their costumes and face paints and gaudy earrings. Simply dressed, they looked ready, at a word from Mistral, for any possibility. The dancer who had caught Arneth's eye under the moonlight and told him to smile was not smiling herself, now.

She asked Mistral worriedly, "Are we in trouble?"

"Tyramin is," Mistral said simply. "There's no way out of the quarter."

"So what should we do?" the red-haired Ney asked, with a glance at Arneth.

"The quarter warden tried to help us. Even he can't get us out. The royal guards are at the Twilight Gate, and the wizards are blocking the river."

Someone whistled. "What is Tyramin supposed to have done besides putting out a fire?"

"The king's daughter is missing," Arneth explained. "Nobody is thinking very clearly."

"Does she have a lover?" Elide suggested practically.

"If she does, she might want to stay hidden for a while since she is about to marry the wizard Valoren."

Ney scratched his curly head. "And all this has what to do with Tyramin?"

"His power is suspect. That's all I know," Arneth said heavily. His eyes went to Mistral. "I don't know what to do for you. There is a point at which even my father, the High Warden, will notice that I'm not just being obtuse and clumsy, that I am seriously evading my duty to produce Tyramin for him. I may have to go into hiding with you. Unless you—or Tyramin—can think of something."

They were all gazing at her by then, their eyes pleading for the master trick that would open the box without a lid, let the trapped birds scatter out of it to freedom. She said slowly, for among them there were those that knew, those close to guessing, those that would never know whose face they would find beneath the magician's mask. "Arneth, come with me. We'll explain all this to Tyramin together. Perhaps he'll find something for us up his sleeve."

"Should we start packing?" Gamon asked.

She gazed at him, already picking through odds and ends of glittering threads, half-formed visions, illusions at the bottom of the magician's bag of tricks. "Pack what you need," she told them. "The rest can stay here."

She took Arneth to the room overlooking the water where Tyramin dressed and rested and dreamed. One of his older masks hung on the wall, with chipped paint and mouse-chewed beard; his boots stood beneath it; his cloak of many pockets lay draped over a stool. An open trunk spilled satin shirts embroidered with stars, dark, voluminous trousers with even more pockets in them. The painted eyes seemed to come alive under the light of Mistral's candle, to watch her as she entered.

She lit other candles, sparking illusions of fire in glass jewels and metallic threads. She felt Arneth's eyes on her as well as Tyramin's painted eyes: both seemed to hold the same question.

"What will you do?" Arneth asked softly.

"I don't know yet," she told him. "You should go. Won't they wonder where you are, the guards, the High Warden?"

"They'll think I'm searching for Tyramin."

"Yes," she said, and let him hear the obvious in her silence: and you have found her. He shifted, shadow falling across his eyes.

"I shouldn't ask you," he said huskily. "And you should not tell me."

She bowed her head. "I know."

"I want you to vanish. I don't want to know how, I don't want to know where you are, I don't want to see you again until this—until—"

"Yes."

"Can you do that?"

She looked at him again, let him hear her silence. Yes, no, maybe, it is not for you to know . . . "No one," she heard herself say then, "outside of my little traveling world has ever seen all of my faces before."

She saw his taut face loosen, the beginnings of his smile. "I'm enchanted by them all," he confessed simply.

"Even this one? My plainest face?"

"Especially that one. All the mysteries are hidden behind it." He didn't move, nor did she. The air itself seemed to become a hand, reach out to touch her.

Her cool voice shook suddenly, spilling stars out of it, tears, jewels. "If I could stay—" she whispered.

"If I could go with you."

"Yes. Yes."

"Find a way," he breathed, so that nothing, not wizards' power, not even the huge, watching face on the wall, could hear what passed between them. She did not answer, only added that thread in her mind of the spell she must work. She raised one hand, opened it. A star burned there on her palm, pulsing crimson fire between them.

She looked at him and smiled. "Thank you," she said softly. "Now go, before neither one of us remembers anymore how to lie, what mask to wear. I will find you again."

His head bowed; he walked out the door wordlessly, his fists and mouth tight. Staring at her star, she heard the door shut. She closed her hand around the fire, hid it somewhere among all the other magic and illusions in her head, where no one else would notice it, or believe it true.

She wrapped the cloak around her, sat down on the stool, and gazed for a long time at the mask on the wall. In the distorted, dirty panes behind her the last star faded; a silver thread in the distance marked the boundary between night and day. After a time, she rose again, went down the hall, hearing, as she walked, the sleepless murmur of voices, soft movements within the drafty, creaking warehouse. She opened the door to the room where she made and mended costumes and wore her most prosaic face.

She sat down among the threads and fabrics, needles, beads, the glass jewels and fool's gold, the tinsel stars and paper moons. From the floor now, Tyramin watched her, the great head she had left there earlier. She gazed back at it, drawing from the vast treasure of illusions stored in the busy, teeming mind beneath that mask.

She picked up needle and thread, began to refashion the world.

EIGHTEEN

Yar, baffled by the sudden lack of a gardener, woke the sleeping Elver, brought him out of the brickwork, where he could see the blinking, dream-glazed eyes.

"Did Brenden tell you where he is going?"

The boy tried to shake his head and look around him at the same time. "Is he gone?"

Yar sighed, loosed him. "Yes. And I won't stop him this time."

"Where did he go?"

"Home, I would guess. I don't know how far he'll get, but it seems best to let him try. I'm going back to the school. Coming?" He paused, watching Elver wake a bit more as he remembered the dilemma he had gotten himself into. "You may have expelled yourself from the school, but I'm sure Wye will allow you a bed until someone can come for you. She'll want to question you, of course. And, since you were with me, so might Valoren."

Elver's voice wobbled slightly. "About what?"

"About your reasons for breaking the school's rules. About that powerful gift for magic you are taking home with you. You brought it here, made it subject to the king's law and the king's use; now you are withdrawing it. Valoren will explain very clearly what you will and will not be permitted to do with it."

Elver swallowed. Yar waited, wondering how far away home was. The boy said finally, reluctantly, "One of my uncles lives here in Kelior. I could go to him."

"Where in Kelior?"

"On Crescent Street. My father told me to go there if I got into—if I needed someone."

Yar nodded. The street was not far from the Royal Quarter, in an old and tranquil section of the city that never saw much excitement. "Do you want to come back to the school with me and get some sleep before you face your uncle?"

Elver shook his head. "I'd rather face him than Valoren."

"I don't blame you. But Valoren will find you when he wants you. Do you know the way? Shall I take you?"

"I can find it. I stayed with my uncle before I came to the school."

"What is his name?"

"Bream. Bream Marsh."

Yar consigned it to memory: another water dweller. "He can send to the school for your possessions. Wye may want to talk to you when things are calmer. If you can't find your uncle, or run into trouble, come back to the school."

"I will," Elver said, beginning to shiver again. He took a few heedless steps to the corner and was brought up short by the motionless line of guards across the gate. He tiptoed back to Yar, asked softly, "Will they let us out?"

"I'd walk through the wall if I were alone," Yar said. "But I'll have to explain you."

"You could teach me —" the boy began eagerly.

"I wish I could," Yar said with sudden intensity. "I wish every student in the school had such a bright and curious and fearless mind as yours. But as things stand I would only get us both into deeper trouble."

Elver smiled at him ruefully and slid back down next to the warm bricks of the fire pit. "I'll wait here until the guards change, and sneak through with them when they ride out. I won't make the horses as nervous then when they smell someone invisible passing by."

Yar hesitated. But the boy seemed in no hurry; his eyes were already drooping again. And it would be much quicker for Yar to melt through stones than to talk his way out of the gate, since he saw no sign of Arneth. He fished a coin out of his pocket and unclasped his cloak.

"Here," he said, consigning both to Elver. "You can bring my cloak back to the school when you come for your things. If you happen to remember it."

He startled another smile out of the boy, who promptly vanished into its voluminous folds. "Thank you, Master Yar."

"Be careful."

"I will." His face popped out again. "I'll come and talk to you again before I leave."

"I will be breathlessly waiting."

Yar, visible only to the wind, eased himself through the stones in the wall and took the shortest way back to the school.

He expected, after being thoroughly questioned by Valoren and the king, to be sent back out to search for the princess, whose disappearance, Yar suspected, had more to do with her impending marriage than with Tyramin. He hoped that he would not have to persuade her out of some unfortunate lover's bed. He emptied his mind of such thoughts when he entered the school, and resigned himself to whatever fate he encountered in Wye's chambers when he reappeared under Valoren's bleak eye.

But something intruded into the stillness where his thoughts had been, just before he made his way upstairs. He stood in the silent hallway, listening with both his mind and his ears. The students were still sleeping; shadows clung stubbornly to the walls, while the high windows in the vast upper regions grew filmy with encroaching dawn. Images teased him, tugged at him, as though someone called soundlessly to him without knowing his name. A student, he thought, awake and playing with power. But he lingered, struck by some elusive quality in the magic, something not quite familiar. Or was it, he wondered, the mind behind it that was unfamiliar?

And then a narrow, darkened stairway that went down instead of up caught his attention. Someone, he realized, had ventured into the labyrinth to work magic in the night. It wouldn't be the first time. He debated ignoring it. But again the hint of strangeness, of familiar music played on an unfamiliar instrument, drew at him. He turned to it finally, followed the beckoning power down into the labyrinth.

It didn't riddle with him long. He took a step or two into it, and a name flowed into his mind. Smiling, he followed the thought of Ceta and found her at the heart of the maze. And there with her, he found the heart of the magic. Dark, disheveled heads together, they watched a candle flame, one of many stuck and burning on the center stone. Their faces were pale with sleeplessness; they must have been there all night, he realized. An odd assortment of buttons were strewn among the candles, along with tangled string, strips of cloth, rings, a jeweled shoe, an intricately ornamented goblet, half a loaf of bread, and a little pile of carefully arranged bones.

Ceta turned her head and saw him. He saw the relief in her eyes, and then her smile. Still entranced within her own spell, the princess said a soundless word to the flame. It grew, fluttered, then detached itself from the wick and floated a moment in the air before Yar's astonished laugh made it fall again, missing the candle wick to dance among the bones.

Startled, Sulys turned. She said uncertainly, "Yar?"

"Yes."

Unaccountably she loosed an exasperated huff of air. "I give up."

Illumined, he guessed, "You were summoning Valoren."

"She has been trying to get his attention," Ceta explained.

"For days." The princess sighed and sat down on the stone among bread crumbs, buttons, and wax drippings. Ceta blew out the little flame before it caught at her skirt.

"What were you doing with those bones?" Yar asked curiously. "And whose were they?"

"They belonged to a roast chicken, which I begged from the kitchen," Ceta answered.

"Is there more of it?"

"We ate it all," Sulys told him apologetically. "But we can offer you bread and cheese." She passed him the bread; Ceta rummaged in a basket for cheese, added half a browning pear to her offerings.

"The bones?" he prompted, and took a ravenous bite, still standing to remind himself that he should be elsewhere.

"It was an experiment," the princess explained, gazing

perplexedly down at them. "Of course, my great-grandmother didn't encourage me to play with my food, even for magical purposes. But she said that she knew someone, long ago in Hestria, who could tell fortunes with bird bones."

"Perhaps not chicken bones," Yar suggested. "They rarely leave the ground."

The princess regarded him thoughtfully. "They don't soar," she agreed, "beyond the present."

"So it was your great-grandmother Dittany who taught you this secret magic?"

She nodded, her mouth tightening a moment. "I hoped it would attract Valoren's attention. We badly need to talk."

"Yes, I see you do," Yar murmured. He reined in his own thoughts, which were roaming curiously among the oddments the princess used like flint to spark her spells. "It was your absence that caught his attention first."

"Really. How unusual."

"And the king's." Her brows went up; her eyes widened, glimpsing, he saw, the first intimations of trouble.

"My father noticed I was gone? He never notices me when I'm around; I didn't expect him to notice that I wasn't."

Ceta, who read his expressions like a language, said abruptly, "Valoren could have found her easily."

"Valoren didn't think to look for her in the school. He and the king are convinced that some power within the Twilight Quarter—perhaps Tyramin's—has stolen the princess away. The royal guard has closed the Twilight Gate, and I suspect that the wizards have engaged the full force of their powers to set a guard along the riverbank so that no one can enter or leave the quarter. They are all searching in the wrong place."

"Tyramin!" Sulys exclaimed incredulously. She stood,

looked down at her bare feet and reached impatiently for her shoes, one of which for some reason held a candle in it. She shook it out. "It is so like them both—Valoren and my father—to blame some innocent trickster for what they failed to see under their own noses." She dropped the shoes, stepped into them. "Where are they?"

"I last saw them in Wye's chambers," Yar answered. "But that was in the late afternoon, when Valoren sent me out to search for our missing gardener. I doubt that the king is still there at this hour."

The women looked at one another, then back at him. "At what hour?" Sulys asked warily.

"It's nearly dawn."

She sucked in a horrified breath. "It can't be."

"Time plays odd tricks in the labyrinth, especially when you bring magic into it. Spells take their own time, here."

"You've been out all night looking for the gardener?" Ceta said incredulously. "When I heard that the king was angry, and you were missing, I thought—" She checked, a little color rising into her face. "I couldn't guess what you might have done."

"Nothing," he said softly. "Yet. I looked for you before I left, to tell you not to wait for me. I gave the librarian a message for you."

"I had gone up to your chambers to look for you. I didn't return to the library; I came here with Princess Sulys. I didn't talk to the librarian until much later. He told me then where you had gone. Did you find the gardener?"

"Yes. And no."

"You found Tyramin."

He looked at her silently, added the question in her eyes,

the water in the goblet, and the princess's magic together. "Yes," he said again, "and no. Somehow the gardener became confused with Tyramin, so I went to look for him among the Illusions and Enchantments. Did you really think I would offer my talents to a traveling magician?"

"Not to the magician," she answered simply. It was one of the rare moments that he saw her face without a smile anywhere in it. "Down here, I realized that I don't know anymore what you might or might not do."

"Strange," he breathed. "Up there, so did I."

He felt the princess's tension then, and stepped very close to Ceta to study the map on the stone underneath all the odds and ends scattered over it. "I've never used this, but it might be easiest for you if—"

He was interrupted by something resembling a snort from Ceta.

"That will get you anywhere but out," she said roundly; her voice sounded less strained. "But, Yar, look—I think it has more to do with—"

"It really doesn't work?" he marveled. "No wonder the students get lost down here. What was she thinking?"

"It does lead somewhere. Look at this." She brushed a few buttons and bones off the stone, tapped the carving beneath. "Yar, I think this pyramid in the center is Skrygard Mountain, and the path is the way to it."

He looked at her. Then he closed his eyes, held them closed, trying to follow the labyrinthine path of her logic and failing utterly. "How," he demanded, "could your mind make that leap from the depths of a school in Kelior to a mountain in northern Numis?"

"I can't quite remember at this hour of the morning how I got from here to there, but I bet I'm right."

The princess cleared her throat. "I don't really care where we go," she said uneasily, "but I suppose we should go somewhere. Yar, can you lead us out?"

"I can try."

Ceta blew out flames, swept everything off the stone into the basket, leaving some candle drippings and a lighted candle for each of them. "In case we get separated," she told them. The corner of her mouth slid upward faintly as she handed Yar his candle. "Lead us into morning," she suggested, and, with no small amount of astonishment, he did.

He took them both to Wye's chamber, since neither showed any sign of wanting to go elsewhere. He felt the power within as he opened the door, like air so massed and fused it seemed about to transform itself into a different element. The princess seemed aware of it as well; her weary face grew paler, set as against a coming storm.

Nearly all of the teaching wizards were in there, silently weaving thought and will together, so still they didn't seem to breathe or even see. Some of them had slipped out of their human shapes, to come closer yet to their makings: one had blurred into the half shadows of dawn, another's face seemed roughly shaped out of the uneven bulges and cracks of stone. Valoren, gazing at the interruption out of wide, unblinking eyes as it entered, seemed, to Yar, oblivious of them all. But Sulys gave a little, startled gasp at the predatory stare, and Valoren blinked. The dense air, trembling as with some low, immense sound too deep to be heard, seemed to thin a little as his thoughts frayed out of it.

"Sulys," he breathed, a cob strand of sound, but enough to tangle the threads of the spell around them like a stone thrown through a web. His eyes went to Ceta, then to Yar. "Where have you been?" he asked. "Where did you find the princess?"

Color flared into Sulys's face; she took a step toward him, catching his attention again, though for a moment she seemed unable to speak.

"You might ask me," she said when she could. "I am, after all, standing in front of you. I've been down in the labyrinth, doing everything I could think of to get your attention."

"The labyrinth?" he said bewilderedly. "Why didn't you just come up here?" He turned again to Yar. "Then where have you been?"

"Doing what you asked me to do," Yar said tersely. "Looking for the gardener."

"You didn't find him."

"I found him, and lost him again."

"You lost him! How could you lose him? Is he with Tyramin? Is he, himself, Tyramin? And powerful enough to elude even you?"

Yar hesitated, trying to find the simplest way through that tangle. "No. Brenden Vetch is not Tyramin. He is our gardener. Or was, until he frightened himself with his own power."

"Why didn't he come back here with you?"

"We frightened him, too, I think. He didn't explain himself, and he didn't tell me where he was going."

The pale eyes slid away from him briefly, as though they saw through walls, across the sleeping city. "I'll find him," the wizard said simply. "What about Tyramin?"

"I don't know. You didn't ask me to find Tyramin. If he hasn't been found, Arneth Pyt must still be looking."

A trace of color fanned across the wizard's sallow cheeks, the nearest Yar had seen to a display of temper. "It shouldn't be that difficult to find a gardener or a traveling magician. Must I look for them both myself?"

"I found the princess," Yar reminded him.

"Apparently she was never lost."

"Apparently," Sulys said abruptly, "I am invisible. You talk around me, you don't see me when I'm under the same roof, even when I'm in the same room—"

"You were hiding from me," Valoren said slowly. "So it seems."

"I wanted you to find me—I wanted to talk—"

"Yes. There are simpler ways to do that than to play games and worry the entire court." Sulys drew a breath sharply; he held up his hand. "Now, perhaps, is not the time."

Sulys held her breath; so did everyone, it seemed to Yar, in that precarious moment. Then the princess turned, pulled open the heavy door, and went through it without a word, slamming it so hard behind her that Yar winced and Wye, on the far side of the room, put her hands over her ears.

Ceta broke the spellbound silence. "You," she said crisply to her cousin, "are going to lose her."

He looked at her, then at the door, as though he were trying to figure out why it had made such a noise. "Nonsense," he said absently. "We are bound by contract and by our fathers' wishes. We'll have time to discuss this later."

Ceta rubbed her eyes tiredly. "Talk to her, Valoren. Go after her."

"I haven't time," he protested. "There are dark powers loose in Numis, and we must find them. I am going to the Twilight Quarter myself to search for Tyramin. Yar, come with me; I want to question you. And you can take the magician back to face the king when we've captured him. I'll find the gardener then, if I have to track him all the way to the north country."

"What do you want us to do?" Wye asked resignedly.

"Bind the Twilight Quarter again. Tyramin may have slipped through our net when the princess interrupted us, but it's unlikely he has had time."

Yar put a hand on Ceta's arm, met her rueful smile with his own. He would have bid her farewell, but Valoren, taking a step toward the door, paused as though he sensed the unspoken words behind his back.

"Yar."

Yar bowed his head, not trusting himself to speak, and followed.

NINETEEN

Arneth Pyt watched the sun rise over the Twilight Quarter through a bleary smudge of cloud and river mist. Around him the streets were empty but for a cat slinking through an alley. Somewhere a shutter banged shut against an obtrusive finger of light. A torch along the wall guttered out. Arneth heard one of the motionless guards stifle a yawn. His own eyes felt gritty. He was waiting, ostensibly, for the change of guard to relieve the tired men at the gate who had been there all night. When relief came and positioned itself, then he would continue his futile searching for a gardener whose face he had never seen, a princess who probably did not want to be found, and a magician whom Arneth had no intention of finding if he could avoid it.

He wondered how Mistral could possibly hide herself, let alone her performers, from the entire school of wizards. She couldn't hide her mind, Arneth thought, straining his own mind to the limits as he tried to imagine what went on in her head. She might hide her face, but how could she hide her magic from the likes of Valoren? It could not be possible. The captain of the guard said something to him. He pulled himself out of his nebulous speculations and turned.

"What?"

"I hear the relief guard coming."

Arneth grunted, recognizing the sound of two dozen horsemen moving across the cobbles beyond the gate. "Good," he said. "Take the night guard out first so they can get in."

"Yes, sir. Do you want me to stay and help you search?"

"No. Go to bed."

The captain nodded and turned his mount. He signaled to the guards; they fell in behind him. Arneth shifted to give them room. He watched the last of the riders disappear into the archway. His thoughts strayed again to Mistral as he waited for the captain of the relief guard to ride into the quarter. There was silence on the other side of the wall. With sudden impatience he urged his horse forward, wondering if they needed an invitation.

Two figures emerged from the shadows of the gate: men on their feet, moving noiselessly as wizards knew how to do, seeming to balance on air. Arneth's jaw clenched as he recognized Valoren. The other, a tall, dark-haired man wearing a dour expression like a piece of armor, he had seen before but could not name.

Arneth heard the horses begin to move through the gate behind them. He dismounted, went to meet the wizards while the relief guard ranged itself along the wall.

"This is Yar Ayrwood," Valoren told him. "He has come to help us search. I take it that you do need help."

Arneth gave a cautious nod. If the imperturbable Valoren had been anyone else, Arneth would have suspected him of holding his temper on a very short leash. "My lord," he answered as crisply as he could, "I intend to resume my search as soon as the relief guard is positioned and instructed."

The wizard favored him with a curdled glance that reminded Arneth of his father. "You have been looking all night and found—what, exactly?"

Arneth thumbed his brow, looking for some tactful word for nothing. He found the wizard Yar's eyes on him, a disconcerting clarity in them. "My lord, I have never seen the gardener's face."

"Never mind the gardener," Valoren said shortly. "You were told to find Tyramin."

"He is proving extremely elusive."

"Elusive! He performed last night! You could have dragged him off the stage then."

"My lord, you were the one who counseled discretion," Arneth pointed out mildly. "I was trying—"

"You tried and failed. Show us where he keeps himself."

"I doubt that he's still there."

Something close to a healthy color flowed across Valoren's face. "Don't tell me what you think, just do as I tell you," he snapped, startling Arneth. He apparently startled himself as well; he closed his eyes briefly, drew a long breath, while Yar contemplated a pair of squabbling starlings on a nearby roof. "Take us," Valoren said finally, tersely, "to the place where you saw Tyramin perform."

"Yes, my lord," Arneth said, and turned to mount again. Feeling safer above the wizard, he risked a question. "Should I send part of the guard to look for Princess Sulys?"

"The princess has been found," Valoren said, so shortly that Arneth decided not to ask where.

The wizards, who could have flown over the rooftops as far as Arneth knew, walked quickly beside his horse. They spoke quietly enough, but did not seem to care that they were overheard, for which Arneth was grateful. He would have grown a third ear to listen after Valoren asked Yar, with bewildered asperity, "Why did she slam the door like that? What did I do to make her so angry?"

"She needs to talk to you," the wizard answered.

"Now? She needs this precisely when the dangers to Kelior are demanding the whole of our attention?"

"She was in the labyrinth all night; she had no idea what was happening in the rest of the world."

"What was she doing in the labyrinth, of all places?"

Yar did not answer. Arneth glanced at him curiously; so did Valoren, but more like an owl, alerted and fixed by some prey. Yar chose to answer the look. "Yes. I can tell you. But it's for her to speak."

"Is it important?"

Again, Yar seemed wordless for a moment. Then he said with some force, "If she believes with such passion that it is important, then it most certainly should be to you. You will lose her if you can't figure out how to listen to her."

"She won't defy her father," Valoren answered, which seemed, even to Arneth, completely beside the point.

"Maybe not," Yar said somberly. "But if you have no time to learn to know her before you marry her, why would she assume you would find time afterward?"

"That was why she spent the night in the cellar? So that I would know her better?"

"In the labyrinth," Yar amended. "And yes. If you had been there with her, it would have made more sense than it sounds."

The owl's glare became more focused, even brighter. Arneth could almost see the ruffled feathers. "You presume, Master Yar, to know us both too well."

"I listened and found her," Yar said pointedly. "You didn't. That is why she slammed the door."

There was a silence, during which Arneth, his nape hairs prickling, sensed an imminent display of wizardly pique. Quickly he turned them down a side street, where they could finally see the worn roof of the warehouse. He pointed. "There. That's where Tyramin performs."

Valoren turned his disconcerting gaze to the bulky old building looming at the river's edge. Yar looked at Arneth instead, a dark, enigmatic glance that made the quarter warden shift his own eyes. It was as though the wizard had guessed something, had seen something that passed between Arneth and the magician's complicated daughter. But how could he? Arneth wondered. He had never seen Yar in the Twilight Quarter before.

"Let's go in," Valoren murmured. "We'll find out which of you it takes to arrest the trickster."

Arneth tried to keep his thoughts still, his face impassive, as they rode toward the warehouse. Deliberately not thinking of Mistral's name, he found it constantly in his head like a persistent insect. She couldn't possibly have had time to hide herself. What was the worst that could happen to her if she were found? He had no idea, he realized. Nor did he know what she might consider the worst. Exile, maybe; he had heard of that happening a time or two to unruly wizards. Mistral had spent her life wandering through strange lands; exile would scarcely be a punishment. Being forced to put on a student's robe and to stay shut up in the school while she restructured her magic to meet the exacting laws of Numis would be worse, Arneth guessed. But the worst Valoren could do, Arneth could not imagine. He couldn't help trying though, until, a street away from the warehouse, he heard Valoren say:

"Who is Mistral?"

Arneth felt his skin constrict. He said nothing; Valoren would have to drag an answer from between his teeth.

Unaccountably, Yar came to his rescue. "She is the magician's daughter. She assists him while he performs. So I've heard."

Valoren grunted. "The name strayed into my thoughts."

"From the warehouse, no doubt."

Arneth found his voice, said steadily, "I've questioned her a time or two. She took me to talk to Tyramin. He was disguised for his performance then, but he seemed harmless beneath the mask."

"We shall see," Valoren promised.

The warehouse seemed asleep, like the rest of the quarter, as they approached. There were no packhorses, or oxen, or half-loaded wagons in front. The doors were closed but not locked; they opened easily and without magic, Arneth discovered. Inside, the place was as bare as the aftermath of Tyramin's performance usually left it: not a discarded scarf or a tinsel star anywhere. Just warped, scuffed floorboards, a makeshift stage with nothing on it but a carpet so old its patterns had grown blurred with age; it might have been lying there for centuries.

"I'll search in the back," Arneth said briefly, hoping the wizards would leave him to it.

But Valoren said, "Go with him, Yar." His voice sounded odd, remote, as though he spoke out of a dream. Arneth glanced at him. The pale, unblinking eyes seemed flooded with light, the pupils all but vanished. He didn't move. He didn't have to, Arneth guessed with sudden insight. He searched for magic with his mind as he stood in the silent, empty warehouse. His thoughts could seep through the hoary bones of rafter and post, through closed doors and locked cupboards and chests, through the dark cellar, its beams moldy with river mist. There would be no place to hide.

Arneth, his mouth tight, moved helplessly to search the only way he could. Yar followed silently. The tangle of chambers and corridors behind the vast storage space indicated a certain amount of flurry. Swaths of lace and silk eddied on the floor; forgotten masks stared sightlessly at the intruders. A flock of birds made of feathers and cloth were scattered all over the floor of a dressing chamber, along with a dancing slipper and a broken mirror. In another, costumes had slid from their pegs on the walls to the floor, where they slumped like disembodied sleepers. Another room held nothing but an old mask of Tyramin left on the floor. Paint had cracked on the bright cheeks, the vigorous brow. A clump of beard was missing. Yar spent a moment gazing at it, his own eyes as expressionless as the mask's. More wizardry, Arneth guessed, but the wizard did not say.

They searched every room, every passage, even the grounds at the back of the building. On the river, the fishing boats had gone out; a trade ship with painted sides and a great, carved sea monster twined about its prow, was finding a dock farther up the water. Nothing came close to the dock near the warehouse; the little boat that Arneth had seen before was still there, its sails tightly furled, as though it, too, slept.

"Nothing," he breathed. "They must have all scattered into the quarter." Yar said nothing. Arneth looked at him, asked carefully, "Did you—Did you see something I missed?"

"I doubt it," Yar said, his voice oddly dry. He turned to go back in; Arneth followed, wondering suddenly how much the wizard had seen and if he would tell Valoren.

But Yar only asked Valoren, whose eyes had turned human again as he waited for them, "What did you find?"

"They couldn't have escaped," Valoren answered tightly, "when the princess broke our spell. They had no time. They must be still in the quarter." He paused, hearing the question in Yar's mind, it seemed, and answered it before he was asked, "I sensed no magic. At least nothing I recognize as magic." He hesitated again, looking, to Arneth's amazement, almost uncertain. "Could magic take such form that you or I, trained as we are, wouldn't recognize it?"

Expression startled into Yar's face, fine lines of amusement and bitterness. "How would I know? We only know what we are permitted to learn. If all I ate in my life was cabbage, how would I recognize the fat wooly object in the next field as food?"

Valoren's thin mouth all but disappeared. "This is hardly the time to question the laws of Numis."

"Then when will be the time? When magic as obtrusive as a cloud on our horizon attacks Numis?"

Valoren blinked. "You think that Tyramin—"

"No," Yar said adamantly. "I do not. I'm only suggesting that in the centuries we've spent keeping magic we can't control outside the boundaries of the kingdom, we've left ourselves ignorant of power that we may find useful. Or interesting. Or astonishing. Or—"

He stopped. Valoren's eyes had grown strange again, luminous and remote, as though he were seeing into Yar and out the other side. Arneth, watching puzzledly, found himself holding his breath. In the air between the wizards a star formed and exploded with a minute flash of fire. Arneth started. It seemed oddly like one of Tyramin's tricks. Valoren drew back abruptly.

"Sorry," he said stiffly. "I was trying to see what you are seeing. It seemed simpler than arguing."

"I suggest," Yar said with asperity, "that when you are married you stick to arguing."

"Yes," Valoren agreed. But his wide, unblinking eyes had sighted prey, Arneth guessed uneasily; he had probably not heard a word Yar said. "What was that?"

"What?"

"In your thoughts." He held up a hand swiftly. "I know. I have passed far beyond the pale of courtesy. But for an instant I saw something, felt something that I have never encountered in all my years among the wizards. What is it, Yar? What are you concealing?"

The pitch-black eyes nearly stared Valoren down. "Nothing."

"I felt it."

"You felt nothing beyond my thoughts."

"It seemed very old, very powerful . . . Does it have a name?"

Yar was silent. Arneth, watching without daring to shift a muscle, resisted an urge to slide off his horse, sidle quietly into a back alley before those wide eyes, that sinewy, relentless voice started pursuing what was in his own head.

"Yar," Valoren said softly. "Nothing that powerful should be hidden from the king. You know that."

"It's nothing," Yar insisted, but this time Arneth heard the odd despair in his voice. "It's a dream, an image, a fragment of writing—"

"Whose writing?"

"Od's. There's no danger to Numis in it at all. The writing itself is very old; she was traveling and saw—"

"Traveling where?"

"In the north country. Your own home. If you never noticed it, then there's nothing to notice."

Valoren's eyes changed, narrowing now, and burning within. "The north country. Brenden Vetch's home as well. Perhaps that is where he got his power? Did he speak of them?"

"Ceta showed me Od's writings about them. She found a sentence in the royal library, another in the school."

Valoren nodded briefly. "Yes, I remember. She has been writing about Od's life. But did the gardener speak of them?" He had to wait again; the silence itself, stretching long and fine, became an answer. "So"—the wizard breathed—"that's where we might find the gardener. I want to see those writings, Yar. Will you come with me to talk to Ceta, or must I go alone?"

Yar turned his face away from Valoren, touched his eyes wearily. He said nothing that Arneth could hear. But both wizards grew thin as river mist and vanished, leaving Arneth blinking reddened, gritty eyes that still tried to pick the dark figures out of the empty morning air.

TWENTY

Brenden found his way step by step out of the Twilight Quarter, across the river, out of Kelior. Home drew him, the bare, windswept hills, the marshes where he could sit for an entire day watching a bog lily open and never hear a human word. The stark longing fueled his magic; he shaped it to his purpose, no longer asking how it was that he could do such things but rather how they could be done.

Getting out of the Twilight Quarter was a matter of combining wish and will. Appalled by the confusing and disturbing reactions to his magic, he wished himself wholeheartedly elsewhere. He had made himself invisible before by contemplating a wall. Yar had turned him into an illusion of bricks. When Yar left him to speak to Arneth at the gate, Brenden stood up and contemplated the shadowy predawn air. Soundless as a cat, he walked away from Yar and the sleeping boy, whose soft snores seemed to emerge from within the fire pit. As he walked, he let thought flow out of him, left past and future drifting; he banked the eager flames of the present within the misty dark around him. So he saw himself as he moved: a damp cloud of river mist and waning night. He had no idea whether or not he could be seen. He only knew that when he passed under torchlight, he didn't see his own shadow.

He wended his way through the quiet, unfamiliar streets until he saw the wall at the end of one of them. It was quite high, and very old; houses and buildings hid most of it, some attached to it like snails, using the ancient rise of stones for their own back wall. The wall enclosed the quarter in a horseshoe curve; the river itself completed the mysterious boundary, which, Brenden had noticed from his high garden, existed nowhere else in the city. He wondered if the quarter had shut itself away from the rest of Kelior to pursue its eccentric habits, or if, long ago, the city around it had grown weary of watching them or fearful that such aberrations might spread.

Whatever the vagaries of history, he had to get over the wall or find his way to the river and swim. The wall was in front of his nose; the river was not. He went up to it. A rat sniffing through some debris did not notice him; neither did the mangy dog eyeing the rat. Brenden gazed at the old stones, seeing the north beyond them, the hills of home, the dark, craggy mountain even farther north with its astonishing hint of magic in the snow. He wished the wall were behind him instead of in front of him. He leaned against the stones, asking wordlessly what he must do for them to let him through. Stones slowly filled his thoughts; they were all he saw, all he heard, all he touched; there was nothing else in that moment but the rising of stone between him and his heart's desire. He shifted, impelled by his longing, a stone-man with his mouth and mind blocked by stone, his body stretched over stone, his eyelashes and skin the finest grit, his bones the bulky shape and weight of it. And so he took his ponderous step, felt earth tremble and settle as his foot rose and fell. He took another interminable, mindless step, slower than a walk underwater, hearing minute particles shift as he passed.

He emerged like a statue stepping free of its own stony husk. He opened his eyes, found the wall behind him as he had wished, and before him the broad road that ran along the river's edge until it turned to cross the bridge over the river.

On this side of the wall, Kelior was beginning to wake. He submerged his thoughts in shadow again and moved, quickly and unobtrusively, among fishers and dockworkers, toward the bridge.

He crossed it as the sun rose, whey-faced and desultory, behind the clouds. Beyond it the city fanned like a great, breaking wave over the opposite bank, spreading and thinning until at last it reached its farthest, a scatter of distant fields and farmhouses. The road continued to the river, another, across the water, ran north through the rest of Kelior. Brenden had walked every step of it, not long before; he could walk every step of it back. He had a warm cloak, solid boots, and a little money. Those would take him a good part of the way home; the rest of the way he would worry about when he came to it.

He trudged steadily through the day. Nobody seemed to notice him, whatever shape he was in. The sun, yielding to cloud, cast few shadows. Brenden, his thoughts neither here nor there, only on his next step, had no idea if he was cloaked by invisibility or just by disinterest. Either way it did not matter; he felt as safe. By midday he could see an end to the road he was on, as it left the distant fields behind and dwindled into a path traveled mostly by herds of cows and sheep. That stopped beside a stream, he remembered. A little east of it there was a stone bridge across the stream. And on the other side, an inn, where one road branched east and west away from it along the water, and another road wound through the woods beyond the tavern, heading north.

He had almost reached it, near sunset, when he realized he was being pursued.

He had been nagged for some time by an incoherent notion in his head. Something he had forgotten, something he needed to do, something weighing in his mind, but what it was would not reveal itself. The idea grew stronger as the pallid sun lowered itself toward a sullen bank of cloud. The cloud, he felt, was seeping into his own head, a dark mist spreading slowly through him, making him uneasy, wary, without knowing why. It was, he decided finally, as though he were being watched.

And that stopped him dead in the middle of the dusty, lonely path. He turned, his skin prickling, looking behind him across the empty fields, the coming night.

Valoren.

He had no idea how the mind of a wizard worked when all its intricate, unwieldy powers were honed and trained in orderly fashion on a problem such as a runaway gardener. All he sensed, from what Yar had said, was that Valoren might be capable of anything. He might indeed track a solitary traveler simply by knowing his name and something of his power. How much of him Valoren had glimpsed during their conversation about flowers, Brenden had no idea. Enough to send a guard and a wizard after him into the Twilight Quarter. Enough to want to stop him from leaving Kelior. Enough, perhaps, to pursue him as far as he could run.

Brenden moved again, quickening his pace. How could you hide your own mind, he wondered, from someone who was following it as intently as a fish drawn by the lure of wings? He had no idea. The best he could do, he decided after some time, was to move fast. Faster than the wizard. Faster than he had ever moved in his life.

That thought crossed his mind just as he crossed the threshold of the ancient, tidy fieldstone inn at the crossroads on the other side of the bridge. He went in anyway, and asked the plump, comely innkeeper for a bed. A scattering of faces, most of them solitary travelers, glanced up idly from their ale and beef to listen.

"I do have a bed for you," she said. "Sit and have some supper; you look as though you could use it."

Brenden nodded, sliding the pack from his shoulder to find a coin for her. The others, their eyes drifting over him and away, finding nothing to hold their attention, went back to their own musings. The innkeeper's daughter, a solemn, red-cheeked child, brought him bread, beef, roast onions, and ale. He ate quickly, expecting Valoren to appear in the doorway at any moment, while outside the thick, smoky windows the prowling dusk peered in, drawn to the light.

How? he thought. How to outrun the speed of thought. How to hide while you are doing it.

He finished his supper, asked to be shown his bed, for he was very tired and must be on the road by dawn. The innkeeper sent her daughter to light Brenden's way upstairs. She set a candle beside a pallet on the floor near the warm chimney stones. He sat down on it, began to remove a boot. When she had gone downstairs, he let his boot be and stood up again. Cloaked, pack in hand, he tiptoed down the stairs and out the back door, past kitchen garden and stables. He could see the wood, a vague blur in the twilight, and a twist or two of road that led up to it. He was used to sleeping among the trees and animals. There, in the crumbling hollow of a fallen trunk, he would find his bed for a few hours. He would empty his mind the way he did when he watched a plant grow, or a mushroom push itself up out of the bracken. Maybe Valoren would mistake him for a tree, if he did not dream . . .

So he spent that night curled up with the animals in the wood, and if anyone inquired about a young, pale-haired young man traveling alone, he would be upstairs asleep upon his pallet. That would not stop Valoren, Brenden guessed. But it might puzzle him to find his quarry unpredictably slipped away into the night.

He woke before dawn, ate a heel of bread and an onion he had dropped into his pack from supper, while he tried to think about traveling from a wizard's point of view. When he could see, he followed the slope of the wood uphill, keeping the road visible but at a distance. He saw nobody else going north in that season.

When he reached the top of the hill, he could see the road more clearly, a chalky white slash through scrubby fields and flowing plains growing sere in the autumn. Walking across that plain, he would be clearly visible. Unless he traveled by night. If he learned to see in the dark. Or unless he learned to fly like a bird. Or the wind. Or to leap across distances somehow, make them closer than they seemed. He lingered, considering possibilities, all of which seemed equally improbable.

A chill wind flowed over him, into his mind, it seemed; all his speculations scattered like leaves. He crouched down instinctively, alarmed and helpless; for a stark moment he had no idea what to do. And then he did it, seemingly without thought: he gazed down at the red-capped mushroom with the snow-white speckles on it like a warning. He let his mind fill with mushroom, become something small, fibrous, damp, and utterly wordless.

After a time, during which the invisible sun moved fully into morning behind the tumbling gray clouds, he found a coherent thought in his head.

He will drag me back to Kelior if he finds me, and I might never see home again.

The thought alone was enough to move him. He cast longing like a hook on a rope across the landscape, toward a hillock in the distance with an enormous boulder on its crown ringed with brush like an egg within a nest. He hauled himself upon a wish through air and time, knowing nothing except his terror and his need. When he could see again, he found himself standing beside the boulder, blinking at the edge of the wood he had left, almost expecting to see himself still there, rising to take a giant step across the world.

Air screamed and beat around him. He flung up his arms, fending off a flurry of fierce golden eyes and outstretched claws. The eyes, too like Valoren's, stunned him breathless for an instant. Then his thoughts, outrunning his own body to escape the wizard, pulled him after them; in the next breath, he knew he was elsewhere, he had done something, but he was not certain what. The ground was flowing under him like water; the terrible eyes had vanished. Borne on the wind, or on the frantic rush of his own thoughts, a bird, a dead leaf, a wisp of smoke, whatever shape he had made for himself fled with him until the threat in his head diminished and he began to feel for his own shape again.

He tumbled to earth then, rolling over and over until he smacked into a tree. Groggy, but still alarmed, he pulled his face out of the bracken and sat up. He saw the hill rising through scrub, farther away than he would have guessed. A bird circled the boulder, huge and dark; he could still hear its faint warning cries.

He sat up, catching his breath. Not Valoren, then, he thought with relief. He wondered what shape his fear had made of him. Sitting in the wild emptiness, with the clouds scudding above him and the wind soughing through the brush, he concentrated. A juniper bush spangled with its round red berries caught his eye. Old habits of stillness, solitude, silence pervaded his bones, freed his mind from language. He drew green into himself, sharp, stubby needles, smooth waxy garnet, tough branch and trunk that clung close to earth and weathered the worst of winter. He drew its smell into his skin, let the needles prickle through his thoughts, his eyes, until he felt himself rooted to the harsh land around him, so deeply that he could have tapped its hidden waters while he stretched his thousand windblown fingers out for light.

When he found his own shape again, driven there by some submerged impulse, he was startled at how high the pale sun burned behind the cloud. He stood up unsteadily. Then he felt what had roused him out of his hiding place. The chill, nagging dread, the sense of being watched in secret, of being silently followed, gusted through him, seeped into his thoughts. He hunkered down quickly, looking around him for the shape he needed: something that moved close to earth, that could travel swiftly, tirelessly, and unobtrusively, and that knew how to hide at the crack of a twig. Wind brought him a scent before he glimpsed it: a silver fox hunting nearby in the brush. He watched it, let the shape flow into him for a long, timeless moment. Then he rose and padded away quickly, nose to the rich, redolent wind that came down from the north.

So he moved across Numis, hardly sensing time pass, sometimes forgetting what shape he had taken, sometimes impelled, by the constant harrying of the menace at his heels, to fold the landscape into great, thin swaths in order to keep a pace ahead of terror. In this piecemeal fashion, he crossed a land he seldom saw out of human eyes, and certainly never passed a human word with anyone.

Finally, shaking some animal's night vision out of his eyes at dawn to see if anything was familiar yet, he recognized a jagged, pointed tooth on the horizon. Its bare dark peak glowed under a rare finger of sun. He stood gazing at it, feeling its ancient silence in his heart: the place where time had stopped and magic had found a place to hide itself so securely that even the word itself had vanished.

Skrygard Mountain.

By then he could scarcely remember his own name. Words had become too bulky to carry with him on his desperate flight across Numis; they scattered away from him with each shape he took, each wild eye he looked from that reshaped a wordless world. Night and day meant nothing; he could see as easily in either. Sun and moon became his guides; one kept him on his path as well as the other. Dark and light, warmth and cold, wind and earth and water, he drew into his skin and bones and marrow. Becoming them, he lost the need to name them.

He kept the word for fear. It never left him, for the magic that dogged him across Numis tracked his every turn, recognized him within every shape. Even in that moment, when he paused to see the world for a moment out of human eyes, remember human names, he scarcely took a breath free of fear.

He sensed it almost immediately, the power that pursued him. He remembered that name, too, but it seemed to small a word to contain such magic. Valoren had become as faceless and relentless as the coldest of the northern winds, the one that killed, that froze and broke the hearts of stones. Brenden vanished as soon as he felt it. A small, dark shape that rode the winds took a straight, lonely crow's flight to Skrygard Mountain.

He felt the place before his crow's eye recognized the raw, barren peak. He felt himself drawn to it; the crow angled down toward the little empty plane of snow on the mountain's flank. His heart saw for him, then, glimpsing an ancient, wordless, secret power that had been left undisturbed so long there was no name left in the world for it. He winged toward it; it reached out to him. He felt his shape blur as he neared, peel away from him until it seemed his own shadow had stripped itself free, gone tumbling away on the wind.

He opened his mind to the forgotten mysteries of Numis. With a brief, bright shock, as though he had swallowed a star, or fallen into the sun, he took in their power with their shape.

TWENTY-ONE

Sulys had walked nearly all the way around the Twilight
Quarter before she realized that there was no way in.
The butter-colored satin had drifted away on the school stairs
during her precipitous flight from her betrothed. She had
snagged someone's cloak on her way out the door. The cloak,
dark and massively hooded, covered her from head to foot
and even dragged along the ground. Awkward in the carbun-
cle shoes, she kept tripping over it. But at least she felt hidden, disguised from everyone but Valoren. His eyes kept
finding her in memory, distant and critical, as though she
were a beginning student who had accidentally dropped a
toad into his brightly bubbling cauldron. There would be, she
thought grimly, no living with a mind like that. She would
have to skulk behind her own smiling, agreeable face just to
keep herself safe from his suspicious mind, his probing eye.
She could never tell him the truth.

The line of guards at the Twilight Gate brought her up
sharply. There was no traffic at all in or out of the quarter.

She gazed at them incredulously, and felt the complaints of her pinched, swollen feet. Everyone else, she remembered, was looking for Tyramin, too. She had no clear reason for her own urgent desire to see him, except that he must be everything Valoren was not. He was a different kind of magic, one that might be destroyed if Valoren and her father found him before she did. She turned away from the guard before they saw her, began to search for any chink in the high walls, a forgotten gate, a slump in the old stones that she could clamber over. Once inside, she could use her own small magics—water, maybe a bird—to find the magician, whom she might help escape Kelior, if he helped her escape what looked like a bleak and lonely marriage.

Perhaps, she thought helplessly, I will just run away with the magician, become part of his company. I will travel to the land where my great-grandmother was born and learn what other magic is possible beyond the walls the wizards have built around Numis's magic.

There was yet another wall where the stone wall ended in the river. She had thought she might be able to swim around the old mossy stones where they moldered in the water. The air along the waterfront shimmered dangerously, and she recognized what all the powerful minds weaving together in Wye's chamber had built with their magic. She stared at it, then turned abruptly, her eyes filling the weary tears. She limped from the magic before her mind got caught in someone's stray thought, and she was discovered.

There must be a way in, she thought coldly, blinking back the tears. There must be. I will find it.

But at that moment, she could not think beyond her blistered feet. She took her shoes off, and remembered, at the flash of sullen morning light within the jewel, a kindly face.

With great relief she pocketed the shoes and retraced her path to the elegant river houses lining the water, one of which, she knew, belonged to Ceta Thiel.

Ceta didn't seem entirely surprised to see her, once she recognized the black-swathed, hooded figure that the startled Shera had found pounding at the door.

"I'm glad you came here," she said simply, handing the cloak to Shera. Dressed in thin pastel silks, her own feet bare, she looked as though she must have just gotten out of bed. "Please, sit—that one is the most comfortable. Shera, see what you can find us for breakfast." Sulys sank gratefully into a plump concoction of wood and stuffed tapestry. Ceta gazed down at her, absently twirling a strand of hair. A runaway princess, Sulys realized, was an awkward thing to find on your doorstep, and Ceta was frowning, but more in displeasure than in discomfort. "I can hardly blame you," she said before Sulys could speak. "My cousin may be a shining example among wizards, but he has forgotten how to be human."

"It doesn't matter," Sulys said wearily. "I can't go home to that. What I want to do is find Tyramin, but I can't get into the Twilight Quarter. It's completely surrounded by wizards and guards."

"Tyramin," Ceta said blankly.

"I think he would understand my magic in a way that the wizards never could. At least we could be outcasts together. Which is what I feel like, now. I am too afraid of the man I'm supposed to marry to tell him the truth."

Ceta nodded. "He has turned into something of a monster," she breathed. "I think that's part of what has been troubling Yar."

"Yar." Sulys straightened a little, glancing around. "Is he here? Maybe he could help me get past the wall."

"No. Valoren took him into the quarter to search for Tyramin." She sat down beside Sulys, her mouth crooking. "There does seem to be true magic in the way no one is able to lay eyes on the magician. But Valoren will find him, I'm sure, and it would be worse for both of you to be found together."

"I could hide him, I think," Sulys said very softly. "There's a trick Dittany taught me that's done with threads. It just might work on people. I don't believe a wizard trained in Od's school would know what to do with a needle and thread."

"I'm not even sure I know what to do with a needle and thread," Ceta admitted. "I'm very sure Valoren wouldn't. But I think he would recognize magic in them."

"Would he? If he didn't know to look for it?"

"I don't know." She brooded silently, while Shera set an enormous tray laden with dense, spicy breads and cakes, dried fruit, soft cheeses, pickled eggs, and smoked fish onto a table in front of them. "Thank you, Shera. What happens to people when they grow up, I wonder? Valoren was very sweet when he was younger, and he had a great deal more sense."

"Like my brother Enys," Sulys said, casting a polite glance at the tray. "He used to like me before."

"Before?"

"Before our mother died. Now I seem to annoy him constantly, and he never smiles." She toyed with a dried pear, thinking of Enys's prickly expression. "I suppose grief changes people. But it's as though I have lost them all—my father and Enys as well as—" She paused, put the fruit down very carefully, and swallowed the fire out of her throat. "As well. Only Dittany didn't change."

Ceta poured her a cup of cool water scented with mint; Sulys sipped it gratefully.

"Is there anyone I can send for?" Ceta asked worriedly. "You can't just wander alone around Kelior. Of course you may stay here for as long as you like, though you should let your father know where you are."

"I suppose I should," Sulys murmured, with a bleak eye on her future. "But then nothing would change, would it?"

"Then what will you do?"

"I don't know . . . Sell these ugly shoes, perhaps, and pay a boatman to take me out of Kelior." She leaned back into the silky tapestry, her eyes closing. "Or I could disappear like Tyramin into the Twilight Quarter, use my magic to earn my bread. Find missing things for people, tell fortunes in ashes. My great-grandmother would miss me, but she has Beris, and I could send her crows every day with messages. What do you think?" She opened her eyes again at an exasperated noise from Ceta.

"I wish—" she began, rising and beginning to pace. "I wish my brilliant cousin—"

What she wished for Valoren she did not say, for, turning, she nearly ran into him. He had appeared out of nowhere with Yar beside him. Sulys, frozen in her chair and staring at him, thought with dread: I will never feel alone again, if we marry, I will never feel private . . .

"You might have knocked," Ceta told him sharply. "I'm hardly dressed for company."

"I'm sorry," he said absently, his eyes on Sulys. "We are in a hurry."

"At least tell us that you are searching for the princess."

He sighed, made a visible effort at tact. "I would have, if I'd realized she was missing again. You," he amended to

Sulys. "You were missing. I know that you and I must talk, but there is no time, now. I came to ask Ceta what Od wrote about Skrygard Mountain."

Ceta's mouth opened, closed wordlessly. She gazed at Yar as though, Sulys saw with amazement, he had wantonly broken something precious to her. "You told him."

"I had no choice."

"Indeed he did not," Valoren said bluntly. "I gave him none. I think the gardener has fled to Skrygard Mountain, where those strange, powerful beings I found in Yar's thoughts have hidden themselves. It could be extremely dangerous to Numis if Brenden Vetch is not found before he reaches them. I need to know what Od wrote."

Ceta's eyes pleaded with Yar; he shook his head a little, helplessly. "Show him." His mouth twisted ruefully at her silence. "You wanted to know what they are."

"But not this way—not disturbed—They are ancient, and so quiet no one remembers them, and who knows if they're even still there?"

"Brenden knows," Yar told her gently. "He spoke of them."

"Are those Od's writings?" Valoren asked, looking at an untidy scattering of scrolls and manuscript along one side of the carpet. Ceta moved toward them defensively, but Valoren was there, somehow, before her, already kneeling and rifling through them. He looked up at her, waiting; Ceta spoke to Yar before she took another step.

"Are you going with him?"

"I don't—"

"Yes," Valoren answered for him.

"Then I'll show you what you need to know," Ceta told him reluctantly. "I found another piece of the puzzle earlier this morning among manuscripts I borrowed a while ago from the king's library." She picked a piece of tattered parchment off a table, handed it to the wizard. "I put it aside for Yar to read when he came."

Valoren read it to himself. Sulys, watching him warily, as they all were, was surprised by an expression she hadn't seen before. In anyone else, she might have called it wonder.

"What is it?" Yar asked him.

"'They,'" Valoren read aloud, "'are the forgotten treasures of power. The missing faces of it. The hidden. The secrets of Skrygard must only be found by someone strong enough to wake them and fearless enough to free them. Otherwise, terror will rule over Numis again, and the land will lose its heart.'" He raised his eyes to stare at Yar. "Do you have any idea what these are?"

"No."

"Terror will rule . . . Surely they must not be freed. If Brenden Vetch reaches them—if his power has some root in theirs—"

"If you drag such fears with you to Skrygard Mountain," Yar said sharply, "there may well be the disaster that Od predicts."

"We must hurry," Valoren said, setting the paper down and ignoring what seemed to Sulys to be some very sound advice. "The gardener's powers seem untrained, unpredictable—we have no idea how quickly he can travel, and we must be there waiting for him."

"He probably hasn't even found his way out of Kelior yet," Yar said dourly. "He did walk all the way here."

Valoren ignored that, too. "We should leave now. Yar—"

"Valoren," Ceta interrupted, "at least give us a moment's privacy before you take him to the hinterlands. And I do mean private; don't just make yourself invisible and listen to us."

"I would hardly do that," Valoren said stiffly. "Besides, Yar would sense me." He paused, then lowered his head an inch. "I'll give you an hour. Meet me in Wye's chambers then." He looked at the princess, who had begun to hope that he had forgotten her. "Shall I escort you back to the palace? It will give us a few moments to talk, before I must explain to the king where I'm going. You could tell me what you needed so desperately to say that you spent the night in the labyrinth."

Sulys cleared her throat, said carefully, "I think that now is not the time to distract you with my concerns. And I need far more than a few moments of your time. It can wait."

He seemed suddenly curious, she thought uneasily, as though he scented something trying to elude him. "Are you sure?"

"Yes."

"Then we will talk, I promise, when this is over. Arneth Pyt is at the Twilight Gate now; I'll send him here to escort you back." He turned to Yar. "I'll see you shortly."

He used the door this time. Ceta stepped close to Yar, but did not speak until they heard the sound of it closing behind the wizard. Sulys was about to rise to take her leave; Yar had opened his mouth to speak; Ceta held them both motionless with her sudden, fierce whisper. "Yar. Use the labyrinth. Go now."

"What?"

"I'm sure it will take you there! Warn those—those mysteries about Valoren—warn Brenden. Do what you can. Don't let Valoren disturb them."

"Do you realize," he asked her steadily, "what you are telling me to do?"

"Yes."

"You know your cousin. He fears the worst. He may assume the worst when he finds me missing: that I have taken sides against the king and the school of wizards with Brenden Vetch and these strange powers."

"He may. But you are right: Valoren could very likely be Od's worst fear. Find your way there and protect them."

"He'll come here looking for me," he warned her. "He's very difficult to lie to."

"I do," Sulys reminded them, "all the time. He doesn't see what he doesn't expect."

"Just go," Ceta urged him. "Try the labyrinth. If it doesn't work, you'll have no choice but to go with Valoren. But you must at least try. If he questions me, I'll tell him you left me, as far as I know, to do what he asked."

He smiled a little, tightly, and shifted a strand of hair out of her eyelashes. "You would never have suggested that I keep secrets from king and court before."

"No," she answered gravely. "Perhaps it's Od herself who inspired me to look at things differently. Her way instead of Valoren's. You've been unhappy; you want to change. I had to change a little myself to see that."

He kissed her gently. Sulys watched his wry, kindly, experienced face, and wondered what it would take for Valoren to wear such an expression. Years? Life? A startling and unexpected turn of events that might make him question everything he knew? She found Yar's eyes on her suddenly, and wondered if he had sensed his name in her head.

"Do you want me to take you back to the palace?"

"No," she answered simply. "I want to get inside the Twilight Quarter."

He was startled. But he didn't argue, as she thought he would; unexpectedly, he acknowledged her magic. "It takes you like that," he told her. "You've learned what you can from your great-grandmother; that isn't enough for you. You are drawn to the something in the magician's magic; it calls to you."

She straightened abruptly in her chair. "Is it true?" she whispered. "His magic?"

He did not answer her directly, only murmured, "With Valoren leaving Kelior, it's a good time to find out. I can tell you something that should help you get past the gate. No one else knows this."

"What?"

"Arneth Pyt loves the magician's daughter. Tell Arneth you will do what you can for her, and I think you'll find Tyramin easily. Let him know that I told you this. He'll trust me. I knew that he was protecting her, and I didn't tell Valoren."

"Yar," Ceta said wonderingly. "How can you possibly know such a thing?"

He smiled again. "I learned it wandering around the Twilight Quarter in the dark looking for a gardener."

"Of course you did." She reached out, touched the princess lightly as she tried to make her way unobtrusively past them toward the door. "Wait for Arneth Pyt to come here," she suggested. "You don't want to run into Valoren now. Eat something. I have a pair of boots that may fit you better than those shoes; I'll have Shera find them for you."

Sulys subsided back into the chair, listening for a knock on the door as she nibbled, and hearing the soft voices weaving gently together for a few moments longer, until a final word faded into the air, and the wizard was gone.

TWENTY-TWO

Appearing briefly in the school to put on clothes more suitable to the harsher northern weather, Yar looked for his heavy cloak, didn't find it, and remembered Elver. He found another cloak, older and a bit frayed at the hem, and put that on instead. He dropped some coins into his pocket, forgetting Elver, his thoughts turning to Brenden, wondering how far he had gotten, and then to the labyrinth, which he would reach with his next step, moving so swiftly through the school that no one would realize he had come and gone.

But his chamber door opened before he could take that step. And there was Wye, her seamed face the color of ivory, shadowed with exhaustion. Encounters with the king and the exacting Valoren had shaken her composure badly.

"Yar, where have you been?" she demanded.

"Mostly trying to do what Valoren asked," he answered gently.

"And now where are you going?"

"To help Valoren with Brenden Vetch. Or to help Brenden with Valoren, whichever seems most appropriate."

"I need you more than either of them. Some of the older teachers binding the Twilight Quarter could use your strength. You must persuade Valoren to—" She stopped, seeing something in his eyes, something he had left unsaid; she knew him that well. "Yar."

He stepped out, closed the door behind them, avoiding her scrutiny. The ubiquitous Elver, whom he had left sleeping beside a fire pit at dawn, popped into his mind again. He said, to change the subject, "I've had no time to tell you. The young student Elver followed me into the Twilight Quarter yesterday when Valoren sent me to find the gardener."

"Who?"

"Elver. I explained to him that he had expelled himself from the school, which he accepted without much regret. He's staying at his uncle's on Crescent Street. Marsh was the name, I think—something Marsh. Some kind of fish. When anyone has time to notice him missing, that's where he'll be."

"I don't," Wye said with a touch of asperity, "have any idea what you are talking about."

"Bream. That was it. Bream Marsh."

"Yar, where are you going?"

He paused, meeting her eyes again, letting her see his own filling with distances, with uncertainty, with wonder. "I'm sorry to leave you with all this. I'll be back as soon as I can."

Her white brows puckered; she tried to read his mind without crossing the boundaries of courtesy. "What," she asked softly, "have you discovered that has put that expression back on your face for the first time since you passed beneath the cobbler's shoe?"

"I don't know," he answered unsteadily. "I won't know until I see it. If."

"Well, what—where shall I tell Valoren you've gone?"

"You don't know."

"Yar, be careful," she pleaded.

"I have been for nineteen years. That's long enough."

He felt her eyes on him as he went down the tower stairs. But she left him his privacy; he went unobserved into the labyrinth.

This time it showed him its own path, unentangled by his thoughts. He was astonished how easily he found the center: a turn or two and there he was, blinking away the dark to examine the center stone with a wizard's vision. The map carved into it looked far more elaborate than the labyrinth around him. He could see the pyramid Ceta had described very clearly, again looking nothing like it should. He wondered where Od had begun this labyrinth, what door to open to find it, what road to begin walking, what thread she had left, centuries before, to follow.

It should begin here, he thought, illumined. Within this labyrinth. The first step to Skrygard Mountain should be the step I take from where I stand, looking at this map and seeing where it begins and ends.

He studied it for a while longer, saw no other answer to the riddle Od had set. To find the beginning of the maze, he had to know where it ended. No one would guess that without having pieced together, as Ceta had, the clues in the scattered fragments of Od's writings through the centuries. No student, perceiving the discrepancy in the map at the center of the labyrinth, could have accidentally gone there, for Od had not made anything about Skrygard Mountain part of the common lore or the accepted teachings of the school. Ceta's curious mind and sensitive heart had seen between the lines of Od's writings, pieced a sentence found in the king's library to a faded paragraph in an obscure scroll gathering cobwebs in the school's library. Knowing where the secret labyrinth ended was the center stone of Od's spell.

Yar took a step up onto the center of the stone, and whispered, "Skrygard Mountain."

Shadows swirled around him the instant he spoke. They paled, whirled into mist so thick and close he couldn't see his own boots or the stone beneath them. Standing, it seemed, within a roiling cloud, he had no idea if he were moving as well, or if he had just roused a passing storm in the school's cellar. He waited. The mists did not part to reveal the world; they simply continued around him with a great deal of energy and no point whatever that he could see.

After a while, he stepped off the stone. The mists promptly vanished, left him staring upward at the barren crags and snow-covered flank of a mountain.

He felt the cold then, smelled pine and snow and stone. He turned, his thoughts beginning to form again, as though they, too, had turned into that blinding, churning mist. He looked down the mountain to the fields and marshes of the north country, across them, south toward Kelior, as far as he could see until the mists formed again, the lowering autumn sky hiding the rest of Numis.

Wonder struck him then with the force of wind: Od's magic was still potent, and unpredictable as well, after all those centuries. She was still a force in Numis, finding ways to work her will, even in secret. He looked for her across the colorless landscape, or for Brenden Vetch, for anything, anyone in motion. No one was out in the chill, drab afternoon. In the distance, he could see a cluster of tiny stone houses tucked in a fold between hills, a vague smudge on a hillside that might have been a herd of something. Of fleeing and pursuing wizards he saw nothing, just a bird, a dark fleck moving across the endless cloud.

Something seemed to call to him out of the mountain's silence, request his attention. He turned again, looked up across the field of snow clinging to the steep side of the mountain. Huge trees lined the snow on both sides but did not encroach; bare rock jutted above it, looming crags angling together to form the pyramid at the center of Od's map.

Below it, high on the snow line, he saw the strange, dark shapes.

They looked like jagged, misshapen trees, so old that their limbs had crumbled away, leaving only the suggestion of tree behind. Like stones that someone had begun to sculpt long ago and left for wind and weather to finish. Something, he thought, that once might have been alive, or had a recognizable resemblance to a common word. Now they were wordless, shapeless. Old things in perpetual snow, they seemed to him. He took a step or two up the mountain toward them, stopped as he felt their almost imperceptible withdrawal, the awareness of them fading in him like shadow fading at a sudden cloud.

They were alive, he realized. In their own way, they had spoken to him, told him of their awareness, their alarm. Painfully, as though it had been clenched like a fist for years, his heart opened; wonder spread its wings through him. A word he did not know, something he did not recognize, a power that was not defined within the laws of Numis: these things still existed, despite the king and all his counselors.

But what were they?

The missing faces of power, Od had called them. Its forgotten treasures. Hidden away for centuries, until they could be coaxed back into the world by someone powerful enough not to fear their power.

Do I have enough power? he wondered. Will I be afraid?

He took another step toward them. Another. He felt their tenuous awareness once again, their uncertainty, their waiting. He continued his slow movement toward them, while the pale light of late afternoon dimmed; the snow underfoot grew gray.

When he was close enough to see the dark stains of time or sorrow across their forms, the seams and gashes of weathering, he stopped. Somehow, they had grown huge during his trek upward. At a distance, they had seemed shrunken, dwindled, whittled down to human size. They loomed over him now, immense and silent as the ancient trees, watching him, he sensed, the way wizards watched, aware in thought and breath and skin, however they defined their hard, blackened husks.

"Who are you?" he asked aloud, and with his heart. But he did not know their language yet; they did not answer. After a while he kindled a fire in the snow, having nothing to burn but magic, and sat down to watch night fall over Numis as he waited.

For a long time nothing spoke except his fire. The world grew very dark, very still. Now and then he sensed wind, brisk and noisy, blowing through the valleys below, but on the mountain, in that dreaming place, nothing moved, perhaps not even time. A wizard tended his fire in the night. Yar saw himself from a distance, the way the moon might see him, or something crouched and watching him beyond his circle of light. He started at the thought, was himself again, staring back at the night. It seemed a sentient thing suddenly, enormous and aware, so close around him that he could have turned away from light and looked into its eyes.

That close, he marveled. He felt no fear, though, that these strange, powerful, nameless beings seemed to have crept as close around him as the dark. He might be dreaming, after all. He saw himself again, the wizard tending his fire in the snow, only his face and hands illumined. He looked at himself, he realized then, out of other eyes. They were very close, the forgotten ones, close enough to see the reflection of fire in his eyes. Then he saw himself again, far away now, a distant figure in a circle of fire and snow, on a plane of night.

Eyes closed; the figure vanished. Again he started, trying to regain an inner balance, but this time he couldn't find himself. He saw only the endless dark across Numis, illumined by nothing, no one.

They were that old, he knew then. Older than the name of Numis. They were of a wild magic, as ancient as wind, as night. They had known the force of wind before it had a name; they had become fire before it had been tamed, when it roamed the earth at will, unconfined by hearth, candle, lantern. They, too, had wandered at will, then, power without language, shaping everything they saw, twig, bird, leaf, water, stone, earth, light. The image became the language of power, the language of the heart. No written words, no human law could restrict something that needed no language; no walls could imprison a power that could become the stone it saw, the bird that could fly between the bars. The air that made it soar.

With the ache of longing, Yar remembered glimpsing such power before he walked beneath the cobbler's shoe and the doors of the school closed behind him. On the long road to Kelior, he had seen the possibility of it. Within the school, within the king's laws, he had seen the impossibility of it. There language defined power. The spoken word, not the image itself, became the source. Words could go unheard; words could deceive; words could be imprecise, unpredictable, and forbidden. Words, used against those who had no language, could be devastating.

So he learned, during the night that seemed to last forever. Somewhere beyond the plane of darkness, he sensed a soggy dawn, the passing of a bitter day. Another night. The wordless tale was the history of magic in Numis, when the land had a name and early kings ruled it. The strange, nameless, wordless powers, who had grown seemingly out of the earth itself, caused great fear in the early inhabitants, some of whom had brought their own powers from distant places. They fought to kill; without language, the ancient powers could not explain themselves. They tried, taking the shape of humans to protect themselves, which only made the humans terrify one another, for they could no longer believe what they saw, and so mistrusted everyone.

The ancient face of power had retreated into itself so long ago no one remembered, and only Od had recognized it. Hints survived in old tales haunted by terrible creatures of the night, who could take a human face when they chose. That such power still existed anywhere in Numis, beyond language and beyond law, would have stunned the well-schooled wizards of Kelior.

Somewhere beyond him, snow was falling. Somewhere, he had a name. After a time, he remembered it. His fire had gone out; his bones were growing stiff. Someone had roused him, he thought, but when he opened his eyes to the gray light of day, he saw no one. Only the softly falling snow, and the great, weather-ravaged forces around him, which ringed him like immense, dark flames, or the memory of fire.

Someone said his name.

He stood up, clumsily, feeling his blood flow. Someone knew him; no one was there. He felt the gentle awareness emanating from within the ancient mysteries. Someone among the ring who knew language, knew his name.

He felt his throat close, wordless with wonder. Turning as he looked up, he searched all the blurred, unrecognizable faces of power for the one he knew.

He said, "Brenden?"

TWENTY-THREE

Mistral walked through the waking streets of the Twilight Quarter, wearing her life on her shoulders, in her hair, on the long skirt that would have spun itself into a perfect circle if she danced. It was a simple spell, but one she doubted the wizards of Kelior knew, requiring, as it did, needle and thread. She had sent her company scattering about the quarter, carrying money and the least that they needed with them. The magic in that was that there was no magic. They wore nothing, took nothing that might connect them with Tyramin. Not a silk shirt, not a glass pendant or painted buckle that, glittering in the light, might turn itself to jewel or gold. No masks, no face paint, nothing that might suggest illusion. In the Twilight Quarter, such colorlessness might draw attention to itself, but only from the capricious occupants, who wore their brightest to distinguish them from the night.

The rest of her life: the great masks, the trunks full of costumes, the ribbons and swaths of silk, the mirrors, drums, carpets, curtains, the profusion of oddments Tyramin used for his spells, even the painted wagons, she had hidden within a spell she had learned from a seamstress once when her father traveled through Hestria. How to hide secrets within stitches. How to render a thing invisible even to a wizard's sight, so that all the magic lay in the threads and none in the objects themselves that might betray them to inquisitive minds. She had whispered names of the images in her thoughts as she sewed them into random patterns on her skirt, her tunic, the scarf in her hair. She had left a few things visible, strewn about the warehouse to suggest a precipitous haste in leaving. There was nowhere to go; the royal guards and the wizards would still be searching for them. But they would only recognize Tyramin's illusions; the mundane faces beneath the masks would pass unnoticed in the streets. Mistral doubted that even the most powerful of the wizards would think to suspect magic in the embroidery on a skirt.

The performers had separated, found lodgings anywhere they could throughout the quarter. The oxen and packhorses had been stabled since Tyramin arrived; Mistral didn't bother to hide them, since one ox without its ribbons and spangles looked very like another. She had slipped back into the warehouse after Valoren had searched it. It seemed safest to stay there rather than risk being recognized in an inn or lodging house. She hid herself by day in one of the invisible wagons, which were drawn up in a line in the back of the warehouse. No one went there: nothing to see but the muddy riverbank and old dock posts rising out of the water. There, with Tyramin's great, fearless head for company, she strengthened her spells within a labyrinth of threads and tried to come up with a trick for the magician that would surpass all others: how to transform the king's fear into trust.

She thought so often of Arneth that she was afraid she might have sewn him into her sleeve and made him invisible. He had left a footprint in her heart, a little, restless, curious urge to follow, see what she would find in him when she found his face again. That, too, she must work somehow into Tyramin's master spell: to convince the King of Numis with her magic that she was a harmless trickster, so that he would let her stay in the Twilight Quarter to be near the one man for whom she did not have to wear her masks.

It seemed an impossible task. But so had taking her father's place, wearing his mask, seemed when she had first begun. What can be conceived, he had told her often, can be achieved. So she sat in solitude for long hours, plying her needle and traveling the boundaries of her mind, trying to find a way to turn what she already knew into a spell that would enchant even the enchanter.

She was relieved, after she had vanished out of his life, to see Arneth again, solid, visible, and recognizable on the streets of the quarter. She had slipped out of her wagon under cover of night to walk, gather gossip, find something to eat. The crowds in the quarter were far sparser without the night traffic from the rest of Kelior. But they were no less lively. The occupants, refusing to be intimidated by the guards across the gate, tried to entertain them. Some wore masks and proclaimed themselves Tyramin, pulled eggs out of their sleeves and buttons out of their ears. Some still found their way to the warehouse, hoping that the magician would pull himself out of a hat. Mistral saw them beginning to gather as she left; a few would linger there until dawn. Her hair bundled up under her scarf, her black tunic and skirt swirling with embroidered secrets, the myriad details of her life, she walked past the little crowd without attracting more than perfunctory attention. She found a shadow near them, stayed to listen for news.

Princess Sulys was still missing, she learned. Rumor had it that she had run off with a gardener from the wizard's school. Her betrothed, the king's wizard Valoren, blamed everything on Tyramin. Moving invisibly through the quarter, Valoren was searching it house by house, every tavern and shop and stall, even the stables, to run to earth the elusive magician. Who, everyone knew, must have already escaped through chinks between the stones in the wall, for where else was he? What's more, the princess Sulys had also run away with him to avoid marrying the milk-faced Valoren, who looked more curdled by the day, or would, if he allowed himself to be seen.

Mistral turned away. Nothing new, then. She took a step, heard Arneth's voice, and froze.

When she could move again, she turned cautiously to look at him. He was in the company of a wizard, it seemed: she remembered the dark, hooded robes the pair of them had worn when they came to search the warehouse. She had not expected them to return. But here one was back again with Arneth. Valoren? She wondered desperately what thread of her spell she had left unknotted to snag the wizard's attention.

"It's a place to begin searching," Arneth had said, which made no sense; he had already brought the wizards there. Mistral filled her mind with river mist and shadows, eased deeper into the night. The hood within which the wizard's face had burrowed like a small animal turned this way and that, scenting, revealing nothing.

"You have no idea?" The unfamiliar voice surprised Mistral. It belonged to a woman, young by the sound of it, tense but unthreatening, and hushed, as though she, too, were in hiding.

"How could I?" the quarter warden asked softly. "She couldn't tell me; it's too dangerous for me of all people to know. I can deceive my father, but not Valoren if I ever caught his attention."

"If he bothered to see," the young woman said a trifle tartly. Mistral, startled at her temerity, wished she could see into the hood without being seen. "Well, we're all safe from those eyes for the moment."

"Only until he finds the gardener."

"I think he'll go all the way to Skrygard Mountain with or without the gardener," the young woman said evenly. "Lady Thiel sent me upstairs to sleep this morning after you suggested we wait until dusk to come here. Valoren's voice woke me. He was too distracted to sense that I was still there instead of in the palace. Of course Lady Thiel couldn't hide from him where Yar had gone. But she didn't tell him how. He thought Yar couldn't be very far ahead of him, and he was completely mystified that Yar hadn't waited to go with him as he asked."

"So am I," Arneth admitted. "I wouldn't want that wizard hunting me."

"It's not easy to explain. I only know that Valoren left this morning, and I haven't seen him since. There's a mystery in the northlands that could, he said, threaten Numis. Now he thinks that Yar might have been trapped by its powers, drawn into its snares, perhaps by the gardener, who is also corrupted by it, since he grew up in the north country. Of course, Valoren must go and investigate. So we should be safe from him for a time."

"You're not afraid of this mysterious power? That it might attack your father?"

"They're very old, Lady Thiel said. These creatures of power. Od first wrote about them centuries ago. I can't think what my father might do to annoy them more than any other king has done in all that time."

Mistral's eyes widened. That was the mystery within the hood: the missing princess, who, it seemed, had no high opinion of her betrothed either. But why, she wondered, was Arneth risking everything bringing her into the forbidden Twilight Quarter instead of taking her back to the palace?

He was looking for her, that much Mistral guessed. And he trusted the princess, for whatever reason. Discovered with either of them there, princess or magician, Arneth could lose his position, his reputation, perhaps even his freedom. Yet he had chosen to face those dangers. She spent a moment weighing her own risks, to herself and her company, while Arneth spoke again.

"She could be anywhere within these walls. It may be better if I take you home and search for her myself, let her know you're looking for—"

"No."

"Your father—"

"How many chances to come here do you think I'll get? The last time I tried it, you stopped me as soon as I got through the gate. I'm here, now. You know what I want. I won't leave until I get it."

"I know what you want," Arneth said slowly. "But I'm still not sure why you want it."

The princess's voice grew very soft again. "Yar told me it's magic that calls out to me."

"You, too?" Arneth said incredulously.

The head within the hood nodded briefly, emphatically. "As you can imagine, I need help as well as the magician. Perhaps we can help each other."

Mistral moved. It took only a step or two to reach Arneth, a breath to look into his face, hold his eyes until she saw his expression change. Then she lowered her head, continued past the crowd and down the dark side street that ran to the back of the warehouse, where she waited for them. She led them through the back door of the warehouse, into the little room where Tyramin's chipped and work-worn head watched them from the floor.

Mistral lit a lamp in the windowless room. The princess pulled back her hood, revealing a thin, troubled young face and a mass of untidy dark hair. She gazed at the battered mask, then, uncertainly, at Mistral. She blinked, glanced at Arneth, and back at Mistral, a question in her eyes.

Mistral said softly, "He knows."

"Your threads are showing," the princess said faintly. "Not," she added hastily, "so much that anyone would notice. I only see them because my great-grandmother taught me that trick. I have only hidden small things—a locket and a ring my mother gave me—but I could see the magic in the stitches."

"What threads?" Arneth asked bewilderedly. "What stitches?"

Mistral looked at him. A mistake, she thought, for now she didn't want to take her eyes away from the green eyes that had warmed so quickly to her, the smile that she felt her own face reflect. She answered with an effort, "Some magic I did. If you don't know what it is, you won't have to—"

He shook his head. "It's too late to try to protect me. All we can hope for now is luck. This is Princess Sulys."

"I know. I heard you talking. I listened until I felt safe enough to reveal myself. At first I thought the princess was a wizard."

"When I persuaded Arneth to take me into the quarter this morning, he suggested I disguise myself as one, and he would lead me through the gate when he came on duty again at twilight with the changing of the guard. I had already stolen someone's cloak from the school." The princess's eyes moved again to Mistral's threads; she asked wonderingly, "What—how much can you hide within them?"

"Everything."

Sulys's eyes grew wide; so did Arneth's. He breathed, "What exactly—"

"Exactly what I want," she told him. "For as long as I want, until someone recognizes the spell and breaks my stitches."

"The wizards wouldn't pay any attention to threads," Sulys assured her. "Thread is among the ordinary things the wizards no longer see."

"Along with magic where they don't expect it, I would assume from your betrothal."

The princess nodded wordlessly; her eyes were caught by the black gaze from the massive head on the floor, flickering in the lamplight. "Is that Tyramin's mask?"

"Yes."

"Why—" The princess hesitated, her eyes still on the mask, as though it might, at any moment, utter solemn and powerful words of magic. "If I can help him escape, will he let me see him?"

"Why do you want to see him badly enough to risk so much?"

"Because I'm tired of hiding. Of having no one to talk to, to learn from, to tell me what is possible instead of what is not. A magician powerful enough to elude the entire school of wizards, including Valoren, and fearless enough to do it, would see no harm in my simple magic. And now that I've met you, I know it must be true: you don't have to hide your magic from him. He must have taught you the things you do. He sees the magic in ordinary things, too. And he is not afraid. Maybe, together, we can figure out a way for us all to escape. Maybe —" She faltered suddenly under Mistral's unblinking gaze; her eyes broke from it, went to the mask's dark stare, then back to the magician's daughter. "Maybe," she whispered, "the reason no one can find Tyramin is that he is only a mask. No one sees the magic they don't expect. No one would look for a woman behind his mask."

Mistral opened her mouth; for a moment, no words would come. She whispered, "How did you know?"

The princess took a step toward her, eyes catching the lamp's fire, as Tyramin's did. "I asked Arneth to take me to Tyramin. He brought me to you. From what I've heard, nobody ever sees Tyramin. Everyone sees you. That's the kind of magic I understand. The kind that nobody notices."

Mistral smiled shakily and removed her last mask. She shifted close to Arneth, shoulder touching his shoulder, fingers lightly clasping his wrist. "Can you help us?" she asked the princess. "My greatest wish is to live here with my company in the Twilight Quarter, at peace with the king and Kelior. But he distrusts us, sending Valoren to hound Tyramin, and for very good reason: I have brought forbidden ways of magic into Numis; I am breaking laws. But only to create a few lovely illusions and enchantments that vanish by morning. If there is some way you can think of to get us all out of Kelior, I'll take my company and leave. But I would rather stay."

"If you leave," Arneth told her firmly, "I'm coming with

you. I don't see why I should have to look at my father and
Valoren every day instead of you."

"I don't see why I should have to, either," Sulys told them.
"I'm coming, too."

Mistral, envisioning the rejected suitor breathing fire on
her heels across Numis, pulled her thoughts together. "It
would be better if we all could find a way to live peacefully
together instead of running away."

"Then I could visit you here freely, and you could teach
me things," Sulys said, looking at them both as though they,
not she, were their only hope. "Surely we can think of something? If we put all our spells together? Threads and candles,
buttons and ribbons and bones . . ."

"And wishes," Arneth added.

Mistral was silent. Rich threads stitched themselves
through her thoughts, scarlet and gold, glittering like Tyramin's fires . . . She might lose everything if she pursued these
threads: her company, her freedom, even Arneth. But if she
could show the king the truth about her magic, its innocence
and ephemeral charms, then she might gain everything for all
of them, even the extraordinary princess.

"I think," she told them slowly, watching the golden needle in her vision running through detail after detail, "Tyramin
might have one last trick up his sleeve . . ."

TWENTY-FOUR

Arneth escorted the princess back to Lady Thiel's house sometime in the night and spent the next few hours roaming the streets of the Twilight Quarter, trying to think of a way out of it for Mistral that did not involve the brightly sealed message to the king in his pocket. He would have preferred to toss the entire risky business into the river instead and ride off into the night with the magician's daughter. But as things were, he couldn't even find a way out of the quarter, let alone out of Kelior, for Mistral and her company. So he rode back to the palace with the night guard at dawn, waited for his father to arrive in the High Warden's office, and presented him with the message to the king.

Murat Pyt regarded it with astonishment. "What is this? Where—How did it come to you?"

"It was given to me by Tyramin's daughter. She came to me late last night and told me it was to be given to the king."

Murat turned it over in his hand, studied the gold and teal ribbons caught in a scarlet splash of wax, then turned it over again, as though trying to see through the paper. "Did she tell you what it says?" he asked huskily.

"Yes, sir."

"Well?" the High Warden demanded after a silence. "What?"

"It's a message," Arneth answered fastidiously, his eyes on the far wall, "for the king."

"Don't be ridiculous," his father said testily. "It's your duty to tell me what you know, which has been little enough lately, I might add. It's about time you've produced some proof that Tyramin is still in the Twilight Quarter. What is the message?"

Arneth told him. The High Warden had risen before he finished. He rounded his desk, snagged Arneth's elbow, and propelled him out the door. "Come with me to the palace. The invitation was given to you; you will deliver it with your own hand to King Galin."

They had to wait in an antechamber while Arneth gave his news to a household guard, who sent several pages running. One of the king's older counselors appeared finally, looking gaunt and owlish with the added strain of Valoren's absence. He listened to Arneth's news and reached for the message, which the High Warden shifted adroitly out of his grasp.

"My son was told to give it himself to the king."

The counselor cast a yellow, bloodshot eye at him, but said nothing. He vanished; they sat down and waited again. Arneth's eyes closed. He opened them again, quickly, at a jab from his father's elbow, and got to his feet as the king entered, his heir beside him and the aged counselor on their heels.

He took the proffered letter, looked at it, then at Arneth. "Who gave you this?"

"The magician's daughter, my lord, very late last night; she told me it was to be given to—"

"Where is she?"

"My lord?"

"Surely you arrested her," Galin said impatiently. "Where did you put her?"

Arneth, floundering, pulled his thoughts together swiftly. "My lord, she told me the contents of the message. It seemed wiser not to arrest her then, or threaten her in any way since Tyramin himself was offering to walk onto the palm of your hand."

The king grunted, tearing open the message. The prince offered his opinion brusquely. "We could have taken her as a hostage. We would have had Tyramin by now if you had thought."

Arneth bowed his head. "My mistake."

"Not the first," Lord Pyt said testily. "Sometimes I wonder if—"

Arneth was rescued from his father's suspicions by the king, who slapped the paper in his hand and barked, "Ha!"

The prince and the counselor peered over Galin's shoulder. The High Warden crowded closely behind him, asked disingenuously, "What is it, my lords?"

"Tyramin offers a private performance to the king at his court," the counselor murmured, reading. "To make amends for whatever trouble he has so unintentionally caused to the Twilight Quarter, and as a gesture of goodwill toward the King of Numis." He paused, looking, Arneth thought, as though he had caught of whiff of something unsavory. "I don't like it."

"If he's powerful enough to attack me in the company of my wizards under my own roof, then he can easily attack me from wherever he is now," Galin said briskly. "So far he has done nothing but hide. I like it."

"When does he offer to come?" the High Warden asked.

"He and his performers will gather at the Twilight Gate tomorrow at dusk, during the changing of the guard. If the king desires, the quarter warden will meet the company there to lead them, escorted by the royal guard, to the palace."

Even the suspicious counselor seemed taken aback by that.

"We could simply arrest him then," Murat Pyt suggested. Arneth gritted his teeth to keep himself quiet.

"We could," the counselor said slowly. "But the wizards would learn far more about him by watching him work."

The king nodded. "Arneth, be at the gate and bring them to the great hall, tomorrow, as they offer."

"Yes, my lord."

"I would like to see what the entire quarter has been talking about. I would also," Galin added a trifle explosively, "like to see my daughter. Has she given anyone a message for me? Valoren told me before he left that he had seen her with Lady Thiel. I thought he had instructed you, Arneth, to escort her home."

Arneth cleared his throat. "My lord, she refused to come with me. She is still with Lady Thiel."

"What is she doing there?" the king demanded. "She has a wedding to prepare. Fanerl is becoming unbearable on the subject."

Arneth swallowed a snort of laughter and stared raptly at the floor. The prince thumbed an eyebrow, his stiff face easing, becoming vaguely bemused. "I think," he said slowly, making an effort to remember something, "she needed to talk."

"About what?"

"I don't know."

"Well, why didn't she talk to Valoren?"

"Apparently she tried. They quarreled, I heard, in front of the wizards, instead of talking, and then she disappeared again."

"Where was she the first time?" the king asked. "Hiding in the school cellar or some such morbid place? In the dark with the beetles?"

"Someplace like that."

"And now she's with Ceta, and Valoren couldn't charm her back home? What ails the girl? Doesn't she like him?" The king glanced around him at the silence. "No one knows?"

"Valoren might know," Enys answered doubtfully.

"Valoren is pursuing the rumor of some monstrous power in the north country," Galin said grimly. "A wedding is the last thing on his mind."

The High Warden stared at him; the counselor rocked slightly at the news. "My lord," he said, shocked, "should we prepare for attack?"

"I have no idea. His only source for the threat is a few lines that Od wrote centuries ago. He thinks the powers have been dormant in all this time, but may have something to do with the missing gardener. I don't know," he added restively, "what so many nebulous bits and pieces—a gardener, a trick monger, a sentence in an ancient scroll—will add up to in the end. Valoren will tell us."

"Surely Od would have warned us," the prince said.

"Maybe her way of warning us was to send the gardener here," the king answered. "That was Valoren's suggestion."

"Why didn't she just come and tell us herself?" Enys asked skeptically. "She rescued Kelior once before."

"It would seem more helpful than inflicting a dangerous gardener on us." The king stopped, as though trying to envision such a thing, then blinked and said again, irritably, "I don't know. Nothing makes sense. I can't even understand my own daughter, let alone these obscure threats and portents that may be threatening us and maybe not—Arneth."

"Yes, my lord," Arneth said quickly.

"My daughter is apparently still speaking to you, at least. I want her back under this roof and attending to her wedding before she vanishes out of our lives like her—" He stopped again, rendering himself speechless with what he almost said. The prince eyed him mutely, disquieted. The king tossed his hands in the air, and said it. "Like her mother. I'll give you a message for her and Lady Thiel: that you will escort both of them, together with the magician and his company, tomorrow evening to watch Tyramin perform." He fixed Arneth with a questioning glance, then Enys. "Will that do? Do you think she'll come?"

Arneth, who had been asked by the princess to do just that, let the prince answer. Enys seemed to cast his thoughts back to a young woman he had once known, but now was not certain he would even recognize. "Yes," he said hesitantly. "I'm not sure why I think so. But I think it will please her."

The king was silent a moment, adrift in his own memories; Arneth glimpsed the bewilderment of loss in his eyes. Then he said briskly to no one, "Good. Maybe she'll talk to somebody then, and one thing in this murky confusion of events will begin to clear itself up." He turned restively, made for the door, his entourage falling in behind him. "The rest must wait for Valoren."

TWENTY-FIVE

B renden refused to come out.

Yar, waiting patiently in the snow, could hardly blame him. Words, he discovered early, were of no use. Talking to one of the strange, silent beings was like trying to converse with a boulder. He knew no words old enough, slow enough, for such an ancient thing to hear, when a single word in its own language might begin in one century, end in another. When he let their minds seep into his, tell him what they chose, they filled him with emanations, images. So Brenden spoke to him, in this language older than words. When Yar tried to answer, letting his own awareness venture into the dark, weather-beaten masks of power, he found himself halfway down the flank of the mountain, lifting his face out of the snow.

For some time, all he could see or think or feel was a painful brightness as though he had been struck by lightning, and a force like water plunging over the sheer edge of a cliff. He had barely touched the surface of such power when it flung him and his curiosity away on a spume white surge of motion. When the burning in his head eased a little, he heard his name again, a gentle, persistent awareness of him flowing out of wherever Brenden had hidden himself. He struggled up slowly, staring at mysteries, stunned by their power, and by Brenden, who had opened his mind to them as easily as he might have opened himself to a bog lily, and had lived, Yar assumed, to tell about it.

He walked back up to the bulky shapes circling the place where he had made his fire. He lit another, warmed his sodden bones, and went back to waiting, keeping his mind still, open to whatever chose to enter.

He didn't see what shape Valoren took to reach the mountain. He felt the gentle, wordless company of minds withdraw swiftly as small animals startling away from a hawk's shadow. He stirred, puzzled, oddly lonely, and found that he was not alone. The young wizard had come out of nowhere to stand near his fire. He was staring upward at the faceless, nameless enormities around him. At the touch of Yar's eyes he whirled abruptly, his face as colorless as the snow and wary, Yar saw with surprise, even of him.

"What are they?" His voice trembled with shock or the cold. Yar, searching for words, for a place to begin, couldn't find them fast enough. Valoren reached him at a step, gripped his arms, and hauled him to his feet. Yar sensed the tension in him drawn dangerously fine. "Yar!"

He found words finally. "They are everything you fear."

Valoren's hold on him tightened; he breathed incredulously, "You aren't afraid—"

"They're terrified of you."

Valoren stared at them, then at Yar. He asked hoarsely, "How can you tell?"

"Why do you think they have chosen the most isolated place in Numis to hide themselves?"

"Why did they come to Numis at all? Why did they choose Numis?"

"They were born here."

The young wizard's hands slackened. "No," he whispered. "No. You saw what Od wrote—They brought terror into Numis."

"I listened to them. They told me."

"You let them into your mind? Yar, they could tell you any lies!" He glanced around them suddenly, bewildered, remembering what he had come for. "Where is Brenden Vetch? You said he would be here."

"He is," Yar said briefly, anticipating trouble. But it was past time to hide things from Valoren, even the gardener.

"Where?"

Yar looked up at the circle of dark, rough-hewn shapes around them, all silently listening, he knew, and wondered how much, if anything, they understood. Perhaps, given their disastrous history with humans, they understood only too well what all the shouting was about. Valoren followed his glance; his quick breath whitened the air.

"In there? They took him?"

"I don't think so," Yar answered. "I think he vanished into them to hide."

Valoren was silent, his attention sliding from shape to shape as though he might recognize some part of Brenden, his eye or his hair, in a runnel or a stump. Then his face grew very still, as he focused his thoughts and his powers.

Yar said sharply, "Don't—"

But Valoren did, even as he spoke. Yar, catching at him, was thrown off his feet by the force that tossed Valoren away as easily as a twig in a torrent. Valoren, crying out, landed heavily on top of him. Yar lay in the snow for a moment, catching his breath, then pulled himself free and held out a hand to the ashen-faced wizard, who was blinking as though he had gone blind.

"As I was saying," Yar continued grimly, as Valoren pulled himself up to sit slumped and cradling his head in his hands, "don't go into their minds. Let them come into you. You'll hear them, if you listen. If you invite them in. If they sense that you mean them no harm."

Valoren rolled a bleary eye at him. "If I mean them no harm," he repeated painfully. "If I mean them—Yar, you are mad. These powers have crazed you; you make no sense. They have enough power to—" He stopped himself, gripped Yar's arm again to hoist himself up. "We can't talk here," he breathed. "We must go back to the school, think what to do. Ceta must give us all of Od's writings about them. There may be a hint in them somewhere of how they can be destroyed."

Yar's sigh, dredged from the depths, blew a mist between them. "Of course they can be destroyed," he said impatiently. "Why do you think they've been hiding up here all these centuries? But why would you want to destroy such power? Such wonders?"

"They're lawless, renegade—who knows what they might do?" He gazed back obstinately at Yar, both hands at his brow, pushing against the headache Yar knew he had gotten from venturing into the unknown. "What do you suggest we do to make them safe? Bring them back to the school and put them into a classroom to restructure their magic?"

"I suggest we leave them alone."

"And Brenden Vetch with them? Think what powers a human might have, combining his own powers with theirs."

"What makes you think that Brenden would be more successful than you or I? He's alive; that's all I know. He remembers my name. Other than that, he hasn't spoken a word."

"He's trapped," Valoren said flatly.

"He is terrified. He found what he thought was the safest place in Numis to hide."

"Here? They eat wizards, it seems."

"He was hiding from you."

"Why? If he had nothing to hide?"

"You frightened him?" Yar guessed. "Maybe he thought that, if he stayed at the school and learned what we had to teach, he would turn into you?"

Valoren stared at him. He closed his eyes at a stab of pain, opened them again, and asked heavily, "What's wrong with that? The king is pleased with me. Isn't that the point of the school: to strengthen the powers of Numis? If we let such raw, lawless power exist within our boundaries, it could destroy everything we know."

"I don't think so. I think we could learn unimaginable things from them."

"I can't imagine anything but danger."

"I know you can't. That's why they fear you."

Valoren shook his head, and winced again. "I don't understand you. Od began her school in Kelior with permission from the king; she used her own powers to protect Numis. Her purpose was clear: to bring order to the chaos of unschooled, unruly power by bringing it to submission under the laws of the king. These wild powers have no place in the land that Od chose."

"She calls them forgotten treasures," Yar reminded him.

"She writes of terror ruling Numis if they are freed."

"If they are feared."

"How could they not be?" Valoren exclaimed, looking up at them through snow, which had begun to fall again, lightly, upon the massive, silent shapes, flakes catching on a bulky curve, an upraised stump. He turned to Yar again, the same incredulity in his eyes, as though Yar seemed one of them. "We were taught the same rules of magic at the same school. You were my first teacher. How can we both see exactly the same thing and define it so differently?"

"You are seeing what the king would fear. I see—" Yar paused, felt their attention again, their awareness of him. Wonder swept through him, fierce curiosity, longing. "I see," he whispered, "all the possibilities of magic."

Valoren rubbed his eyes, trying to clear his vision, perhaps, more likely still fighting the headache that Yar's ideas kept fueling. "You think what they want you to think."

"You think what King Galin wants you to think."

"I think I should go now and bring back the entire school of wizards. All the power we possess might be enough to drive them out of Numis."

"I think we should both go back," Yar said. "We can't end this argument because we don't know enough—"

"Go back and do what? Wait a decade or two for Od to come along so that she can explain these creatures more clearly than she did throughout five centuries? I doubt that she knows any more about them than what she wrote. We don't need to discuss; we need to act now, with or without—"

Yar gave a sudden murmur that stopped Valoren. A dark figure was leaning quietly against one of the mysteries, listening to them argue. Yar blinked falling snow out of his eyes, but they kept showing him the same thing anyway. Brenden? he thought at first blink. But, no, the figure was too slight, even allowing for the bulk of the shape looming over it. Valoren, seeing it, too, started and took a surprising step closer to Yar, whose eyes had begun to narrow. The cloak, far too long for its wearer, was dragging in the snow.

"It's the eel," he breathed, stunned.

"Who?" Valoren demanded.

"Elver. The student. He's been following me everywhere."

"A student! How could he possibly—"

"How could you possibly have followed—" Yar stopped, cutting short a sentence and a stride at once. He stood still, not knowing yet what he was looking at, but certain it couldn't be what he saw.

The boy pushed back the hood, and said calmly, "I didn't follow you. I followed Brenden Vetch. He needed to learn a few things, and learn them fast, and he did that very well indeed, thinking that it was Valoren on his heels, harrying him across Numis. But it was me."

Yar heard Valoren's breath stop. Then he heard himself speak again, though he didn't recognize his own voice.

"Od?"

The boy unpinned the cloak; the gray-haired giantess caught it as it fell.

TWENTY-SIX

The princess and Ceta rode with Arneth to the Twilight Gate at dusk to bring Tyramin to the king. Outside the wall, they watched as the guards at the gate parted to let the magician's company through. The wagons, brightly painted with shooting stars, genially smiling suns, full moons with more enigmatic smiles, had their curtains and shutters pulled to, their doors shut. They enclosed their secret worlds as tightly as cocoons, the drab creatures in them busily transforming into marvels, enchantments. The oxen, trailing ribbons and strands of paper flowers from their horns, were led by slender figures in black from hair to heel, their faces masked; the only color about them came from the ribbons braided into their long hair.

Behind the last wagon rode the moon.

So it seemed to Sulys when she appeared. The moon was rising out of the Twilight Gate, her face an oval of porcelain, her eyes black and empty as the night, her hair streaming behind her in great waves, planets caught in it, and shooting stars. Long streamers of silk, the shimmering, half-glimpsed colors of lights in the coldest north, held her to earth by wrist and ankle and throat. Dancers carried the ends of silk, whirling now and then at whim, bright skirts throwing off flickering swarms of sparks.

The moon's eyes turned briefly to watch the princess as she passed with her constellation of dancers. The guards closed around them, a long line on either side. Arneth, followed by the two women, rode to the head of the procession. He led the guards up the road and into the broad, cobbled yard nearest the great hall. There the lines of guards diverged to circle the wagons, which were drawn up close to the palace steps. The broad, massive doors were open wide; the oxen might have pulled the wagons into the hall but for the steps. Ceta and Sulys dismounted. The princess, staring at the iron-bound doors, swallowed a burning in her throat. She straightened the long, dark, filmy scarf around her throat. Its endlessly coiled threads glittered faintly in the torchlight. Her fingers found the threaded needle hidden along one edge, then dropped. Head held so high it seemed balanced precariously and in danger of floating away, she went up the steps and into her father's presence.

Most of the court and the school, including some of the older students, had gathered in the great hall with the king. Predictably, he didn't notice his daughter; he was on the other side of the vast room conferring with some of the counselors. Enys stood beside him, frowning as he listened. There was a startling lack of Valoren in the little gathering. Sulys looked around, hoping against hope that he was still in the north. Ceta touched her lightly.

"Isn't that your great-grandmother?"

Sulys turned, surprised. Dittany had actually come down from her tower for the occasion, with Beris in attendance. Her great-grandmother seemed frosted and scalloped like a confection in strawberry-colored satin and cream lace. Even her lapdog was festooned with ribbons. They were sitting by themselves in a quiet corner under a torch, Sulys noted; not many took an interest anymore in the aged dowager from a distant land.

She said softly, "She hasn't left her tower since my mother's funeral. Let's sit with her. Nobody will see me working there."

But her ladies had seen her; she was suddenly surrounded by women cooing and chattering all at once. Her aunt Fanerl pushed among them, shrilling a dozen questions in one breath and not listening for answers to any of them. Even Ceta looked a bit dazed by the noise and the crush after the tranquil peace of her river house. Sulys gripped her wrist, drew her firmly past her aunt, who rarely remembered whom she talked at as long as there was a face in front of her. Heading in the general direction of Dittany, the princess brought herself face-to-face with her father.

They stared at one another, startled. A din of drumbeats overwhelmed the noise in the hall. Dancers spun like tops through the doors, causing clusters in the middle of the floor to break apart, flee in all directions toward the chairs lining the walls. The king, urged toward the wizards by his counselors, went one way; Sulys went another, to her great-grandmother, who embraced the wayward princess with joy.

"Oh, my dear. You've come back. I was afraid you had run off with the magician, and I'd never see you again. Everyone had you running away with somebody different."

"No. I only needed to run away and think. Lady Thiel kindly let me stay with her."

"Ah. I'm glad you found someone to talk to." She patted the empty chairs on either side of her. "Sit with me." Beris, who had risen from one of them to curtsy, stepped toward a lonely chair behind them. But Sulys, shifting adroitly, claimed it first.

"I'll sit here," she said, drawing the chair close so that Dittany could turn easily to see her. "I have my needlework, and I need the light."

"But, my dear, you hate to sew."

"I will be married soon. Lady Thiel says a woman with needlework in her hands is generally assumed to have no other thoughts in her head and can safely harbor any number of improprieties. That will come in handy, especially when I'm married to a wizard."

"I see," Dittany said, blinking vaguely. "Beris brought some cakes in her handkerchief for us to nibble during the performance. Your father has been beside himself, I heard."

"How dreadful," Sulys said absently, feeling herself grow tense now that the performance was about to begin. She searched the hall for Mistral, but the moon had vanished, it seemed. "One of him is difficult enough."

All the lights in the hall fluttered then, as though wind had swooped in to carry off taper flame, lamplight, torch fire. The doors shut with a hollow boom. Only the dancers' skirts remained visible, wheels of sparkling silk and light seemingly attached to nothing. For an instant the hall was soundless.

A staff struck the floor; lights streamed out of it, whirled through the hall. They broke into pieces, formed a flock of luminous butterflies that turned as one and showered down upon the towering figure standing in the middle of the hall.

The butterflies flew back into his staff. It struck the floor again to illumine the lovely face of the moon, her porcelain mask changed into paint, her eyes like golden fire now, the warm, crimson smile on her lips inviting them all to be as delighted as she with what they saw.

"I am Tyramin," said the hairy, dark-eyed giant with his painted globe of a head and his voice like the rumble of the white bear in the royal menagerie. "Master of Illusions and Enchantments. And this enchantment is my beautiful daughter, who assists me." They both bowed in the direction of the king among his wizards. "We offer you these diversions to make amends, and in hope that you will consider us from this moment friends of the Kingdom of Numis."

Light flooded the room from his staff. Sulys saw Dittany's face turn lavender, then rose. And then the magician made the mundane world vanish around them with marvels, wonders of lights and fires, tricks and transformations, each lovelier and more astonishing than the last. So thoroughly did Tyramin charm the world away, not a sound came from it beyond the occasional gasp. Even the wizards, faced with the captivating power of his charms, watched silently, their eyes reflecting his fires. Sulys, astonished by the wonderful, secret powers of the calmly smiling Mistral, felt her heart change with every enchantment. It turned, like the magician's daughter, into that deep red rose, its petals of fire blossoming wider, wider, until it began to spin, and her heart became the milk white bird that flew out of the heart of the rose. The bird soared; so did her heart. They sang. The bird became a long flowing spiral of colored paper that reached down from the ceiling to touch the floor. Within the spiral the magician's daughter reappeared: first her pale oval face, then her wild hair, and finally her amber eyes, tinged with fire at another pound of Tyramin's staff. Fire spiraled up the spinning paper, whirled around the magician's daughter. Drums beat; Tyramin commanded. Fire consumed paper and disappeared. The magician's daughter stood free, showing them her changeless, impervious smile, unaltered by the kiss of fire.

Sulys picked up her needle then. Mistral could not turn her performers invisible in a hall full of wizards, she had explained to the princess. They must be hidden within thread. Each pattern on the scarf would conceal one performer; Sulys had only to close a pattern with a stitch at the exact moment. Then, depending on the king's reaction to Tyramin's magic, she would either give the scarf freely back to Mistral, or wait to pass it secretly to Arneth, who would take the invisible company out of Numis forever.

Sulys, holding her breath, counting tricks, knew by the order of them when the performance drew toward its end. When it seemed the world could hold no more wonders, Tyramin astonished his rapt audience yet again, turning his dancers, his musicians, his assistants one by one into dreams, illusions, that vanished at a flash of light into some other world. Each time his staff sparked, Sulys stitched. She knotted the thread, and the performer vanished; she broke it, knotted it again, and found another pattern to complete. Finally, only the magician and his daughter stood alone on the floor. He turned her into a flowing fountain of paper roses, then his staff spat light. Sulys stitched. His daughter's crimson smile lingered for a moment in the air, holding everyone's eyes. Sulys turned the scarf to the last unfinished pattern, stitched again. The smile vanished. And with it, everyone realized suddenly, so had Tyramin.

The silence held a few moments longer in the hall as everyone waited for the next illusion, the next enchantment.

Nothing was left of the performers, not a fallen star or a feather. A deep murmur came from the direction of the dais, as though from a beast awakened abruptly, but not sure yet why. Sulys saw her father roused and beginning to wonder where his prey had gone. Around him, the wizards were looking vaguely perplexed. They might have seen magic, their faces said, but then again maybe not; but if not, then what exactly had they seen?

The king opened his mouth; the princess's hands closed tightly over the ends of the scarf she had slipped around her neck. But it was her great-grandmother's voice that broke the spellbound silence in the hall.

She had turned suddenly to stare at the princess's handiwork. "I know!" she cried with delight. "I taught you that trick! You've hidden them all in the threads." Sulys felt the blood leave her face. Dittany put a satin-covered knuckle to her mouth, her eyes growing wide. "Oh, dear," she whispered. "Did I say that?"

The king stood up, frowning at his daughter as though she were some stranger who had wandered into his hall. "Sulys?" The name came out like a bark. "What does she mean? What trick? What threads?"

Sulys, frozen, heard Mistral's deep, cool voice very clearly in her head: Free us.

She stood up shakily. Dittany groped toward her, blinking away tears; Sulys paused to pat her hand. Then she went to face her father and the ranks of wizards around him. The crowd was soundless again, mute with amazement, as though the missing princess had been conjured out of Tyramin's staff.

She curtsied wordlessly, then pulled the cloth from around her neck and began to pull out the gleaming stitches. As the broken threads drifted to the floor, one by one the company became visible again: the dancers, musicians, assistants. After them, the magician's daughter reappeared, though her smile did not. Her face was masked now by its oval of white porcelain, eyes hidden within the seemingly empty dark. Sulys pulled a final, shimmering thread and revealed the magician, discovered in his hiding place, his trick revealed. He bowed to the king, and then to Sulys, but beyond that had no comment.

Sulys cleared her throat. "It's one of the tricks I learned from Dittany," she said to her stupefied father and the wizards. "How to hide little things within threads. Play magic from Hestria, she calls it. The magician's daughter showed me how much more you can hide."

The king made a couple more menagerie noises before he finally settled on words. "Is that where you've been? Hiding with this magician?"

"No. I've been staying with Lady Thiel. I disguised myself as a wizard and found the magician's daughter in the Twilight Quarter. I had—There were things I found I could do from a very early age. Some of it seemed kin to Tyramin's magic. So I went looking for him."

Her father was still staring at her as though he had never seen her before. "Your mother never told me you could do such things."

"She didn't know. Dittany and I kept it secret from her, so that she wouldn't have to hide it from you." She paused, resisted an impulse to wring her chilly fingers. "I tried to tell Valoren. I thought he should know this about me before we married. Unfortunately, he had no time to listen to me. Please don't blame my great-grandmother. She didn't teach me everything I know. Some things, like seeing a gift of peacocks in a candle flame, I was born knowing how to do. They seemed harmless bits of magic. Things too unimportant to attract the wizards' attention. Or to bother you about. Until now. And I was—now—"

"You were what?"

"I was afraid to tell you," she said softly. "And like Valoren, you had no time for me. Always it was Tyramin this, or the gardener that." She gave a small shrug of resignation. "And now, I really don't care what you do to me. The important thing is that you and Valoren know. I suppose you could exile me and my great-grandmother to Hestria. They like our kind of magic there. Or marry me to someone in a strange land where what I know is not forbidden."

Her father's face grew streaked with color as though he were about to erupt. "You grew up among wizards; you know the laws of Numis! You should have studied at the school, instead of practicing proscribed magic with your great-grandmother under my roof. Did that never occur to you?"

Sulys drew breath, loosed it noiselessly, to steady her voice. "Yes. It occurred to me. But I was afraid the wizards would take away everything I know and replace it only with what they know. I do things with threads and buttons and bones. I don't imagine that a needle and thread or the wishbone of a goose is common equipment for a student of Od's school."

"Wishbone?" one of the wizards echoed faintly.

Her eyes moved from the king to the gathering around him of the most powerful in his realm. "If you let magic into Numis instead of shutting it out, your wizards would know what a wishbone can do."

The wizards consulted one another wordlessly. The king swallowed what must have been a thunderbolt, judging by his expression. Sulys waited, still uncertain what the wizards had truly seen in Tyramin's magic and wishing against hope that they would simply turn her out the door along with the performers, since they would have to read between the lines of the laws of Numis to find one that would permit her to use her threads and bones. Around her, every eye was upon her, and not a few mouths hung gracelessly open. Except for her aunt Fanerl, whose mouth was clamped shut at the idea of Sulys's wedding hanging by a thread. Tyramin and his performers were motionless; they hardly seemed to breathe. As though, Sulys thought, if they were just still enough, the king might mistake them for air.

The wizard Balius, harsh lines running deep along his mouth, said slowly, "My lord, there was more magic here tonight than can be accounted for by a simple wishbone. There is more than illusion in those tricks."

"They came here freely," Sulys reminded the king desperately. "They mean no harm."

"Laws were broken," the wizard said inflexibly.

"To make real roses out of paper?"

"For whatever reason, Tyramin has worked forbidden magic in the king's house."

"So have I," Sulys said adamantly. "So have I. What you do to Tyramin, you must do to me."

"There are ways of undoing methods of magic, ways of retraining minds improperly taught, which might be appropriate for one such as Tyramin—"

"You mean, you would go into the magician's thoughts?" Sulys breathed, aghast. "Force him to change the way he thinks of magic?"

"It has been done to recalcitrant wizards. Only in extreme cases. I don't think—"

"I don't think so, either," Galin snapped. "This is my daughter you are threatening, not some renegade wizard!"

Balius inclined his head to the fuming king. "As I was about to say, my lord, I don't think that would be at all appropriate for the princess. The king holds the power of law, of arms, of magic in Numis. It is not for us to say what to do with your daughter. Except for Valoren, perhaps, who would expect his wife to obey the laws of the land, especially when the land is her father's."

"Valoren!" Sulys felt the blood rush into her face, heard something in her voice that sounded remarkably like her father. "I'm not going to change the way I think for Valoren. Or you. Or my father, or anyone else in this land. You will have to exile me or find a way to live with me, because I won't give up a button's worth of magic."

"You just used a thread's worth of magic to conceal magic from me," her father reminded her forcibly.

"Because you are harassing something innocent and harmless! You and Valoren—you want to mold wizards like coins that all look alike; if it doesn't bear your seal, it is worth nothing and must be destroyed. Or it is dangerous and must be destroyed. There's no place for any kind of magic that's of no use to you. No place for charms, or marvels, or enchantments, for anything you or Valoren can't understand. I can't marry someone who would look at me as a threat or an aberration or—or a task to be undertaken—"

She heard a muffled imprecation from Fanerl. Galin, his face mottling, growled pithily, "You will do as you're told, and that's the end."

She thought about that for a split second, answered calmly, "No. I won't. What will you do?"

Galin opened his mouth; nothing came out. She had rendered him speechless, Sulys saw with amazement. He truly did not know. There was no law in Numis to tell him; he had to look elsewhere for an answer. Where would he look? she wondered. How long would he permit this moment of doubt to exist? Long enough to begin to doubt other things as well?

She never knew. Before he could tell her, the huge hall doors opened with a bang that brought the wizards to their feet. The performers whirled, drawing more closely together. Sulys heard guards shouting as they ran through inner doors, swords hissing out of their scabbards. She turned bewilderedly, alone and uncertain in the center of the room, wondering if one of the wizards, impatient with her arguing, had summoned guards to stop her. She heard a sword drawn too close to her and gasped as someone gripped her arm, pulled her into the cluster of performers. It was Arneth Pyt, she realized, standing between her and Mistral with his sword in his hand.

"What is it?" she cried. "Are we under arrest?"

"I don't know," he answered breathlessly, and asked Mistral, "Do you?"

But she only shook her head. "No." Her porcelain face remained untroubled, but her voice trembled. "Something is at the door."

Sulys saw all color and expression flow out of Arneth's face. Magic came in the king's door, stood under his roof. That was the only word she could find in her head for these huge, strange beings that had wandered in from the night. They had no faces, no recognizable limbs; they might have been walking stones or tree trunks. But they were alive, and she could sense their power like silent thunder in the air

Valoren walked among those giants. He looked peculiar, Sulys thought dazedly; his face had lost its aloofness, its certainty. Yar was with him, and so was the strangest woman Sulys had ever seen. She was very tall, big-boned; her hair, ivory streaked with ash, swept past her knees. A bird seemed to be nesting in it. Others perched on her shoulders, peered out from under her ears. Her great horny feet were bare. A green-and-turquoise snake was coiled around one ankle.

She heard a sudden exclamation from Ceta. The guards surrounding the king and his heir still had their swords raised toward the threat. But the wizards were murmuring, wonder Sulys had no idea they possessed flowing into their eyes.

She heard her father's amazed voice crack a syllable into two. "Od?"

"King Galin," the woman said, giving him a friendly nod.

"What are you—what are these—"

"This is the face of the oldest living magic of Numis. They've been hiding up in the north country since the reign of King Telios."

"Telios! That's—that was—"

"A while back," she agreed. "But it never hurts to get reacquainted with the past. Nor," she added after a pause, "to offer a guest welcome. If that's the case, of course."

"Of course," the king agreed hastily. "Every door in my house is open to you. As Numis's savior and great friend, you are always welcome."

"Thank you, King Galin. I would like to keep my welcome certain here."

"Has anything," Galin asked carefully, "occurred to make you less than certain?"

"A great deal," she answered amiably. "I paid a visit very recently to the school to see how I would fare in it if I were a student there. I got myself expelled within the first week."

Sulys, feeling sound bubble up in her, put her hands over her mouth; others didn't catch their barks of laughter so gracefully.

"It seemed to me," Od continued, "that the students are lacking a certain vision. So I brought these here to remind the teachers what magic looks like before it becomes words on a page." Her broad, homely face turned to Valoren; Sulys saw her eyes then, tranquil, gray as cloud and as impenetrable, filled as they were with centuries of seeing. "Tell them what it looks like to you, Valoren."

"Like nothing," he said hoarsely, "I've ever seen in my life."

"And you've been studying magic nearly half your life. Your face shows it. You are the face of the magic that comes out of my school. You were, anyway. And now look at you. Look at all of you." She gestured toward the wizards massed behind the king; even the most severe of faces, Sulys saw, looked melted and vulnerable as they stared back at Od and what she had brought with her. "Now," she told them, "you are wearing the faces I had hoped to see come out of my school."

"What are they?" Balius pleaded. "Please tell us."

She nodded. "I interrupted another argument on Skrygard Mountain earlier. It seems the day for it. The argument was between Yar and Valoren, about whether or not these should be destroyed. They're very old, and they only want to live in peace. I've known about them all my life, though it took me a century or two to find them. Long ago, when they lived freely in the land before it became Numis, they took any shape that caught their curiosity, that kindled their wonder. They never knew the words for what they shaped; their magic is that old. Humans came to fear them in their dangerous shapes, and killed them when they discovered them in defenseless shapes—songbirds, small animals, wildflowers. To protect themselves, they sometimes took a human shape. Some even learned a few words. That only terrified most humans, since who could ever tell if the stranger they saw was truly human?"

She paused to catch a mole dangling precariously out of her pocket. The room was soundless again. She looked at the king. "Not everyone feared them. Some loved them. Saw the wonder and beauty in them. My mother, for instance." One of the wizards made a sound like a mouse's squeak. Od continued mildly, "You may have wondered where I got my powers. My mother told me to keep an eye open, through my wanderings, for such as these, and there I would find the face of my own power."

Sulys heard the king's voice above the rest: an explosion of gabbled words through which Od waited patiently, until the hall was almost quiet again. "I recognized them when I saw them, rooted by time among the snow and trees and stones of Skrygard Mountain. If it was one of them who loved my mother for a time in human shape, I have no idea. So long ago, so many shapes ago, perhaps he—it wouldn't re-member. Or forgot the words for such a thing. That's why I've lived so long. I thought it was time you all met what I was thinking about when I started the school. Power shaped by wonder and curiosity, even love. Not by fear and laws that shut out instead of inviting in.

"So I brought these along for a visit. I hoped that Valoren, being among your most gifted, might try to find a way to talk to them."

Sulys watched the wizard sway a little, like a reed in the wind. "Me."

"Let them know they can live without being afraid."

The king found his voice again, asked incredulously, "Afraid of what?"

"Of you." Her eyes turned to the wizards again. "You

might learn something from them. I hope so. Because if you can't find a way to understand this ancient, wild magic that came out of the heart of Numis, then I will have to move my school to some other land that has learned how to hear it. That would be a pity. As well as a great bother. I would like to think that the rulers of Numis and I can continue to get along."

King Galin shifted abruptly, as though he had been bitten by the idea of such power abandoning his kingdom to belong to somebody else's. "Yes," he said quickly. "So would I. Perhaps you'll take some time to explain to the teachers in more detail the changes you would like made in the school."

Od cast a glance upward toward his roof. "I began my school in a cobbler's shop. Somehow, through the centuries, it has become part of your house. You make rules for your house; you make rules for my school. I need to explain a few things to you, too, before I go wandering off again. Change must come from within the laws of Numis as well to keep my school here."

Galin cleared his throat, looking for once almost helpless himself. "Yes," he said gruffly; his eyes flicked at Sulys under his lowering brows. "My daughter was explaining something like that to me when you came in." His attention wandered away from her, drawn again toward the dark, looming shapes emanating power throughout the hall as a river exudes mist. "You're going to leave these here?" he asked huskily. "What if Valoren can't control them?"

"Oh, he can't," she answered cheerfully. "No one can. But he should be able to come to some kind of an understanding with them, so that you can all live peacefully together. If not, I'll hear about it, I'm sure, wherever in the world I am."

The king opened his mouth; for the second time that

evening nothing came out. He looked at Valoren, whose sallow face had grown waxen.

"May I," Valoren asked faintly, "ask for help among the wizards?"

"Oh, I think you should," Od assured him. "I think you'd better. Yar, for instance. He has a gift for recognizing odd magic. And for listening. And the new gardener, as well."

"The gardener," the king echoed, mystified. "I keep hearing about the gardener. But I never see him. Where is he?"

Od looked up at one of the mysterious shapes, then another, inciting a flurry of comments among the wizards. "Which one is he in? Yar, can you tell?"

Yar shook his head, looking up as well, as was everyone in the hall, searching for a sign of the elusive gardener. "Maybe," he suggested gently, "you should ask him to come out. Now that it's safe."

Od smiled. "There's a thought. The simplest magic: make a wish. Brenden, will you join us?"

TWENTY-SEVEN

He did not understand the words, but he felt the wish. It drew at him, like a door opening in the night, spilling light and warmth into the vast dark he had become. Words meant nothing to him; it was what lay within them, around them, the forces that shaped them, that he heard. His name was one more noise among many around him; it could have been an insect's chirr or a birdsong, for all it meant to him. What he comprehended was all that it meant to the one who spoke it.

That stirred memory, gave the amorphous force he was an image, a definition. He shaped all that the image contained: the passions, the experiences, the memories, colors, sounds, shapes, and textures, and finally, all the words.

So he became Brenden, standing in a great hall full of people who were all staring at him. He had felt the passions buffeting the shell he hid within, emotions flung hither and yon amid torrents of words. Now, it seemed, nobody was left with a word to say; he had startled them all away.

Looking around, he recognized a few familiar faces: Yar, Od, Valoren, Mistral. All in the same place, he thought with wonder, and at the same time. He found comfort in Od's smile, her calm eyes. Yar, who was also smiling, bowed his head to the burly, fair-haired, richly dressed man flanked by wizards and guards.

He said, "You sent me to find Brenden Vetch, my lord. It took me longer than I anticipated. This is the missing gardener."

"I don't think so," King Galin breathed. "I don't think he's a gardener any longer."

Brenden sensed an odd tangle of emotions spilling out of Valoren. He met the light, stunned eyes and was startled by what he saw in them.

"How much of their power," Valoren asked raggedly, "did you take into yourself?"

He considered the question, felt himself drift toward that raw, shapeless force that could shape anything. He confined himself to the gardener's shape, answered slowly, "I don't know. I'd have to use it to find out." Then he put a word to what he felt in Valoren, what was flowing out of the gathering of wizards: no longer fear but wonder, filling the hall like air and light, minds opening like windows and doors shuttered and barred for centuries.

Od felt it, Brenden saw; she drew it in with a breath, let it out again in a smile that seemed to shine out of her bones. "That's better," she said softly. Even the ancient shapes around them seemed to loose some attention outward: open a hidden eye, send out a tendril of curiosity.

"Will you help me?" Valoren asked the gardener huskily. "You learned nothing in the school; you found all your power elsewhere. And you alone of all of us understand these—these beings. I tried to see into them—so did Yar—we both failed. It was like trying to swim up a raging cataract, or reason with fire."

Brenden looked hesitantly at Od. She nodded. "I've asked him to find a way to talk to them, so that they can live where they will at peace instead of hiding in fear."

"I'll do what I can," he told Valoren. "Though I don't know how much I understand about them. Except that they weren't afraid of me. I was something desperate trying to run out of the world, trying to hide; they must have understood that much."

A little color tinged the wizard's face. "I put that fear into you," he said softly. "But it wasn't me pursuing you across Numis. It was Od herself."

Brenden stared at her; she said tranquilly, "I had to see how much power you possessed before I let you risk yourself with these. You ran farther than I intended; I couldn't have stopped you, in the end."

"What are you saying?" the king asked incredulously. "That he is more powerful than you?"

"At that moment, he was."

"And he learned this—where?"

"From bog lilies, by the sound of it. Earth. Rain. Seeds."

Galin struggled, incoherent for a moment. "Then why bother with walls? Why books, teachers—"

"Most are the better for them. A few can do without. Magic will spring up where it wills, King, and even in a lifetime you couldn't make enough laws to stop it, any more than you can put out all the night fires in Numis with a breath, or contain the wind within four walls. Trust your wizards; let them come and go. What they find outside these walls and bring back to you may be worth more than you can imagine."

Galin cast a glance at the wizards, whose attention remained riveted on what had walked into his house. "I think I have no choice," he murmured and inclined his head to Od. "Make your changes. I must trust you as well, it seems."

"Good," she answered simply. Then she looked at the performers clustered around Tyramin, watching the complex and unexpected performance going on around them. "We interrupted other important matters you were attending. This can wait while you finish them."

Galin found his daughter's face among the performers, asked a trifle dazedly, "Where were we?"

"You were deciding what to do with me," the princess reminded him.

The king looked at her silently a moment, then at the ancient shapes of a magic that had found its way, despite all his laws, across his threshold.

He shook his head, said heavily, "What's standing in our midst makes the question of what to do about your magic an exceedingly moot point. I have no idea what to do with you. Except to hope that you won't leave us."

The gusty sigh of relief she loosed could be heard throughout the hall. "Thank you, Father," she whispered. "It was the last thing I wanted." She cleared her throat, asked more clearly, "And Tyramin?"

The king's eyes moved to the silent, masked magician. "I can only repeat to you what I said to my daughter about her magic. I'll assume that yours is as you describe it: illusions and enchantments. Beyond that, as long as you do no harm in Numis, I don't want to know."

"My lord, I do," Valoren pleaded. "If there is magic in the magician that I haven't learned, it may help me to try to understand these creatures. There is a power in concealment, even if it is not magic. I need—I need all the help I can get. Even from the most unlikely places. Please. Ask him to reveal his face."

There was a long rustle of silk and shifted shoe and breath around the hall as everyone leaned toward the magician. The king looked at the silent giant, who seemed more kin to the enormous, faceless beings than to the humans around him.

"As a gesture of friendship?" Galin suggested.

One huge, gauntlet loosed the staff; the magician's daughter caught it as it fell. Both hands rose, wrestled with the painted head. Finally, the great globe parted company with the shirt; the gauntlets brought it down and tucked it under one arm.

There was nothing beneath it. The hall sounded suddenly like the king's menagerie when every bird and animal clamored in it at once; Dittany's lapdog bounced on her knee with the force of its barking. Then the powerful giant slowly crumpled and folded like a puppet onto the floor.

The magician's beautiful daughter took off her flawless porcelain mask to reveal the weary, smiling, human face of magic.

"My lord," she said to the king, "I am Tyramin."

Galin stared at her, stupefied. Then he threw back his head and laughed, the sound booming like Tyramin's laughter off the walls, and the hall erupted once again, with shouts and applause at the magician's final trick.

"Because of you," the king said when he could speak, "my counselor Valoren nearly had Kelior up in arms. Things must change indeed, when a traveling magician and a gardener can throw my city into turmoil."

"I'm sorry," Valoren said to him, his shaking voice nearly inaudible.

"You did what I expected you to do," Galin said briefly, and went among the performers to his daughter's side.

Brenden, standing quietly as a tree in an ancient, weathered grove, asked Od, "Where should we take these?"

"I think they'll feel safe among the old trees near the menagerie. They'll follow you, if you ask them. It's peaceful out there, and full of wild things." She paused, studying him thoughtfully, and added, reading his mind, "I know you'll want to be off, testing your own powers, seeing what you can do with yourself. But I hope you'll stay a while, help Valoren, and try to show the wizards how you learned what you learned."

"I'm not sure I know that myself. I never thought about it."

"Well, try and put it into words. That is the language the wizards of Numis know best, so far."

"I'll try," he said, and was silent a little, watching Yar find a lovely, dark-haired woman in the crowd, and Valoren drift uncertainly toward the king's daughter. He felt his own loneliness then, and knew he had become completely human again. But the grinding weight of sorrow had left him, he realized, and he could face his own powers with a great deal of curiosity and only a prudent amount of fear.

Od laid her hand on his shoulder, patted it. "I'll be away then. I think Galin and the wizards can sort things out themselves. Watch over Valoren for a while; make sure he doesn't accidentally kill himself."

"Where are you going?"

"Where else? To find another gardener."

He watched her leave. Turning again, he saw familiar faces drawing toward him: Valoren, grown almost unrecognizable without his arrogance, Yar with an arm around his love, the wizards, even the king, his daughter's hand tucked securely under his elbow as he crossed the hall. Brenden drew his peace from within the oldest magic in Numis and let the uncertain future come.